THE DIEHARD WARRIOR

JENNIFER YOUNGBLOOD

ARBOR
HOUSE

OTHER BOOKS BY JENNIFER YOUNGBLOOD

Check out Jenniferyoungblood.com to save on bundle deals or visit Jennifer's Amazon Page.

The Honeysuckle Island Series

Chasing Whispers

The Fragile Truth

The Secrets We Treasure

False Illusions

To Steal A Heart

A Twist of Fame

A Sliver of Doubt

Comfortable Lies

Billionaire Bodyguard Romance

Protecting the Heiress

Protecting the Journalist

Protecting the Diva

Good Girls Don't Come Last (Romcom)

Cold Feet

Practically Perfect

High Heels and Big Deals

Weddings, Lace, and Cake in the Face

The 101 on Love
The Comfort Romance Series
Christmas in Comfort
Big Secret in Little Comfort
My Italian Love Disaster
Romeo Family Romance
One Perfect Day
One Way Home
One Little Switch
One Tiny Lie
One Big Mistake
One Southern Cowboy
One Singing Bachelorette
One Fake Fiancé
One Silent Night
One Kick Wonder
One More Chance
Billionaire Boss Romance
Her Blue Collar Boss
Her Lost Chance Boss
Georgia Patriots Romance
The Hot Headed Patriot
The Twelfth Hour Patriot
The Unstoppable Patriot
The Exiled Patriot
O'Brien Family Romance
The Impossible Groom (Chas O'Brien)
The Twelfth Hour Patriot (McKenna O'Brien)
The Stormy Warrior (Caden O'Brien and Tess Eisenhart)
Christmas
Rewriting Christmas (A Novella)
Yours By Christmas (Park City Firefighter Romance)
Her Crazy Rich Fake Fiancé
Her Christmas Wedding Fake Fiancé
Navy SEAL Romance

The Resolved Warrior
The Reckless Warrior
The Diehard Warrior
The Stormy Warrior
The Jane Austen Pact
Seeking Mr. Perfect
Texas Titan Romances
The Hometown Groom
The Persistent Groom
The Ghost Groom
The Jilted Billionaire Groom
The Impossible Groom
Beach Island Romance Series
Love Him or Lose Him
Love on the Rocks
Love on the Rebound
Love at the Ocean Breeze
Love Changes Everything
Loving the Movie Star
Love Under Fire (A Companion book to the Hawaii Billionaire Series)
Kisses and Commitment Series
How to See With Your Heart
Angel Matchmaker Series
Kisses Over Candlelight
The Cowboy and the Billionaire's Daughter
Romantic Thrillers
False Identity
False Trust
Promise Me Love
Burned
Contemporary Romance
Beastly Charm
Southern Romance
Livin' in High Cotton

Recipe for Love

The Secret Song of the Ditch Lilies

Short Stories

The Southern Fried Fix

Falling for the Doc Series (Co-authored with Craig Depew, MD)

Cooking with the Doc

Dancing with the Doc

Cruising with the Doc

Winning the Doc's Heart

Saving the Doc

Jackson Hole Firefighter Romance Series

Saving the Billionaire's Daughter

Saving His Heart (Co-authored with Agnes Canestri)

Saving Grace (Co-authored with Amelia C. Adams)

Saving the Rookie (Co-authored with Stephanie Fowers)

Saving the Captain (Co-authored with Jewel Allen)

Saving Forever (Co-authored with Shanna Delaney)

The St. Claire Sisters Series

Meet Me in London (Co-authored with Haley Hopkins)

PROLOGUE

Maddox clutched the bundle of flowers as he willed his feet to move forward. Interesting that he'd gone on scores of SEAL missions and none of them made him as nervous as he was right now. His throat tightened as he swallowed. Maybe it was a mistake to come here. He looked at the large double doors of the resort, forcing himself to relax. For all he knew, Addie might not even be here. She didn't know he was coming, probably thought he was still overseas. He pushed a hand through his hair. What would she think of his ragged appearance? He'd lost a good thirty pounds due to his imprisonment in Syria. His clothes hung on him but he refused to buy more, vowing that he'd gain weight and rebuild his muscle. If it was the last thing he did, he'd take back his life.

What he wanted more than anything was Addie. An image of her flashed through his head, his favorite memory, the one he'd lived by when he was stuck in a filthy cell in Syria. He saw her deep-brown curls blowing in the wind, the tenderness in her smile as she looked at him with fiery green eyes.

He stepped inside the foyer and looked around. There was a woman at the front desk, helping an older couple. He didn't want to ask for Addie and draw attention to himself. Better to see if he could find her. He walked toward her office, stopping in his tracks when he spotted her from a distance. His breath froze in his throat. She was a vision—part fairy, part angel, part vixen—the silky fabric of her emerald dress hugging her curves. It occurred to him that she was overdressed for work. Then he saw a guy in a sport coat and slacks striding toward her, carrying a bundle of red roses. His posture was erect, a confident grin plastered over his face.

Maddox's heart dropped when the guy leaned in and said something as he handed her the roses.

Addie tipped her head back and laughed, gazing adoringly into his eyes.

Nausea rolled in Maddox's gut, and he had the urge to charge forward and punch the guy's lights out. He'd make the guy bleed, make him wish he'd never laid eyes on Addie.

He clutched the flowers. No, he wouldn't do that. Maddox was no longer a prisoner in Syria. Heck, he wasn't even a SEAL anymore. He was a member of polite society—the place where people buried their wounded hearts under polite trivialities and wooden smiles.

His heart thudded dully in his ears as the foolishness of this endeavor flooded through him. Addie didn't want to see him. She'd ended their relationship before he even went to Syria. She was probably glad when she thought he was dead.

No doubt. Maddox was dead to her now.

He dropped the flowers on the floor and turned on his heel, walking swiftly away, before the raging part of him succumbed to the temptation to rip the guy's head off.

ADDIE'S SKIN prickled with the sensation of being watched as she pulled her attention away from her date. She looked toward the foyer, scanning the faces of the people surrounding her. Crazy. For an instant, she'd felt Maddox's presence.

She forced a smile. "Would you please excuse me for a minute? Oh, and can you hold these?" She handed him the roses.

He nodded. "Of course."

Even as she walked in the direction of the foyer, she laughed at herself.

She'd lost count of the number of times she mistakenly thought she'd spotted Maddox in a crowd. Her heart clutched, the longing for him nearly unbearable. She'd thought he was dead. Two days ago, the news came that he was still alive. She'd been waiting on pins and needles, hoping he'd contact her. So far, nothing.

A few paces ahead, she saw a bundle of yellow calla lilies on the floor, wrapped in green ribbon. She hurried forward, picking them up.

Her heart began to pound.

No one except for Maddox knew those were her favorite.

1

SIX WEEKS LATER ...

Addie gritted her teeth as she tightened her hold on the phone, fighting to keep her voice even. "I wish I could just drop everything and leave for San Diego this minute, but I can't. This afternoon a trove of executives from Watermill, Inc. are due to arrive for their conference."

"Are you talking about those water filter guys?"

"Yep," she snipped. "It's the conference I've been planning for six months." She hoped adding that tidbit drove her point home. She couldn't just up and leave. Sure, she was excited about the baby, but she had responsibilities.

Pops let out a long sigh. It had the same effect on Addie's nerves as a pick axe scratching metal. "Isn't there someone else who can fill in for you?"

Addie barked out a laugh. "No, there isn't." Technically, Pops was her grandfather, but he was more like a father. He and his late wife Lou Ella raised Addie and Corbin, her older brother, when their parents were killed. She loved Pops more than anything, but he was the most stubborn man on the planet. This conversation was irritating the heck out of her, especially with everything else she'd dealt with this morning.

"It would be nice if you could be here to support your brother and Delaney." Pops lowered his voice. "Corbin's putting on a good face, but I can tell he's worried about the pre-eclampsia."

Addie pushed a curl away from her eye. Arguing with Pops was as futile as having a shouting match with a fence post. "I thought Delaney was doing better."

"Her spirits are good, but she's really swollen. The doctor's got her on some medicine to stabilize her blood pressure in the hope that she can carry the baby until at least thirty-five weeks."

"That's two more weeks, right?" They'd all been super worried about Delaney. She and Corbin had been through the wringer. They deserved some happiness in their lives. *Please let Delaney and the baby be okay,* Addie prayed silently.

"Yes."

No way could Addie take off work right now. As much as she wanted to be there, it was smarter to wait until the baby was born and then go and visit for a few days. After this week's conference, there was a lull of about two weeks before the next rush was scheduled to begin. Addie planned to go to San Diego then. The baby and Delaney would be okay. They had to be!

She pulled the phone away from her ear when she saw her assistant Sadie rushing towards her. The look of panic on Sadie's face caused Addie's chest to tighten. What was it now? It had been one of those mornings where everything had gone wrong. Half the staff had called in sick. The drain in the sink of the main kitchen was clogged, and it took forever to get a plumber to come out. There was a mix-up with the shuttle service picking the water filter executives up from the airport. Addie called to confirm the appointment, but the office manager had no record of it. The woman went on to add in a snippy, condescending tone that all of her shuttles were booked. It had taken Addie two, long hours of frantic calling to find replacements. When she finally got all the fires put out and had a minute to take a breather, Pops called, hounding her about going to San Diego.

"The caterers are here. They're setting up in the Alpine room," Sadie said breathlessly.

Addie groaned. "No, that's not right. They're supposed to be in the Skyline room. We've already set up the computer equipment for the presentations in the Alpine room." It had taken several hours and a carload of computer geeks to get everything working correctly. No way were they going to tempt fate by switching rooms.

"Who's supposed to be where?" Pops questioned.

"That wasn't meant for you. I was talking to Sadie," Addie explained. She felt like a ping-pong ball zigzagging between two different conversations.

"How's Sadie doing?" Pops asked. "I saw her mother at the grocery store the other day. She said Sadie had just gotten engaged to Buddy Franklin."

Seriously? Pops wanted to talk about that right now? Addie huffed a breath. "Yeah, Sadie's doing great."

"No, I'm not," Sadie countered, wide-eyed. "We have to get the caterers squared away."

"Did you tell them to set up in the Skyline room instead?"

"Yes, but the woman in charge of the catering insists on being in the Alpine room because it's closer to the kitchen." Sadie rolled her eyes, shaking her head.

Addie fought the urge to scream. Sometimes running a resort was like refereeing a bunch of children with sulky attitudes. She gritted her teeth. "The caterers will set up where we want them to. End of story."

Sadie grimaced. "All right. I'll let you tell her that. She's kind of intimidating."

"Intimidating my foot," Addie muttered, her blood running hotter.

"What's going on with your foot? Speak up. It's hard to hear you." Pops' voice was laced with irritation.

Addie rubbed her forehead, thinking how she should've just stayed in bed this morning. "Sorry, Pops. Things are nonstop here right now. I'm gonna have to call you back later." She looked at Sadie. "I'll be right there."

Sadie threw her hands in the air.

Addie held up a finger, her voice ringing with authority. "Tell them to wait for me," she ordered.

Sadie nodded and hurried away.

"I love you, Pops. Bye."

"Wait a minute!"

"Yeah?"

"I thought you'd like to know that Maddox stopped by yesterday to check on Corbin and Delaney."

The air left Addie's lungs as her pulse ratcheted up several notches. It was crazy how the very mention of Maddox's name sent her heart racing.

"He asked about you."

Her mind whirled. "Really?" she sputtered and was instantly frustrated with herself for getting into such a tizzy. She swallowed, sucking in a breath. *He asked about me! What does that mean? That he still cares? No, he was probably just being polite. If Maddox truly cared, he would've contacted me by now.* "How's he doing?" The question left her mouth before she could call it back. She clenched her hand, awaiting the answer.

Pops let out a throaty chuckle. "Pretty good for a dead guy."

Addie's forehead furrowed. "That's not funny, Pops." Her world had come crashing down when she got the news that Maddox and his fellow SEAL members had gone missing while on a mission in Syria. A few weeks later, they were presumed dead. It was her greatest fear coming to pass. She attended his funeral, mourned his death, beat herself up for breaking up with him. Then, like a phoenix rising from the ashes, the news came that Maddox was still alive. Oh, how she'd wanted to run to him then. To tell him that breaking up with him was the biggest mistake of her life. She assumed he'd reach out to her, but she'd heard nothing from him. He'd been back in the states six long weeks and nothing.

She'd learned from Corbin, her older brother, that Maddox had retired from the SEALs and now worked for the same private security company as Corbin. That news didn't come as a surprise. Corbin and Maddox were as tight as brothers. In fact, it was through Corbin that she'd met Maddox. An unbidden image of Maddox Easton flashed before her eyes. Unruly hair, almost as curly as hers, deep blue eyes that held a mischievous twinkle, prominent dimples, and his larger-than-life smile. The captivating Southern twang that made her go weak in the knees. She appreciated Maddox's zest for life and how he never took himself too seriously. The longing for Maddox was so strong, she could taste it. Her throat was drier than sandpaper as she swallowed, trying to clear her brain. It was over between her and Maddox. She'd made sure of that. The all-too-familiar regret pinged through her as she sighed heavily. Yeah, she was an idiot!

"If you were here, you could see Maddox yourself."

A surprise laugh tickled her throat. "Okay, now I'm connecting the dots. You don't want me there because of Corbin and Delaney, you're trying to get me back together with Maddox." The thought sent traitorous tingles circling through her. Instantly, she was irritated at herself. Curse her treacherous body! She'd always been super attracted to Maddox. It was better that it was over between them. She couldn't live in constant fear that something might happen to Maddox. Sure, he'd made it out of Syria alive, but that didn't mean he'd make it out of future scenarios. She wasn't brave enough to love a man like that. She needed stability—a guy she could count on to be there. Not some foolhardy ex-Navy SEAL off chasing danger, so he could delude himself that he was making the world a better place.

She'd made the only decision she could, and she had to stand by that. No matter how much it hurt.

"You miss him, Addie. You're just too dang stubborn to admit it."

She was surprised at the mist that rose in her eyes as she flexed her jaw. "I don't have time to talk about this right now."

Pops' voice grew intense. "Then I suggest you reexamine your priorities and make time. Nothing in this life is guaranteed, Addie. It could all be over tomorrow. Look at poor Delaney, hoping and praying that all will be well with her and the baby. You have to let the people in your life know you love them. Life can change on a dime." His voice quivered as the words lost their air.

Addie knew Pops was talking about Lou Ella, his late wife and

Addie's grandmother, who'd spent the last few years of her life in a care center battling Alzheimer's and then, in a cruel twist of fate, died of brain cancer. Gram's death had left a Grand Canyon-sized hole in all their hearts, but that had nothing to do with Maddox. "I've gotta let you go, Pops."

"I'm not done talking—"

"Bye. Love you," she squeaked, ending the call.

With a heavy sigh, Addie shoved her phone in her pocket and rubbed her sweaty palms against her slacks. Would she run into Maddox when she went to San Diego? The thought rattled her to the core and excited her more than she cared to admit. *Enough thinking about Maddox! Geez.* She was getting all worked up at the mere mention of his name. Not good! She couldn't go down that rabbit hole again. Supposedly time was the cure-all and would help ease the hurt. She grunted. Yeah, that was probably true. In about thirty years or so, she'd be completely over Maddox.

Okay, time to focus on the task at hand. She straightened her shoulders and walked briskly towards the Alpine room. The catering lady had better watch out because Addie wasn't taking any prisoners today!

An hour later, Addie was rushing across the foyer of the Bear Claw Ski Resort. She was headed to a local printing shop to pick up the name tags and lanyards for the water filter execs. Sadie had offered to go, but Addie needed a break from the hustle and bustle of the lodge. Just as she reached the double doors at the entrance, a man called her name. She stopped and turned. "Jordan? What're you doing here? I thought you'd be getting ready for your cruise to the Bahamas. Aren't you flying to Florida tomorrow?"

Jordan Phelps crossed the distance between them with a few long steps and embraced her in a quick hug. "Yes, I'm headed back to New Jersey in a few hours and then Piper and I will leave in the morning."

She looked behind him. "Is Piper with you?"

"No."

He glanced around. "Is there somewhere we can talk?"

Addie groaned inwardly. Of all the days for Jordan to show up unannounced. The executives were due to arrive in less than two hours. It was tempting to tell Jordan that she didn't have time to talk right now, but the words died on her lips. She and Jordan had a long history together. In fact, Addie had been the one who introduced him to his wife. Piper and Addie had been close friends ever since they met several years ago at a support group for caregivers of Alzheimer's patients.

It wasn't in Addie's DNA to turn her back on a friend. She forced a smile. "Sure. Are you hungry?" Her stomach growled as she asked the question. She'd planned to grab something to eat while she was out. Now, there'd be no time for that.

"No, I'm good."

"Okay, let's go out on the terrace. You can get a drink from the café and I'll grab a sandwich to eat, while we talk. I'm starving."

He nodded.

"I was headed out to grab some things for a conference," she explained. "Let me call my assistant and ask her to pick up the items for me."

"I don't mean to intrude on your day," Jordan protested.

She waved a hand. "No worries. Sadie can handle it. I just need to call her right quick." She reached in her purse for her phone.

Jordan nodded again, but she could tell from his distracted expression that he'd barely heard her. She laughed inwardly. *Same old Jordan, his mind always somewhere else.* Lanky with blonde hair and dark eyes, framed by trendy glasses, he reminded her of an absent-minded professor—brilliant, but caught up in his own world. A pharmaceutical scientist with a background in biochemistry, Jordan was the most intelligent person Addie had ever met. The last time she'd seen him, he was on top of the world, telling her that the new drug he was developing at his research facility had the potential to reverse Alzheimer's. Had anyone else made such a bold claim, Addie would've laughed. With Jordan, it was different. He'd made it his life's ambition to eradicate Alzheimer's. He'd lost his mother to the disease. She was in the same care center as Addie's grandmother, which is how she and Jordan first met. They'd formed a strong bond of friendship that had turned into something more. Once Maddox stepped into the picture, however, everyone else, including Jordan, paled in comparison.

After Addie's call to Sadie, she and Jordan went to the café where Addie selected a pre-made chicken salad sandwich and bottle of water. Jordan also grabbed a bottle of water. Next, they went to the terrace and sat down. Addie unwrapped her sandwich and took a large bite, relishing the creamy taste of the mayonnaise combined with the crunchy walnuts and tangy grapes. "I'm so glad you stopped by," she began. "It's always great to see you. I just wish Piper had come with you." As fond as she was of Jordan, she was closer to Piper.

Addie reached for her water and unscrewed the top, taking a large swig.

She looked across the table. Jordan had pushed his bottle of water aside. Hurriedly, she took another bite and put the sandwich down, feeling a smidgen of guilt for being so concerned about eating when it was clear that Jordan wanted to talk.

"How've ya been?" she prompted. It was then that Addie got a good look at Jordan. His face was pale and drawn, worry lines carved deep around his eyes and mouth. A sense of alarm shot through her. "Are you okay?"

He offered a strained smile. "Don't worry about me. I'll be fine."

She sat up straighter in her seat. "What's going on? Is everything okay with the new drug? Uh, what was the name of it?" She took another bite of her sandwich.

"PZT," he inserted.

"Yes, PZT." It was an acronym for a long, technical word that she couldn't remember. "I asked Piper how things were going. She said you're in the final phase of the lab trials and are getting ready to submit an application to the FDA."

"That's the plan."

"It sounds like things are right on track."

He nodded.

"I'm so glad." Emotion welled in her chest. "I only wish you'd developed it soon enough to save Gram and your mother."

Regret flashed in his eyes. "Me too," he said quietly as understanding passed between them. It had been their frustration over the disease, and how it stripped away the essence of the victims, that had first drawn them together and sealed their friendship. Both knew the depth of loss that came with Alzheimer's.

"You did what you could. Now, untold others will be blessed." She reached across the table and squeezed his hand, surprised to find it ice cold. In a deft movement, he flipped his hand over and clasped her hand in his. The close contact made her uncomfortable, but she didn't want to come across as rude by snatching her hand away.

His eyes held hers. "Thank you."

She blinked a couple of times. "For what?"

"For believing in me."

"Of course. I've always believed in you."

A shadow crossed his features. "I know you have. It means the world."

Something flitted in his eyes—sadness, regret? She couldn't pinpoint what the emotion was.

His voice grew reminiscent. "I often wonder what would've happened ... if things had been different," he cleared his throat, "if you and I had ended up together."

She stiffened.

He gave her a wistful smile. "Before you fell head over heels in love with the military guy."

She removed her hand, irritation prickling over her. Was Jordan hitting on her? Surely not! She didn't know what angle Jordan was playing, but she wasn't about to apologize for breaking up with him for Maddox. That chapter of their lives closed eons ago, and she didn't know why he was bringing it up now.

"You're the only one I can trust," Jordan continued.

For a second, she wondered if she'd heard him correctly. She gave him a hard look. "What about Piper? She's your wife ... your business partner." Aside from the fact that Addie knew Jordan and Piper would be perfect together, she introduced them because Piper's father Hamilton Gentry was a renowned brain surgeon turned researcher. Like Addie and Jordan, Piper lost her mother to Alzheimer's. Just as Addie figured, Hamilton took a keen interest in Jordan's work. He secured financial backing from investors and helped Jordan and Piper form a partnership. After Jordan and Piper were married, they, along with Hamilton, moved to New Jersey and opened a research facility.

"Yes, Piper too," he said absently.

"She loves you very much." Addie eyed him, daring him to disagree. She was fiercely loyal to her friend and didn't want Jordan saying anything negative about her.

"Piper's a good woman." He hesitated. "She just doesn't understand."

She frowned. "Understand what?"

He shook his head, an apologetic smile touching his lips. "Never mind."

She could feel nervous energy radiating off him. It was both concerning and confusing. What in the heck was going on? "Are you and Piper okay?"

A tight smile stretched over his lips. "We're great. One of the main reasons I stopped by today is because I'd like to get the earrings and bracelet that match my mother's necklace. I want to give them to Piper on the cruise. I forgot to pick them up when I grabbed the necklace."

Relief surged through her. Jordan and Piper were fine. Of course they were! The two of them were the perfect couple—a match made in heaven. Besides, if something had been wrong, Piper would've told her. "Shoot. You can get the earrings, but the clasp on the bracelet broke. It's at Steinway Jewelers being repaired." She wrinkled her nose. "Sorry."

He waved a hand. "No worries."

A coy smile curved her lips as she crossed her arms and sat back in her seat. "So, how did Piper like the necklace?" A month ago, Jordan called saying he was in town. He asked if he could stop by her house and grab his mother's necklace to give to Piper. Addie was at work but gave him the okay to get them from Pops.

When Jordan's mother Maxine died, Jordan gave Addie her jewelry. At the time, Addie and Jordan were dating, so it seemed logical that he would give her his mother's jewelry. Then they broke up and Jordan married Piper. Addie asked Jordan if he wanted to give the jewelry to Piper, but Jordan declined saying that even though the situation had changed, his mother thought the world of Addie and would still want her to have the items.

"I haven't given Piper the necklace yet. I wanted to wait until we were on our cruise."

"Good idea. I'm glad I didn't say anything to her."

"Me too. It would've ruined the surprise."

Addie made a zipping motion with her lips. "No worries. Your secret's safe with me."

Jordan scooted back his chair and stood. "Can we go now? To get the earrings? Maybe we can stop by Steinway's and grab the bracelet too?"

"Sorry, I can't leave. I have a group of executives arriving shortly."

"Is Wallace home? I can just stop by—"

She winced. "No, sorry, Pops is out of town. Corbin and Delaney are expecting their baby any minute. Pops went to check on them."

"Oh." Disappointment settled over Jordan's features.

"You can take my key and get into the house. The jewelry box is in the top drawer of the dresser in the closet." She reached for her purse and fished for her keys.

"That would be great."

"Just leave the key under the mat after you're done." She removed it from her keyring and handed it to him.

"Thanks."

"Would you like for me to call Mr. Steinway and tell him that you want to pick up the bracelet?" She made a face. "That is, if he's finished repairing it."

"That would be great. Thank you."

She also stood. They embraced as he kissed her on the cheek.

"It was good seeing you, Addie."

"Good seeing you too. Have fun on your cruise." Was it her imagination, or did she detect a note of despondency in his voice?

Her phone buzzed. She reached to retrieve it, but in the process, accidentally knocked over her purse, sending the contents spilling out. "Dang it!" she muttered.

She bent down to pick up the items. Jordan squatted down and helped her put them back into her purse. Her cheeks flushed over how messy her purse was—popcorn kernels had fallen into her purse at a movie she'd attended a week prior and there were scraps of paper and gum wrappers. To her dismay, there was even a tampon. She grabbed it and shoved it into her purse. "Sorry, you had to see all that," she laughed nervously as they stood.

Jordan's features went rigid, fear flashing in his eyes as he looked past her.

She turned to see what he was looking at. The terrace was crowded with people, making it impossible to tell what had jolted him.

"Thanks for everything," he mumbled, walking away so fast that he was nearly jogging.

Addie sat down to finish her sandwich, her mind replaying Jordan's strange behavior. Then she remembered she was supposed to call Mr. Steinway about the bracelet. She'd lose her head if it weren't attached.

She was reaching for her phone when she heard gasps, followed by murmurs.

"Someone's been hit," she heard a woman say.

Her heart in her throat, Addie ran through the foyer and out the front doors. She clutched her chest, holding her breath when she saw a group of people encircling a person on the ground. She caught sight of a brown shoe and blue dress pants—what Jordan had been wearing. Dread screamed through her as she stepped closer. It took a second for her mind to register that the broken man on the ground was Jordan. She rushed to his side. His head was covered in blood, his hand cradling his ribs.

Tears sprang to her eyes as she dropped down beside him. "Oh, my gosh! Call 911," she cried. "Jordan, what happened?"

"He was hit by a black sedan that sped off," a man said.

Jordan gasped for breath, a dazed look in his eyes.

Addie's pulse pounded against her head in hard thrusts. *Please let him be okay*, she prayed. "Hold on. Help is on the way." A burst of dizziness overtook her, and she had the feeling none of this was real.

The cloudiness dissipated from Jordan's eyes for a split second as he focused on her. "Addie," he breathed.

She reached for his hand. "I'm here." Panic rose thick in her throat as her chest constricted to the size of a pea. "He needs help," she screamed, looking around wildly.

"Help is on the way," a woman assured her.

"I've—" Jordan made a gurgling sound as his shoulders convulsed.

"Don't try to talk," she implored.

He coughed, a thin line of blood bubbling from his lips.

A wave of nausea rolled over Addie. She suspected that Jordan was bleeding internally. Tears spilled down her cheeks as she watched his chest go up and down in a futile effort to get air. Jordan was dying before her very eyes, and she was incapable of helping him.

"I've—done—things," he managed to say.

"Rest. Don't talk."

The anguish in Jordan's eyes seared through her like a red-hot knife.

"Please— " he coughed "—forgive me." His eyes glazed, and she felt his hand go slack as life left him.

"No!" she cried, sobbing.

2

Addie knew she needed to call Piper and tell her about Jordan. A part of her wanted to shrink back and let events run their course. Sheriff Hendricks would get around to it in the next few hours.

No, she couldn't wait for him. The news needed to come from her.

Crazy how a few hours ago she'd been going about her life as normal, fretting over the details of the approaching conference. Jordan had done the same—coming to see her so he could get the jewelry to give to Piper. Tears glistened in her eyes. Hopefully, it would bring some comfort to Piper to know his last thoughts had been of her. Addie's heart clutched. That wasn't exactly true. Jordan's last words kept replaying through her mind. What things had Jordan done? Forgive him for what? She pushed her hair out of her eyes and tucked her curls behind her ears as she took in a deep breath. She could do this! She had to hold it together to call Piper!

A knock sounded at the door the second before it opened. Sadie stuck her head in, her wide eyes radiating compassion. "How ya holding up?"

A lump formed in Addie's throat. "Okay," she croaked.

Sadie nodded. "Don't worry about the conference. I've got everything under control. The execs just finished lunch and are headed into the Alpine room for their workshops."

"Thank you." She forced a smile. "What about dinner tonight?"

She raised an eyebrow, a hint of reproof in her voice. "I told you. I'm handling it. We're shuttling them to the Center Street Grill."

Normally, Sadie second-guessed everything, running every insignificant detail past Addie. However, the woman standing before her seemed to have newfound confidence. Or maybe Addie was just hoping Sadie could handle it. Either way, she had no choice but to leave things in her hands—at least for today. "I appreciate all that you're doing."

"You're welcome," she said briskly. "I'd better get back to it." She offered a reassuring smile. "Hang in there." She closed the door.

"I'm trying to," Addie said to herself, "but it's certainly not easy." Was the hit and run an accident? Had the person driving the sedan panicked when realizing he or she hit someone? Or was Jordan murdered? A chill slithered down her spine. Jordan had been frightened when he rushed from the terrace.

Sheriff Hendricks and his deputy had questioned Addie right after the accident. She told them all she knew, which wasn't much. She could tell that the Sheriff was way out of his league. Nothing like this ever happened in the sleepy town of Birchwood Springs, Colorado. Addie grunted. Well, the only other major crime incident that Addie could remember taking place in Birchwood Springs happened a couple of years ago. Her brother Corbin brought Delaney here and her ex-husband's psychotic brother came after her. Why did all the bad things seem to revolve around Addie's family? She shook off the negative thought. Now was not the time to feel sorry for herself. This wasn't about her. It was about Jordan and Piper.

Addie's first impulse was to call Corbin and tell him everything that happened. Corbin had connections in his private security company. No, she couldn't call him now. He had his hands full with Delaney's pregnancy. Maddox! He could help. No sooner had the thought surfaced than she squelched it flat. No way was she calling Maddox. She gritted her teeth.

Okay, she couldn't put it off any longer. She had to call Piper. She reached for her phone. Her heart pounded against her ribcage like the march of doom as it rang. For a split second she thought it might go to voicemail, but Piper answered.

"Hello."

Tears clouded Addie's eyes. A sob rose in her throat as she coughed to clear the emotion.

"Addie? Are you okay?"

"No," she croaked.

"What's wrong?"

Her mind scrambled to find the words. She knew what she needed to say, but couldn't seem to force her tongue to get them out.

"Addie?" Piper asked impatiently.

"It's Jordan," she managed to squeak.

Concern sounded in Piper's voice. "What?"

"He's been killed."

This was met with stunned silence.

The words fell out in a tangled heap. "I'm so sorry. He stopped by the Bear Claw Resort today. As he was leaving, he was hit by a car that sped off."

Piper gasped. Then her voice went shrill. "No, that's not true! Jordan left for work this morning at the research lab. He wasn't even in Birchwood Springs."

Addie's heart felt like it was splintering into pieces. "He was."

"No, that can't be right. There must be some mistake."

"I'm afraid it's true." Her voice sounded small in her own ears. She wanted to crawl into a hole—anything to escape the present.

"No!" Piper made a strangled sound. Then she started weeping.

Tears streamed down Addie's cheeks. "I'm so sorry." She put a fist to her lower lip to stay the quivering. The only sounds were Piper's ragged grief. Addie wished she was there with Piper. It was so cruel to have to tell her this over the phone, but she wanted it to come from her instead of a stranger. "Piper, are you okay?" It was a stupid question. Of course Piper wasn't okay, but what did one say to another person during a time like this?

"I've—" She choked. "I've gotta let you go."

Panic fluttered through Addie. She didn't want to end the call right now, not when Piper was in such a terrible emotional state. "Are you home?"

Silence.

Her voice rose. "Piper, are you home?"

"Yes," Piper finally uttered.

"Are you alone?"

"Dad's here."

The tone of Piper's voice was flat, devoid of emotion like she was in shock.

Addie let out a relieved breath. At least Piper wasn't alone. "I'm so sorry." Her voice broke. There were no words sufficient for this. "I love you. Know that I'm here and will help in any way I can."

"Thanks," Piper croaked as she ended the call.

Addie just sat there, clutching the phone with both hands as she stared into nothing, her mind spinning a million miles a minute. She had to tell Piper everything that happened. However, now wasn't the appropriate time. Jordan was from Birchwood Springs. His funeral and burial would most likely be here. Piper and her dad would come into town. She'd wait and talk to Piper in person, after Piper had a few days to digest the tragedy.

Addie gulped, an avalanche of emotion engulfing her.

Jordan was dead. How was it possible? One minute he was talking to her and the next, he was killed.

Or was he murdered?

BY THE TIME Addie arrived home that evening, she was physically and mentally exhausted. She wanted nothing more than to fall into bed and go unconscious. *Crap!* She gave her key to Jordan and hadn't thought to get it back...after his accident. Reflexively, her hand went to the doorknob as she turned it in frustration. It was unlocked. Had she forgotten to lock it this morning? She never did that.

She pushed open the door and stepped inside, then gasped at what she saw, her hand clutching her throat.

The cabin had been ransacked.

Her knees went wobbly as she backed up against the door and leaned on it for support. She surveyed the damage. Bookshelves were face-down on the floor, books scattered everywhere. Pillows were thrown from the couch, chairs overturned. The refrigerator door was open, the contents spilled over the floor. Cupboard doors were open, food boxes half pulled out. She didn't need to check the other rooms to know that every single household item had been rifled through. This was like something out of a horror movie. With trembling hands, she reached in her purse for her phone. Was someone still here? She looked around, her skin crawling as she feared an attack. She'd put off calling Corbin earlier, but desperate times called for desperate measures. *Please answer*, she prayed.

"Hey, sis."

She realized she'd been holding her breath, waiting for him to answer. "Hey. I'm so sorry to bother you right now with all that you have going."

"No worries. What's up?"

She couldn't keep her voice from shaking. "Jordan Phelps was killed today outside the resort." Tears filled her eyes as the terrible events came rushing back.

"What? How?"

"It was a hit and run."

"Wow. I'm sorry to hear that."

"There's more."

"What else?"

Her heart thudded in her chest like a bowling ball bouncing on concrete. "Someone broke into the cabin and ransacked everything."

Instantly, Corbin went into SEAL mode, firing questions at her. "Are you okay?"

"I think so. I just got home and realized." Her voice dribbled off.

"Where are you now?"

"At home," she said irritably. Had Corbin not heard her the first time?

"I mean, where are you in the cabin?"

"Standing beside the front door."

"So, you don't know if anything was taken?"

"No." The thought of going into the other rooms was more than Addie could take right now.

"Has the intruder left?"

She shuddered. "I'm not sure."

"Get out of there now! Call 911."

Her head began to spin. "Okay." She rushed to the car, her heart sputtering a sickly beat as she jammed in the key with a shaky hand and opened the door. She got in and locked it, looking around at the empty space surrounding her. Shakes started in her hands going down to her toes. Her pulse was making whooshing sounds against her ears. "I'm in the car. Now what?"

"Call 911. They'll come out and search the house and file a report. This is crazy. Why would someone ransack the cabin?"

She let out a harsh laugh. "I have no idea."

"Do you think it's connected with Jordan's death?"

A headache pounded across the bridge of her nose. "I don't know." She rubbed her forehead, letting out a humorless laugh. "I don't know anything anymore. One minute Jordan was talking to me on the terrace, the next he walked out of the resort and got hit by a black sedan that sped off."

Corbin blew out a breath. "Can you get a room at the resort?"

"Yeah, we're not booked at full capacity."

"Okay. Do that. I'll be there first thing in the morning."

"No!" she exploded. "You can't! What about Delaney?" The silence on the other end of the line spoke volumes. "Delaney needs you there. You can't desert her right now." She clenched her jaw, eyes narrowing. If she called Corbin away and something happened to Delaney while he was gone, Addie would never forgive herself. "I didn't call you so you'd come here. I called because I was hoping you might be able to use your connections to find out what's going on."

Long pause. "Okay, I'll see what I can do. In the meantime, call 911 right now. Then call me back so I'll know you're okay."

"Will do." She ended the call and did as Corbin instructed.

As she was calling 911, Addie glanced at the darkening sky. It occurred to her that she was alone in a remote area. Pops rented cabins to tourists who visited the Bear Claw Ski Resort and the nearby hot springs. He and Addie lived in one of the cabins. Just this morning, Addie had appreciated the coolness in the fall, Colorado air and how the leaves were starting to change colors, but now everything seemed ominous and threatening. Shivers snaked down her spine. If someone wanted to harm her, now would be the perfect time. The police wouldn't be able to get here fast enough. While being on the phone with Corbin helped calm her, there was little he could do from San Diego.

Should she leave right now and go to the resort? No, she wanted to be here when the police came. That way, she could see if anything was missing. Her jaw hardened as anger took hold. She had to remain strong—see this thing through.

"911. What is your emergency?" a professional-sounding dispatcher asked.

"Someone broke into my home... Please hurry," she added after she'd given her name and address.

3

A feeling of exhilaration swept through Maddox as the water came up over the sea kayak and splashed him in the face. "Woo hoo!" he yelled, loving the blast of cold wind that whipped through his hair. The kayak nose lifted in the air with the oncoming wave, then dropped a good ten feet down into the ocean with bone-jarring intensity as the wave rushed passed them. "Hold on," he yelled to Felicity, who was sitting in the front.

Felicity shrieked and then cursed. "My hair," she lamented.

"Don't worry. You still look great."

"Yeah, right," she smirked.

It was true. Felicity was beautiful. Too bad he couldn't be as complimentary about her attitude. From the time he picked her up this morning, she'd complained about everything. At the diner, the coffee was too weak, the toast stale. Maddox thought she was going to have an out-of-body experience when she saw the wet suit that the guy at the rental place gave her to put on. "You really want me to wear that grimy thing?" she scoffed, wrinkling her nose in disgust.

"You don't have to wear it," Maddox responded with a casual shrug.

"Good," Felicity sniffed.

"If you want to go into the freezing cold water with nothing more than a t-shirt and shorts, it's your choice."

He swore he could see steam coming out her ears as she snatched the wet suit from the employee and stomped into the dressing room to put it on. A minute or so later, she called out to him saying the wretched thing didn't fit. As it turned out, she had it on backwards.

Maddox leaned forward, paddling with all his might to get them past the breaking waves. Getting the kayak into the water was the hardest part. Once they got past the break, it would be easier to navigate. Splatters of rain hit his face. He looked up at the leaden sky. The water was choppy, the wind picking up. In retrospect, it probably wasn't the best day to come out here. Felicity claimed to love kayaking, but watching her reaction to a few waves and rain, he wondered if she'd only said that to impress him.

Felicity was slapping the water with her oar. An incredulous laugh gurgled in Maddox's throat. "What're you doing?"

"Rowing. What does it look like?" she grumbled.

"Certainly not rowing," he responded under his breath. "Dip your oar down deeper into the water. Use smooth strokes. Put some muscle into it."

He used his oar as a rudder to turn them in the direction of the La Jolla Sea Caves. The seven caves all had their own names and unique features. Maddox never grew tired of exploring them. "Paddle on the right side now," he instructed. "Your other right," he said dryly when she kept rowing on the left. Finally, she switched.

When they got turned in the right direction, Maddox placed his oar in his lap, letting the motion of the current push them forward. "Okay, you can relax a bit," he said when he realized Felicity was still paddling.

She stopped and looked back at him. He did a double-take. She had streaks of mascara running down her face, and her hair looked like blonde glue, matted to her head. Unfortunately, she caught the startled look on his face before he had time to recover.

"What?" She touched her hair. "I look awful, don't I?"

"You look fine." He hoped lightning wouldn't strike him down for telling a lie. No wonder Felicity didn't want to get wet. She looked like a drowned poodle that had black zigzags running down her face. Addie's face flashed before him and with it came a longing that ached through his entire body. He'd brought Addie kayaking. Like him, she was in her element and couldn't get enough of the stories about the folklore and legends surrounding each cave. Addie had whooped and laughed when the waves rushed over them. She'd looked stunningly beautiful with her flawless olive skin, water droplets nestling in her corkscrew curls and shimmering like diamonds in the sun.

He'd not been back to Birchwood Springs since that fateful evening when he saw Addie with another man. Despite everything, he still found himself hoping that Addie would reach out to him. Several times, he'd been tempted to call or text her to see how she was doing. Then he reminded himself that she'd dumped him—said she couldn't handle being with a guy who ate danger for breakfast. "Every time you get deployed, I live in constant fear that you won't come back," she said.

Maddox almost didn't come back. The mission to Syria where he and his fellow SEAL members were captured and tortured by ISIS operatives nearly turned out to be his undoing. The horrors of the ensuing torture at the hands of his captors still haunted Maddox. He'd gone through several rounds of therapy, including eye movement desensitization and reprocessing psychotherapy or EMDR. Surprisingly, EMDR had been the most helpful of all his treatments. While focusing on a repetitive motion or sound, he revisited the upsetting memory. This technique was repeated until Maddox could process the trauma so that it wasn't as distressing.

He'd first heard about EMDR from Creed, a fellow SEAL member who'd been in Syria with him. It seemed like a crock of crap to Maddox, but Creed kept raving about it, so he finally tried it. He was grateful to find something that helped ease his PTSD. Too bad he couldn't find a treatment that would stop him from comparing every girl he went out with to Addie. Talking to Addie's grandfather, Wallace, yesterday brought everything back. It made him miss Addie so much he could hardly stand it. Wallace hinted that Addie missed him and suggested that he reach out to her. He scowled. As much as he wanted Addie back, a relationship required the cooperation of two people, hence the old saying, *It takes two to tango*. Addie had made it crystal clear that she wanted nothing to do with him.

"What is that in the water?" Felicity asked, her voice crackling with tension. "Please tell me it's not a shark."

He looked to where she was pointing and saw a fin. It dipped under the water and back up. He spotted another fin about two feet behind the first. "Those are dolphins."

Her voice grew shrill. "No, they're sharks! Oh, no. What're we going to do?"

Maddox laughed. "Nothing. Just enjoy them. It's not every day you get an up-close look at dolphins."

She shuddered, hugging her arms. "I knew we should've just gone to the movies like normal people. I can't believe I let you drag me out here. It's freezing." She groaned. "And raining!"

Maddox glanced up. It was raining, or rather sprinkling. He'd gotten so caught up in thinking about Addie that he hadn't noticed. "Oh, yeah," he said absently. "Sorry." He chuckled inwardly. What had he been reduced to? Apologizing for the weather? *Sheesh.*

His gaze went up to the mansions perched on the edge of the seventy-foot, craggy cliff running parallel with them as they made their way to the sea caves. He pointed. "See the mansion at twelve o'clock?" Whenever Maddox needed to take the edge off a conversation he went into trivia mode. Before becoming a SEAL, Maddox had worked as a freelance travel writer and photographer, storing up a trove of seemingly insignificant details about people and places. Although, the facts had served him well in Syria when dealing with the guards that held him prisoner. Maddox's motto was, *If you want to get to know the person, get to know his culture.*

"Which one?" Felicity asked dubiously.

Maddox rolled his eyes. Felicity probably had no idea what twelve o'clock meant. She was a total airhead. "The sand-colored mansion directly in front of us." He had to fight to keep the condescension out of his voice. He didn't want to come across as a *know-it-all.*

"Yeah? What about it?" she said in a bored tone.

Why was he even bothering to carry on a conversation with Felicity? She lived in his same condominium complex. When they first met, she seemed fun and upbeat, a nice diversion from his heartache and frustration over Addie. The more time he spent with Felicity, however, the more he realized this was a dead end. They had nothing in common, and her diva attitude was getting old.

"It used to have a guest house below it. Last year, it crashed to the beach."

"You're making this up."

"No, I'm one hundred percent serious. The land is constantly eroding. Where people used to have twenty or more feet of land beyond their decks and pools, the structures are now teetering on the edge. In another fifty years, there's a good chance that all the mansions you see right now will be gone. If investors were smart, they'd buy up the homes one row behind the ones on the edge. Then as soon as their neighbors' homes crash to the beach below, they'll have an unencumbered view of the ocean." He'd hoped for at least a courtesy laugh for his joke, but she remained quiet, an awkward silence descending over them.

He pointed. "See that mansion three houses to the right of the sandstone one?"

"Yep."

"The children's author Dr. Seuss was friends with the owner. Legend has it that Dr. Seuss loved to attend parties there. He'd stay late into the evening. And his—"

She let out a loud sigh. "Is there a point to this story?"

Maddox flinched like he'd been slapped. Had she really just said that to him? "I was getting to the point, before you so rudely interrupted me."

She grunted. "Fine. Continue."

For a second, Maddox almost didn't tell her the rest, but then he decided to be the bigger person. "His wife didn't like going to the parties. She'd stay home and get irritated that her husband was gone so long. She'd call and nag him to come home. The experience gave him material to write *The Grinch that Stole Christmas*."

"Huh. Interesting," she said in a flat tone.

Maddox made a split-second decision. "All right. Date's over. I'm taking you home." And *I won't be asking you out again*, he added mentally.

"Finally!" she exclaimed. "I'm ready to get out of this horrid wet suit. I hate to even think of the germs lurking inside it."

When they were back at the rental company changing into their regular clothes, Maddox got a call from Corbin. He answered on the first ring. "Hey, man."

"Hey," Corbin clipped.

Maddox's pulse jumped up a beat. "Has Delaney had the baby?" During his visit the day before, he could tell that Corbin was worried about her delivering too early. If she'd gone into labor this soon, it could be precarious for the baby.

"No, not yet. Thankfully, the medicine seems to be controlling her blood pressure."

"Good. I'm glad Delaney and the baby are okay. What's up?"

Slight pause. "I'm calling to ask a favor."

"You got it. What can I do for you?" Maddox and Corbin had first met when they were both in the SEALs. Even though they were never in the same platoon, their paths kept crossing. They hit it off instantly and became fast friends. When Corbin married Delaney, another connection was added to their friendship. Like Maddox, Delaney was from Alabama. Also, Maddox was a big fan of Delaney's music, listening to it long before he'd ever met her. Now that Maddox was working for Sutton Smith's security company—same as Corbin—the two were closer than ever.

"Addie's house was broken into last night. She's in trouble. I need you to protect her. I'd go, but I can't leave Delaney right now."

The air left Maddox's lungs. The urge to get to Addie was all-consuming.

"I can't get this stinking thing off," Felicity complained from the dressing room stall. "I hate this putrid thing! Maddox, help!"

He moved the phone away from his mouth. "Just a minute."

Felicity countered with a string of complaints, but Maddox ignored her, moving to the other side of the dressing room.

He turned his attention back to the conversation. "What's going on?" As Corbin gave him the rundown, his muscles tensed. If anyone dared to hurt Addie, he'd shred him to pieces.

"I spoke to Sutton. He's going to check into Jordan Phelps. Sutton's getting a plane ready for you."

Maddox calculated the time it would take to drop Felicity off and then gather his things. "I can be wheels up in less than two hours."

4

Addie felt like a zombie as she went through the motions of taking care of the Watermill conference. Thankfully, Sadie had picked up the slack, coming through like a champ. When all this was over, she needed to give Sadie more responsibility and a raise.

She glanced at the large stack of unpaid invoices on her desk. Betty Burnell the payroll clerk and part-time bookkeeper handled the actual payment of the invoices, but Addie liked the invoices to cross her desk first, so she could check everything before payment was issued. As manager, the buck stopped with her, and she wanted to make sure she was aware of all taking place on her watch.

Blowing out a long, resigned breath, she settled into her chair and picked up the invoices. She'd go through these and return several phone calls. Tomorrow, Piper and her father Dr. Hamilton Gentry were due to arrive in town. Preparations were underway for the funeral, which would take place next Wednesday, a week from today. Addie planned to talk to Piper about Jordan tomorrow. The home invasion the night before added to her tension, making her eager to speak to Piper in the hope that she could shed some light on the strange things Jordan had said just before he died.

Thirty minutes later, Addie was done with the invoices and calls. She sat back in her seat, twirling a pen in her fingers, her thoughts going to the break-in at her home. When the police arrived, or rather Sheriff Hendricks with his young deputy in tow, Addie sifted through the wreckage trying to figure out if anything was missing. From what she could tell, nothing had been taken, which made the situation even more puzzling. What had the person or people been looking for? Her room was the worst. Documents, books, magazines, and photos were strewn over the floor. Her clothes and undergarments were removed from her dresser and heaped on the floor like garbage. She felt so violated and vulnerable. Every time she thought of someone going through her things, she felt sick. And it wasn't just her things, Pops' too. It was all Addie could do to keep going. What she really wanted was to curl up in a ball and cry.

Tears glistened in her eyes as she swallowed. She still couldn't believe Jordan was gone. Her stomach growled, reminding her that she'd not eaten breakfast or lunch, and it was two o'clock. The easy thing would be to grab a sandwich at the café. She recoiled at the thought. She couldn't do it, not while Jordan's death was fresh on her mind. The café and terrace were the last places Jordan had been. No way could she get a sandwich from the café as she had yesterday. Even if she took it back to her office to eat, it would still be too painful.

She reached for her purse, slinging the strap over her shoulder. She'd run out and grab something. Getting away from the resort would do her good. Despite Corbin's protests, Addie planned to go home after work and spend a few hours putting her house back together. She assured Corbin that she'd go back to the resort to sleep. She grimaced. Staying at the resort was like being at work 24/7. She gritted her teeth, anger surging through her. She refused to be cowed by whomever was doing this. Corbin insisted on installing a topnotch security system that he could access on his cell phone. The guys were scheduled to come out tomorrow. As soon as the new system was installed, Addie was going home.

Autumn was Addie's favorite time of the year. Nothing was more glorious than Birchwood Springs with the splendor of the changing leaves and the snow-capped, hazy blue mountain range in the distance. However, Addie hardly noticed the scenery as she walked to her car and unlocked the door. She stopped, the hair on the back of her neck lifting as she looked around the parking lot. Not another person was in sight, but she felt like someone was watching her. A shiver ran down her spine as she quickly got into her car and locked the door. From the safety of her car, she felt a little bolder as her eyes combed the parking lot.

Nothing.

Maybe she was being paranoid. How could she not be? Jordan had been mowed over in front of the resort. It had taken her a half hour and some fancy talking to ease the water filter exec's safety concerns. This morning, she'd held a special meeting with the staff, instructing them what to say to ease guest concerns, especially the front desk personnel. Just as Addie feared, many of the guests bombarded the front desk, asking about the hit and run.

Addie clutched the steering wheel with both hands as she drove into the downtown district and turned into a parking space in front of a popular deli. Normally, there were long lines, but with it being after two o'clock, she hoped to be in and out quickly.

As she walked from her car to the deli, her skin crawled with the suspicion that she was being watched. Her pulse throbbed against her neck as she looked around. A young mother, pushing a stroller, came toward her. The woman offered a polite smile and nodded as she passed.

"Hello," Addie said, pushing out a tight smile. An elderly man and woman were walking arm in arm. The man held a cane, using it for support as they trudged forward.

The wind picked up, cutting through Addie's lightweight sweater and raising goosebumps over her flesh. She looked up at the leaves on the nearby trees, dancing in the wind, their soft rustle filling the air. Her gaze went to the parked cars. Empty. She scoured the surrounding area, finding nothing amiss. Was she being paranoid because of everything that had happened? Probably.

She folded her arms over her chest, continuing into the deli.

"Welcome to Grater's. Sit anywhere you'd like," a short-haired blonde said with a friendly smile.

"Thanks." The woman must be new. Addie didn't recognize her. She sat down at a table by the wall. Out of habit, she retrieved a menu from the stack behind the metal napkin holder and perused the menu, knowing all the while she'd decide on her usual—a turkey club and fries.

The server approached removing her pen from behind her ear as she took Addie's order and scribbled it on her pad. "Good choice, hon."

Addie bit back a smile, not wanting to tell the woman that she'd been coming here for years. She probably knew the menu better than the server. She glanced at her name tag, committing it to memory. *Cindy.*

"Would you like anything to drink?" Cindy asked in a singsong voice.

"Just water with lemon."

"Sure thing," she quipped.

"Thanks, Cindy."

"You're welcome." A large smile filled Cindy's face as she nodded in appreciation. "I'll be right back with your water."

In the hospitality industry, Addie had learned the value of using people's names. It created a sense of familiarity, letting the person know you cared. As Cindy strolled away, Addie sat back in her seat, taking in a deep breath. She had to laugh at herself for thinking of something as trivial as hospitality tips in a time like this. It was engrained in her. Maybe she was trying to concentrate on something other than the fact that her former boyfriend, the husband of her best friend was killed. And someone had ransacked her home, yet didn't take anything.

Corbin assured her that he would look into the situation and call her as soon as he knew something. Addie had not heard from him today. In this instance, no news was not good news. She glanced across the room and caught eyes with a familiar face. *Crap!* Madison

Wells, the last person Addie wanted to speak to right now. Madison had been crushing on Corbin for years. Addie used to get great delight out of teasing Corbin about Madison, which was fine because it was Corbin dealing with Madison, not Addie. Madison was eating lunch with a couple of her girlfriends, former high school cheerleaders, the same as Madison. The adage, *Birds of a feather flock together* ran though Addie's mind. She'd never particularly liked any of the girls. They were too superficial and snotty for her taste. Madison smiled brightly and waved. Addie held up her hand in a stiff half-wave. That's all it took for Madison to stand up and trot over. Addie groaned inwardly. It didn't take a brain child to guess why Madison wanted to talk to her. Madison always had an agenda.

"How are you?" Madison cooed, giving her an over-the-top concerned look.

"Fine," Addie said tersely.

Madison touched her arm. "That's terrible about the accident at the resort."

"Yes, it was." The idea was to keep her answers short and sweet, without providing additional information Madison could use as fodder for gossip.

Madison sat down across from her. "What exactly happened?" Her eyes went large as she leaned forward, intent on catching every word.

"Jordan was hit by a car." The words sounded so plain and impersonal. In an instant, Jordan's life had been snuffed out and Piper's was changed forever.

"Yes, I heard that part," Madison said impatiently with a wave of her hand. "Was it a random thing, or was he targeted?"

"No one knows at this point."

"It's terrible," Madison lamented, shaking her head. "Wasn't he a friend of yours?" The tone of her voice was innocent, but the perceptive look in her eyes spoke otherwise.

After the past two days she'd had, Addie was in no mood for silly games. She folded her arms over her chest, eyeing Madison. "Cut the crap. You know he was. And you also know that he married Piper, my best friend." Madison knew every scrap of gossip in Birchwood Springs, including the fact that Addie and Jordan used to date. Addie felt a little guilty for being so blunt. Pops and Corbin were always cautioning her to temper her sharp tongue. It only took a second, however, for Madison to come back swinging.

"Oh, yeah. I remember now. Geez. You're so sensitive," Madison blustered, flipping the ends of her shoulder-length, platinum hair. "His death is a tragedy, for sure. I hope it doesn't hurt business at the resort," she said in a sugary voice, a smug glitter in her light eyes.

Addie's eyebrows shot up. "Why would it?" she demanded. The comment struck way too close to home. The hit-and-run was bound to cast a negative light on the resort. Hot prickles pinged her like a thousand needles. This could be a PR nightmare. She'd worked hard all these years and finally landed her dream job as manager. Now this was happening! Addie pushed aside the negative thought. She had to focus on one thing at a time. The first order of business would be to find out what had been going on in Jordan's life—why he asked for her forgiveness. Hopefully, Piper could shed some light on the situation when she arrived in town tomorrow.

Cindy returned with the water. She turned to Madison, a perplexed expression crossing her features. "Weren't you just over there?" She rolled her eyes in the direction of the table across the room where Madison's girlfriends were sitting.

Madison chuckled. "Smart girl," she quipped, her voice coated with condescension.

Cindy was not amused. She just stared at Madison with a deadpan expression. Addie smiled inwardly watching Madison squirm.

"I just wanted to come over and say hello to my friend," Madison trilled.

It was all Addie could do to keep from bursting out laughing. *Friend? More like frenemy.*

"Your food will be ready shortly," Cindy said, moving to the next table.

Madison instantly went back to the topic at hand. "Like you said, no one knows if the incident was directly related to Jordan or if he happened to be at the wrong place at the wrong time." She shrugged. "Maybe the resort is being targeted."

"No, I don't think so." This had to be tied to Jordan. Why else would someone break into her home and search through her things? What was someone looking for? Jordan had never given Addie anything important. Well, except for his mother's jewelry. She'd checked all the pieces last night. Everything was still there, right down to the earrings Jordan wanted to give Piper.

"You know something you're not telling."

The accusation jerked Addie out of her thoughts. Madison was assessing her with the eyes of an eagle on the hunt.

She laughed lightly. "I've said all I'm at liberty to say on the subject."

Madison's brows furrowed as she harrumphed. "I see." She brightened. "How's Corbin?"

Addie chuckled inwardly. "He's good. He and Delaney are expecting a new baby any day." *Take that, Madison Wells! What further proof do you need that Corbin isn't interested in you? He's having a baby with another woman.*

A scowl overtook Madison's features, then she shuddered placing her hands over her flat stomach. "I don't think I could ever put my body through that torture. It would never go back to normal."

"I'd hardly call it torture," Addie laughed. "Corbin and Delaney are deliriously happy and can't wait for the baby to be born." The pinched expression on Madison's face gave Addie a twinge of satisfaction. She was so grateful Corbin hadn't ended up with Madison. That would've been disastrous. Addie adored Delaney, almost as much as Corbin did. Even though Delaney was a country music superstar, who had every reason to be uppity, she was the most down-to-earth person on the planet with zero guile. Not competitive in the least, as opposed to Madison who felt the need to chomp everyone down to size to make herself feel superior. Addie knew she shouldn't rise to the bait where Madison was concerned, but she couldn't seem to stop herself.

The light in the room shifted as the door to the diner opened. Addie glanced as a man entered. There was something familiar about his carriage and stride. Her heart leapt in her throat as she did a double-take. She'd recognize those unruly curls and the determined set of his chiseled jaw anywhere. The room did a quick spin. Addie had the feeling that her chair was falling out from beneath her as she fought to regain her bearings.

Everyone else in the room vanished as he strode toward her with quick, purposeful steps like a man on a mission. "Hey," he said, a bemused smile tipping the corners of his lips.

Funny, the things her mind captured in an instant—his cut biceps, the definition of his pec muscles underneath his navy t-shirt, how he exuded masculinity. She glanced at his long legs encased in Levis as heat crept up her neck. "Maddox," she squeaked, clutching her throat. "What're you doing here?"

5

Maddox pulled out a chair and sat down across from her. He'd wondered if Corbin would tell Addie he was coming. Judging by her bug-eyed look, Corbin hadn't. He allowed himself a moment to drink in Addie's exquisite features. How many times had he dreamt of running his hands through her thick tresses of curly hair? Most often in his dreams, her lively green-gold eyes held a twinkle of mischief. Today, however, they were shadowed with concern. There were faint circles under Addie's eyes, and she looked pale. The temptation to reach out and place a comforting hand over hers was so strong that he clasped his hands together, instead, so he wouldn't make a fool of himself.

Addie gave him an intense look that bordered on irritation. "Why're you here?"

He tensed. *No, Happy to see you. I'm glad you're alive. I'm sorry I carved out your heart and stomped it into the ground.* Was Addie really so heartless? Disappointment pummeled through him. What had he expected? That she would fall into his arms? Tell him that she made a big mistake by breaking up with him? That she still loved him?

Only in his dreams. Anything he and Addie had shared dried up months ago. He'd do well to keep his emotions contained. He was here because of Corbin. He'd do what it took to protect Addie before getting the heck out of Dodge.

Maddox realized Addie was awaiting his answer. He cleared his throat, glancing at the woman sitting beside Addie. "Can I speak to you in private?" He gave the woman an apologetic look. "No offense."

A seductive smile snaked over the woman's lips. "None taken." She gazed into his eyes with a star-struck expression, like she'd just seen her first Corvette. "Your accent is adorable," she gushed. "What part of the South are you from?" she asked, mimicking his accent.

He cringed. One of Maddox's pet peeves was when people poked fun at his accent. A phrase from the movie *Sweet Home Alabama* ran through his mind. *Honey, just 'cause I talk slow doesn't mean I'm stupid.* He caught Addie's amusement from across the table. She knew exactly how he felt about the topic. The distance between them shrank, and they shared a silent exchange. For an instant, the connection between them ran stronger than steel. Then Addie seemed to realize what was happening and quickly looked down.

"I'm sorry. Did I say something wrong?" The woman looked back and forth between Maddox and Addie, a befuddled look on her face.

Maddox shook his head and chuckled under his breath. The woman obviously meant no harm. "No, you're good." He tried to catch Addie's eyes, but she wouldn't look at him.

"The name's Madison. What's yours?"

"Maddox."

The woman leaned in, an open invitation brimming in her light eyes as she brushed her hand against his. "Are you new in town?"

An embarrassed laugh hiccuped in his throat as he looked at Addie. Her face had turned darker than an eclipse, and she looked like she wanted to scratch the blonde woman's eyes out. A jolt of surprise raced through Maddox. Was Addie jealous? The notion kindled hope in him. Normally, he'd give the man-hungry Barbie the brush-off. However, this could work to his advantage and be payback for seeing Addie with another man. Of course, Addie had no idea that he'd flown in to see her. Still, it hurt all the same. Maddox flashed a large smile, which he was sure looked goofy. "Yes, I just arrived."

The woman let out a throaty laugh as she made a point of panning over him with an appreciative eye. "Oh, honey. From the looks of it, I'd say you arrived a long time ago."

Maddox's skin crawled, and he felt like a piece of slimy meat.

Addie's eyebrow shot up, her features twisting in a hard amusement. "Maybe I should leave you two alone."

"Maybe you should," Madison agreed, touching Maddox's arm. Inwardly, he recoiled. Forward women always turned him off. Madison was obviously on the prowl. He second-guessed this plan to make Addie jealous. It was working, but no way could he stand to be around Barbie for any length of time. She made Felicity look like the catch of the century, and she hadn't impressed him. The sad truth was that no woman could compare to Addie. Not only was she beautiful, she was spunky and smart. Simply being in her presence made him feel more alive than he'd felt in a very long time. Too bad she wanted nothing to do with him. He wondered about the guy he'd seen with Addie. Were they involved? The notion sent a fireball of jealousy spiraling through him.

A server approached with a plate of food. She placed it in front of Addie, but her eyes remained trained on Maddox. "Hey," she said, interest lighting her features.

Oh, no. Not her too! "Hey, how ya doing?" Maddox said with a curt nod. What was it about the women in this town? They acted like they'd never seen a man before. If only Addie were one-tenth as enamored with him. Even when they were together, she'd played it cool, always making him work for her affection. As frustrating as it was, he liked that about her.

"Can I get you something to eat?" the server asked.

A wicked idea took root in his mind. "Just an extra plate." He looked at Addie. "I'll share with her."

Her eyebrow lifted. "Oh, no you won't."

"Come on, Addie," he drawled, laying his Southern accent on thick. "It'll be like old times." He reached over and grabbed one of her fries and plopped it into his mouth.

"Fine," she relented, rolling her eyes.

"One extra plate coming right up. What would you like to drink?"

"Club soda with lime."

"You got it," the server clipped, walking away.

"My name's Madison, by the way."

"You said that already," Addie said dryly. "But in your defense, it must've flown right out of your head." She wrinkled her nose, a cheeky smile curving her lips. "All that air."

Maddox coughed to cover his startled laugh. He put a hand over his mouth, feeling like a louse, especially when he saw Madison's downcast expression.

She managed to hitch the corners of her smile up quickly though. "You should come over and let me introduce you to my friends. I'm sure they'd love to meet you," she chirped. He followed Madison's look and saw the women at the table. They flashed gargantuan smiles and waved. He nodded and waved back. *Awkward.*

Madison stood and tugged on his arm. "Come on."

This was getting out of control fast—a runaway train with no brakes, headed for a cliff.

"Thanks, but I came here to speak to Addie."

Madison's lips turned down into a pout. "That's too bad."

It was fun watching the triumphant expression on Addie's face.

"Nice meeting you, Madison," he said, signaling that their conversation was over.

She touched her hair, uncertainty creeping into her eyes. "Would you like my number?"

His lips turned down. "I'm afraid not. My girlfriend wouldn't like that very much." He glanced at Addie as he spoke and saw a flicker of surprise before a curtain veiled her eyes.

Madison's smile faltered. "Who's your girlfriend?" Her hand went to her hip. "Addie?" She asked the question like it left a nasty taste in her mouth.

A beat stretched long and tense as Maddox looked across the table at Addie. Her expression was unreadable. "No," he finally said. "That ship has sailed." The finality of the words clunked against his insides like nails in a coffin. "Her name is Felicity."

Madison flicked her hair. "Too bad. If you ever change your mind, look me up." Her gaze lingered on him long enough to make him feel uncomfortable.

"Sure thing." He offered a polite smile.

She turned on her heel and sauntered back to the table across the room.

Addie took a large bite of her sandwich. She chewed and washed it down with a drink of water. "It looks like you made quite an impression on Madison Wells. Congratulations. She's been chasing Corbin for years. Now that she realizes he's taken, she's setting her sights a little lower."

"Ouch. You know how to hit a man where it hurts, don't you?" A grin slid over his lips. "Admit it. You were jealous."

Color seeped into Addie's cheeks, making her look adorable. "Was not!"

He laughed. "You were and you know it."

Her eyes flashed. "You wish."

Well, he couldn't argue with that. Addie's feistiness was one of the things he loved most about her. He winced inwardly at the word *love*. Somehow, he was going to have to find a way to rid her from his system.

The server returned with the club soda and extra plate. "If you need anything else, let me know."

Maddox smiled. "Thanks."

Addie kept eating. He motioned at the food. "Are you gonna share, or what?"

She pursed her lips. "I suppose." He slid the empty plate towards her. She reached for a handful of fries and plopped them on his plate. Then, she placed half a sandwich beside the fries—the half she'd eaten from.

He laughed in surprise. "Seriously?"

Her eyes met his in defiance. "Seriously. You charge in here unannounced and interrupt my lunch." She shoved the plate in his direction. "Beggars can't be choosy."

Man, Addie had moxie. Never a dull moment with her. "All right. I guess I'll take what I can get." He took a bite of the sandwich. It was very good.

"You never did answer my question."

"Huh?" He took a drink of the club soda, appreciating how it burned down his throat.

She leaned forward. "Why're you here?"

He rolled his eyes, growing tired of Addie's accusatory attitude. "It shouldn't take a genius to connect the dots. Corbin sent me to protect you."

She'd been about to take a bite of a fry. Instead, she threw it down. "Are you kidding me?"

"Nope." He put a fry in his mouth and made a point of chewing it slowly. He wasn't going to let Addie get him riled. He'd promised Corbin he'd help and that's what he was here to do.

She scoffed, shaking her head. "This is just like my brother to use Jordan's death as an opportunity to get us back together."

He tensed. "Don't flatter yourself, darlin'. This has nothing to do with our past relationship. Yes, I was upset when you dumped me, but I moved on."

Something indiscernible flashed in her eyes. "With Felicity."

He had the urge to laugh uncontrollably. Felicity? Couldn't he have come up with a better option than her?

Her eyes widened. "You know why I broke up with you."

"Yes, you explained your reasoning very thoroughly." The hurt and anger rushed back with a vengeance.

She clutched her napkin. "I thought you were dead."

"Sorry to disappoint you."

He was surprised to see tears glistening in her eyes. "I went to your funeral. Mourned your death."

A gush of tenderness crowded out the anger. This time, he couldn't stop himself from touching her hand. Electricity zinged through him when their skin connected. He could tell from her startled expression that she felt it too. For a second, he forgot about his own heartache and thought about everything Addie had been through. In her defense, it would be hard to love someone with a dangerous profession. He'd come very close to not coming back from Syria. While he and his fellow SEALs had escaped, they were still living with the emotional scars. Even though he was no longer a SEAL, his profession was still just as dangerous. "I'm sorry for all of the turmoil I've put you through."

She jerked like she'd not heard him correctly.

"I mean that." She'd not moved her hand from underneath his. Warmth from her skin seeped into him and he felt like time had been peeled away, that they'd never been apart. Then in the time it took for him to take his next breath, something changed. She removed her hand and sat back, drawing into herself. What in the heck had just happened? Sometimes, Addie completely mystified him. There was only one way to make this job work. He had to clear the air once and for all, put her at ease about their relationship.

"Look, you don't need to worry. I didn't come here to try and start things up with you." *Liar*, his mind screamed. "I came because Corbin said you were in trouble. He couldn't come, so I took his place."

Her lips formed a tight line. "I see."

"I'll always care about you as a friend." The words rang false in his own ears. "Like I told Madison, I'm with someone else now."

"Felicity."

"Yes." He forced a smile. "So you see, you have nothing to worry about."

Her eyes went harder than granite. "That's good to know." She scooted back her chair and stood. "You know what? I appreciate you coming, but I don't need any help."

He jumped to his feet. "How can you say that?" He lowered his voice. "You don't know why someone killed Jordan or why your home was broken into. Corbin's worried sick about you. Even as we speak, he's getting his boss to check into the situation."

"You mean the billionaire philanthropist Sutton Smith. Who's also your boss."

"Yes." He didn't know how much Addie knew about Sutton's

private security company, so he figured it was better to keep the conversation generic.

She raised her chin. The look in her eyes reminded him of a headstrong horse about to bolt. "I'm sorry you wasted a trip, but I don't need your help."

He caught hold of her arm. "Don't be ridiculous, Addie. This is a serious situation. From the sound of it, you need all the help you can get."

Fire flashed in her eyes. "Not from you." She jerked her arm out of his grasp. "Go back to your girlfriend," she muttered as she stomped out.

Crud! He couldn't let her go like that. He needed to keep her in his sight at all times. She was the most stubborn, infuriating woman on the planet. He thought she'd be relieved if he told her he had a girlfriend, but she was acting ticked about it, which made no sense. Addie had broken up with him, not the other way around.

He pulled his wallet from his pocket and slapped down a twenty-dollar bill before rushing after her.

6

_____

Addie's mind was on fire as she drove away from the diner. Too furious to go back to work, she headed for home. When she turned onto the highway leading to the cabin, she reached in her purse for her phone. Holding the steering wheel with one hand, she called Corbin with the other.

He answered on the first ring. "Hey, sis."

"How dare you get Maddox to come here!" she exploded. "You had no right to interfere with my personal relationship."

There was a stunned silence on the other end of the line. She clutched the phone tighter. "Are you there?"

"I'm here," came his curt reply. "You called me for help, remember?"

She blew out a breath. "Yeah, that was my first mistake."

"Seriously?" Corbin barked out a laugh. "What crawled up your shorts? You need to take it down a few notches, so we can discuss this like adults."

A hysterical laugh bubbled in her throat. "You're telling me to be an adult? Ha! That's ironic."

"What do you mean by that?"

It was on the tip of Addie's tongue to unload on Corbin, rehashing events from their past like how when Gram got sick, Corbin left, leaving her holding the bag. She stared at the ribbon of road ahead, tears stinging her eyes as she clutched the steering wheel with both hands, the phone cradled on her shoulder. She and Corbin were in a good place now. She couldn't keep blaming him for the past. Corbin had done a one-eighty, turned his life around. He was worried sick about his wife and baby. She didn't need to add stress to the situation.

Concern sounded in Corbin's voice. "Are you okay?"

She gulped, trying to keep a lid on the avalanche of emotion building in her. "I'm sorry. I'm just so frustrated about everything." Tears spilled down her face.

"I know. This isn't something you can handle alone. You need help, which is why I sent Maddox."

She gritted her teeth. "Surely there's someone else who—"

"I trust Maddox," he inserted. "Him being there with you is as good as me being there." He paused. "Look, whatever's going on between the two of you ... well, my advice is to table it until this ordeal is over."

"Excellent advice from an outsider looking in." She barked out a laugh.

"I don't exactly qualify as an outsider, sis."

She drew in a ragged breath, trying to calm down.

Corbin switched gears. "I'm glad you called. Sutton's guys were able to gather some intel on Jordan."

Her breath caught as she swallowed. "What?"

"I was going to wait and tell you and Maddox this at the same time, but I'll go ahead and tell you now. Jordan was working on a new drug for Alzheimer's."

"PZT."

He sounded surprised. "How did you know?"

"Jordan told me."

"Jordan and Piper were joint owners of a company called Therapia."

Addie knew all about the company. "Yes, it's a derivative of the Greek word for cure. Piper's dad, Hamilton Gentry, is heavily involved in the company as well. Hamilton's in charge of securing financial backing to fund the research. Shortly after Jordan and Piper got married, they started a research facility in New Jersey."

"That's correct." Corbin's voice was factual and to-the-point. "Therapia is in the final phase of their laboratory trials on PZT and is getting ready to submit an application to the FDA."

"Yes, I know all that," she said impatiently.

"I'm impressed."

She rolled her eyes. "Duh. Piper and Jordan are two of my closest friends. I know just about everything about them. Plus, Piper and Hamilton still have their home in Liberty Falls. They travel back and forth. I get together with Piper whenever she's in town."

"Did you know they were having serious marital problems?"

"What?" Her head began to spin. "That's not true. They were supposed to leave the day after Jordan was killed for a cruise to the Bahamas. I talk to Piper on a regular basis, the two of them were good."

"Not according to Sutton's investigators."

"Then the investigators are wrong," she nearly shouted.

Silence.

"Corbin, are you still there?"

"I'm here. Look, I'm sure this is hard to process, but you've got to remove your personal feelings. According to Sutton's investigators, Jordan and Piper were on the verge of divorce. Jordan had already spoken to an attorney."

Addie felt betrayed and confused. Why would Piper and Jordan not tell her they were having problems? Something Jordan said came rushing back. *"You're the only one I can trust."* Was that Jordan's way of hinting that things weren't right between him and Piper?

Her throat constricted to the size of a straw as she swallowed. "Do you think PZT had something to do with Jordan's death?"

"At this point, it's merely a theory. If PZT really can cure Alzheimer's..." He let out a low whistle. "Think of the billions upon billions of dollars it would be worth. That's certainly motive enough for someone to kill."

"Yeah, but why kill the developer?"

He paused. "I don't know. There are still too many missing pieces to form a clear picture."

"Why did someone break into my house? They didn't even take anything."

"You were the last person to see Jordan alive. Maybe someone thinks you know something."

"Well, I don't," she barked. "All I know is that I'm getting sick and tired of the whole situation." She swallowed. "I just want this to be over, so I can get on with my life."

"Hang in there, sis. I'm working on it from this end. In the meantime, you need to stay close to Maddox so he can keep you safe."

She let out a humorless laugh thinking of how she'd sent him packing. "Sorry, bro, but I'm afraid my meeting with Maddox didn't go so well. He's probably on his way back to San Diego by now." *With Felicity*, she added mentally.

Short pause. "No, Maddox is too diehard to let a few harsh words stand between him and a mission."

Diehard! She rolled the word around in her head a couple of times. Maddox might be a diehard former SEAL, but it was too bad he wasn't as diehard when it came to relationships. Fickle was what he was!

A thick layer of ice encased her heart. This was merely a job to Maddox. He'd made that very clear. When he'd strolled into the diner, she thought she was imagining things—her brain conjuring up her greatest desire. Then he touched her hand, evoking a longing she could hardly contain. For a moment, she'd let her guard down when she saw the tenderness in his eyes, then she thought of Felicity. Her eyes narrowed. Maddox had only been back from Syria a little over a month and he'd already replaced her with another woman. She was unprepared for the hurt that pummeled through her like a battering ram. Fresh tears stung her eyes. He was probably grateful that she'd broken up with him and saved him the trouble of dumping her.

"Don't make Maddox's job harder, sis." There was a hint of teasing in his voice. "I know it's hard for you, but can you try to be a little accommodating?"

She grunted.

"He's trying to keep you safe." Corbin's voice caught. "With all I've got going right now, I need to know that you're okay."

Addie felt like a louse. Corbin had a mountain of his own troubles right now. She was adding to his list. "Okay, I'll play nice."

"That's good," he breathed in relief. "After this is over, you and Maddox can go your separate ways."

"Yeah." Her heart felt like lead in her chest. She didn't want to talk about Maddox anymore. "How's Delaney doing?"

"So far so good. We just keep praying for time. It's like walking a tightrope—making sure Delaney's health is okay, while trying to keep the baby in her womb long enough to be out of the danger zone."

She could hear the strain in his voice. "I'm sorry, bro."

"It's not your fault. Just life."

Both Addie and Corbin knew how unfair life could be. Their parents had taken an anniversary trip to Mexico. They were mugged and killed outside their hotel for a few measly dollars. Thankfully, Pops and Gram had stepped up to the plate and raised them. Then Gram was diagnosed with Alzheimer's. Unfortunately, fate couldn't leave it at that. Gram also developed brain cancer, which ultimately killed her. Addie and Corbin knew all too well that bad things could indeed happen. "I meant that I'm sorry for adding to your stress."

"If you'll listen to Maddox and do what he says, that will help tremendously."

"I told you I'd play nice," she grumbled. "What more do you want? My signature in blood?"

He chuckled. "Your word will have to do." He sighed. "All right. That's all for now." He paused. "I love you."

She felt a rush of tenderness for her older brother. "I love you too. Give my love to Pops and Delaney."

"Will do. See ya," he said, ending the call.

Addie dropped her phone in her purse and clutched the steering wheel with both hands, her mind trying to digest all that Corbin had said. Were Piper and Jordan having problems? Why hadn't they told her?

Her thoughts went back to the last conversation she'd had with Jordan. He was edgy, an undercurrent of negative emotion running through him. Addie had worried for a blip that something might be wrong between Jordan and Piper. Then, when Jordan assured her that all was well, she believed him. Jordan said Piper was a good woman, but that she didn't understand. Addie wrinkled her nose. *Understand what?* She had much to ask Piper tomorrow.

Maddox. What to do about him? Should she call and apologize? Her jaw tensed. No way! She'd rather spend a week buried in an avalanche. She'd be cordial to Maddox, just as she promised, but that didn't mean she had to seek him out. She glanced in the rearview mirror. Her heart clutched. A silver car was following her. It was an American car, a Chevy, maybe. There was a man driving. His sunglasses prevented her from seeing his face. Her pulse thrashed against her neck as she gripped the steering wheel. This was a lonely stretch of highway. The side-road leading to the cabin was a couple miles up on the right. Did she dare turn onto it with this car tailing her? She pressed the gas pedal to the floor, increasing her speed. To her relief, the Chevy maintained the same speed, staying far behind.

As she turned a curve, she increased her speed again. The Chevy disappeared from her view. She turned onto the side road, hardly slowing her speed. Her tires squealed. Panic shot through her veins as she felt the Jetta shift before the wheels regained traction with the road. She glanced in her rearview mirror. The Chevy drove by, still on the highway.

She slowed to a safe speed, cursing herself for her stupidity. Her fear and paranoia had almost caused her to wreck.

When Addie pulled into her driveway she was shaking. She turned off the engine and pushed her hair out of her face before rubbing her palms on her pants. Maybe it was a bad idea to come here before the new alarm system could be installed. She clenched her fist. No, that was ridiculous. She needed to come. She couldn't let her fears overwhelm her. Whomever had broken into the cabin hadn't found anything. Maybe the person would get a clue that Addie knew nothing about whatever was going on and leave her alone.

She sucked in a breath, trying to calm her rattled nerves as she walked briskly to the door. The empty space around her felt menacing as she pushed the key into the lock. The cabin next door had long-term renters, the Ridleys, an older couple. Unfortunately, they were currently in Florida visiting their grandkids. Two-thirds of the other cabins were temporary renters, people who'd come to enjoy the fall colors or the hot springs. Technically, Addie was alone. The knowledge sent a shiver down her spine. She pushed open the door and stepped inside, closing and locking the door behind her. It was then she realized she'd been holding her breath. She exhaled slowly, her gaze flitting over the cabin.

In the light of day, the mess looked worse than it had the night before. Anger surged through her veins. She felt an intense hatred for whomever had done this. A part of her wanted to crumple in a heap and weep, but that wouldn't help. Instead, she offered a silent prayer asking for strength. A couple minutes later, she felt better.

With a resigned sigh, she put her purse on the kitchen table and got to work cleaning up the place.

An hour later, she was in her room, reorganizing her papers and getting her desk back in order, when she came across the framed picture. The glass was broken, but the picture was unharmed. It was taken when she and Corbin were still in high school. Pops and Gram had taken them to Disneyland a couple of weeks before the end of summer break. Addie and Corbin had complained that they were too old for Disneyland. To their surprise, they had a wonderful time. Addie rubbed a finger over Gram's face. She looked so happy as she grinned at the camera, her arms around Addie and Corbin. Pops was standing to the far left, on the other side of Corbin. Instead of looking at the camera, he was looking at Gram, an expression of pure adoration on his face. Tears rose in Addie's eyes. Everything changed when Gram got sick. Pops and Addie tried to pick up the pieces while Corbin joined the military to escape. At least now, they had Corbin back. And, he'd brought Delaney into their family. Soon, they'd have a new baby girl. Addie hoped everything would be okay with the pregnancy. *Please let Delaney and the baby be okay*, she prayed.

Addie placed the photo in its rightful place on her desk and bent down to retrieve more papers. She heard a noise.

She froze, her pulse jumping into overdrive. Ever so slowly, she went to her bedroom door and peered out. Relief surged through her when she saw that the hallway was clear. Gaining more courage, she stole down the hall toward the living room. Her eyes scoured the combination living room and kitchen. It was also clear. This was getting ridiculous. She had to stop jumping out of her skin at the slightest noise. She was about to turn and go back down the hall when strong arms grabbed her from behind.

She let out a yelp, horror twisting through her as she fought against the arms. "Help!" she screamed. A hand went over her mouth. She ground her heel into her attacker's foot. He grunted and released his hold.

Addie darted for the door. Before she made it a foot, she was tackled from behind. She hit the wood floor, but hardly felt a thing as she rolled over, clawing and hitting. The man backed away and stood. It registered in her mind that he was wearing a black ski mask. She didn't know why the man had paused his attack, but it gave her blessed time to escape. She scrambled to her feet and was about to run when he pulled out a gun.

"Stop, or I'll shoot," he ordered.

Her heart sank. This couldn't be happening!

"Hands up!"

Slowly, she lifted her hands in the air. "What do you want?" Her knees were so wobbly, she could hardly stand.

Terror rattled through her like a freight train as he came towards her.

She shrieked when he grabbed her arm and viciously twisted her around, so that he was behind her. He jabbed the barrel of the gun in her back. "Put your hands together."

"What?" she cried.

"Make any sudden moves, and you're dead," he growled in her

ear. "Put your arms together behind you. Now!" he thundered when she didn't react fast enough. He grabbed her hands. She felt a thin band of plastic around her wrists and heard a zipping sound. He opened the door and thrust her through it.

Her mind raced, trying to figure a way out of this. The urge to live was overwhelming. She didn't want to die. Not here. Not today.

He pushed her forward across the front porch. A cry of dismay gurgled in her throat when she saw the silver Chevy. She should've listened to her instincts that screamed the car was following her. How stupid she'd been to push Maddox away. "Who are you?"

"No talking!" He thrust the gun further into her back. Instinctively, she arched her back trying to relieve the pressure of the gun at her spine.

They went down the steps and to the car. She felt movement and heard a click. The trunk opened.

A new terror seized her as she realized what was happening. "No!" she cried. Adrenaline surged through her as she went nuts, twisting and fighting. He grunted in surprise, dropping the gun. She bolted. Better to be shot running than to be placed in a trunk, only to face who knew what horrors. She made it across the gravel driveway before he yanked her hair and pulled her back. She howled in pain as he grabbed her arms and carried her back to the trunk. She lifted her feet kicking and screaming, fighting him for all she was worth, but she was no match for his strength. He heaved her in the trunk and slammed it shut.

Darkness engulfed her. With that darkness came a sinking despair.

7

A mind-numbing panic throbbed through Addie's brain, rendering her powerless to act. She tried to remember what she'd learned about being locked in a trunk. Wasn't there supposed to be some lever in newer models? How was she supposed to pull a lever when she couldn't use her hands? She strained against the plastic that held her hands, but it was futile. Sweat beaded across her nose as a suffocating heat surged through her. Her lungs were bound with iron. She couldn't breathe! A prayer for help went through her mind. *Please, help me.*

She had to be strong. She had to think of her family. Of Maddox. Her last words to him had been spoken in anger. Why did everything have to be so complicated with him?

It occurred to her that the car had not moved. She kicked as hard as she could. "Help!" She heard a muffled pop. She went still, straining her ears as she tried to figure out what was happening. Hope sprang in her chest. Was someone else out there? She jerked into action. "Help!" she screamed. "I'm in the trunk!" She kicked again and again on the side and the top. Maybe she'd imagined the pop. There was probably no one out there except for her attacker. Still, she had to do something!

A lifetime seemed to pass. Addie kicked and screamed until she grew hoarse.

The trunk opened. She sat up, ready to give her attacker the fight of his life. Then she saw his face. "Maddox," she uttered, a cry wrenching her throat.

"I'm here," he said, gathering her in his arms.

THE SIGHT of Addie bound and stuffed in a trunk had unleashed something dark and primitive inside Maddox, making him want to pummel her attacker to mush. He probably would have, had he not needed to keep the man intact so he could be interrogated. The man in question was tied up, gagged, and stuffed in the closet of the guest bedroom. Right after Maddox rescued Addie, he called Corbin, updating him on the situation. Corbin freaked when Maddox told him about the attack and how close Addie came to being kidnapped. The only thing that kept Corbin from hopping on a plane and heading this way was Maddox's assurance that from this point forward, he wouldn't let Addie out of his sight.

Maddox and Corbin then got on a conference call with Sutton. He instructed Maddox to keep the man there until picked up for interrogation. A part of Maddox wanted to conduct his own version of "interrogation," but Sutton assured him of his foolproof methods of obtaining information. One thing Maddox learned in the SEALs was that it was better to leave the interrogations to the "experts." He'd never had the stomach for that sort of thing.

Maddox's main priority was Addie's safety. Whether she liked it or not, he was stuck to Addie like glue. He thought back to the moment when he rescued her from the trunk. She threw her arms around him and buried her head in his shoulder. Even amidst the terror of the moment, he couldn't deny that it had felt right having her in his arms. The softness of her springy curls had brushed against his skin, tickling his face. The familiar scent of her light floral perfume mingling with the fresh smell of her shampoo enveloped his senses. *Stop it*, he commanded himself, balling his fist. He couldn't let this hang-up on Addie continue.

In retrospect, it was good that he mentioned Felicity at the diner. "A girlfriend" was the very thing needed to put a safe barrier between him and Addie. Things could get confusing right now with emotions running high, but then where would he and Addie be afterwards? The obstacles between them weren't just going to disappear. He had a dangerous profession, and she was opposed to it, end of story.

Maddox couldn't allow himself to get close to Addie knowing, that in the end, she'd dump him all over again. He surveyed Addie's bedroom, annoyance resurging at the sight of the scattered papers, books, and clothing. Someone had done a number on the place. Addie was making a valiant effort to put the place back together, but there was still a ton to do. He bent over and picked up a handful of books, stacking them on the bookshelf above her desk. A smile pulled over his lips when he saw the guitar songbook. Addie was teaching herself how to play. He loved that about Addie—how she was always learning new things. His gut tightened. Her guitar. Had it been damaged? He spotted it in the far corner of the room, intact. He relaxed.

His eye caught on a burgundy book with the word "Journal" embossed in gold lettering across the front. He picked it up. First, he thought he couldn't dare look at it. No way could he invade Addie's privacy. He reached for more books, stacking them on the shelf above her desk. Then, he looked at the journal again, noticing a corner of what looked like a picture sticking out the side.

None of your business, Maddox. Keep stacking books! It's one little peek. What could it hurt? He opened her journal to the picture. His heart came to a screeching halt. The picture was of him and Addie, a selfie taken on the summit of the mountain they'd hiked. They were arm-in-arm, their heads close together. They wore triumphant grins, having reached the top in record time. The sheer joy on their faces caused his heart to clutch. They'd been happy together ... so happy. His finger traced Addie's features. She'd taken the trouble of printing this picture and putting it in her journal. He wasn't sure what to think about this.

He jumped guiltily when he realized the water in the shower had stopped. Quickly, he tucked the picture back into its place and closed the journal just as the bathroom door opened.

"Hey," he said, his voice sounding too cheerful in his own ears. Her hair was wet and hanging in ringlets over her shoulders. She'd changed from her dress slacks and blouse into jeans and a t-shirt. Yeah, she looked good in those snug jeans and a form-fitting t-shirt that emphasized her tall, slender figure.

A crease formed between her brows as her eyes went to the journal. "What're you doing?"

"I figured I might as well be of some help, instead of just sitting here like a lump on a log waiting for you to get out of the shower." There was a window in her bathroom. It was locked, but that didn't mean someone couldn't break through it and get to Addie. Corbin was having a security system installed tomorrow, which would make protecting her easier. Still, he wanted to be close enough to hear what was going on, hence him sitting in her room while she showered.

"Have you been reading my journal?" She gave him an accusing look.

"Geez, no." Heat crept up his neck.

She arched an eyebrow, her hand going to her hip.

He held up both hands in defense. "Promise, I wasn't reading it." Guilt cloaked over him. Then again, looking at a picture wasn't the same as reading her journal. He'd answered her honestly...somewhat. "How are you feeling?"

She managed a rubbery smile. "Better."

Right after the attack, Addie was pale as alabaster, a dazed look in her eyes. For a few seconds, Maddox feared she might be going into shock. Thankfully, that hadn't been the case. Addie was a tough cookie. Still, she was wound up tight. Maddox suggested that a shower might help her relax. It seemed to have done the trick.

"Good." The conversation lagged. Maddox missed how it used to be, the two of them having so much to say to each other that they could hardly draw in a breath between sentences. "Are you hungry?"

She shoved her hands into her pockets. "A little, I guess."

He chuckled. "You hardly ate two bites at the diner. Unless you grabbed something afterwards, I'd venture to say you're pretty hungry." The Addie he knew had a healthy appetite. He used to tease her about having a hollow leg because she could eat him under the table and was naturally thin. In fact, Addie had to work to keep from becoming too skinny.

She laughed in surrender. "Yeah, I'm hungry. Starving, actually." The moment slowed as he caught something in her eyes—a longing that matched the fire raging in him. The two of them were here, alone, the memories of how it was before swirling around them like beckoning sirens to unsuspecting sailors. She was a mere two steps away. He could pull her into his arms and crush his lips to hers, drinking in her passion.

She cleared her throat and broke eye contact, scrunching her hair with her hand. Maddox remembered the unconscious gesture as something she did when she got nervous. His gaze took in her thick mane of curls. Everything in him wanted to bridge the distance between them, take her in his arms and explore her soft, sensual lips. "Want me to do that for you?" he uttered in a low tone.

She jerked as she caught the intent of his question. For one agonizing second, he feared that he'd gone too far, but she only laughed. "Thanks, I think I can handle it."

"Is there anything we can fix in the kitchen?" He hoped so. If they ordered takeout, that meant he'd have to vet the person who brought the food. Another ordeal.

Her eyes clouded as she lowered her voice. "We're supposed to eat and go on like normal with that guy tied up in the guest bedroom?"

"Sutton's men are due to arrive in the next couple hours."

She nodded, her lips vanishing into a thin line.

"Are you sure you don't recognize him?"

"No, I've never seen him before." She clenched her hand, the words coming out in ragged strips. "Do you think he's the one who killed Jordan?"

"I don't know." He clenched his jaw. "But you can rest assured that Sutton will beat it out—get to the bottom of it," he amended when he saw her stricken expression.

The kidnapper was in his early thirties. An average looking Joe with hard features and thinning hair. Maddox punched him a couple of times, demanding to know who he was and who'd sent him, but the guy sat in stony silence. He had no identification. No phone. Nothing. He snapped a picture of the guy and texted it to Corbin and Sutton, knowing that Sutton would run it through a database.

Addie shuddered, her eyes taking on a haunted look. "I keep thinking about what might've happened if you hadn't shown up when you did."

Maddox didn't like to think about that either. "I'll stay right by your side until this thing's over. You have my word."

"Thank you," she said softly.

His mind went back through the events that had led them here. Maddox left the diner in search of Addie. Unfortunately, she'd gotten too much of a head start. He assumed she was going back to the resort. When he realized Addie wasn't there, he headed to her cabin. He saw another car in her driveway with no license plate. He parked a short distance away and jogged back. He reached her yard just as the man was shoving her into the trunk.

Addie stepped up and touched his face. Her finger trailed lightly down his skin, sending a jolt of awareness through him. He gave her a questioning look. "You have a bruise," she explained, frowning, "from your fight with that horrid man."

"I do?" A wry grin twisted his lips. "I hadn't noticed."

Her eyes lit with amusement. "Tough guy, huh? The weasel was obviously no match for your hotshot, ninja, Navy SEAL skills." There was a touch of admiration in her voice.

He laughed in surprise, not sure how to answer.

A shadow darkened her features. "When I heard the gun, I wasn't sure what to think ..." She shivered. "I'm so glad you were there."

"Me too." The attacker had an elementary level of combat skill, but he was no match for Maddox's SEAL training, meaning he wasn't Special Ops.

After they got some food in their systems, Maddox planned to question Addie in hopes that he'd find a common thread to help him figure out why she was being targeted. "Is there something in the kitchen we can fix for dinner?" he prompted.

"We have a few cans of soup. I can make us some grilled cheese sandwiches." She scowled. "Thank goodness I put the food back into the fridge last night after the break-in. Otherwise, the perishables would've been ruined."

He touched her arm as the familiar attraction zinged through him. "I'm sorry for all that you're going through. I know it's rough."

"Thanks," she said, offering an appreciative smile. Their gazes locked as something akin to attraction flashed in her eyes. For one wild moment, Maddox got the distinct feeling that Addie wanted to kiss him. To his disappointment, she took a step back as if to put as much distance between them as possible. *It's for the best*, he reminded himself, even though, he really didn't believe it.

Addie motioned to the shelf above her desk. "I appreciate you putting things away." A sheepish grin tugged at her lips as she rocked forward on the balls of her feet. "Sorry I accused you of reading my journal." Laughter simmered in her eyes. "Read anything interesting?"

His eyes rounded as he coughed. Ouch! The guilt was killing him!

She laughed lightly, brushing his arm. "Just teasing."

This was the Addie that he craved—the playful one who kept him on his toes. He motioned with his head. "Shall we?"

"Sounds like a plan." She held up a finger. "As long as I'm the one doing the cooking."

"Hey." His face fell. "My cooking's not that bad."

"No, it's great," she paused, her mouth giving way to a grin, "if you don't mind Mohave Desert dry and charred like a brick."

He rolled his eyes. "I burn the pancakes one time and never hear the end of it. Just like a woman to never forget."

"Never," she uttered, her eyes holding his.

What in the heck was happening here? A part of him wanted to call Addie out, demand to know why she was sending him mixed signals. But he didn't want to throw a monkey wrench in the gears. Better to let it ride ... see where the road took them. He offered a slight bow and flourish of his hand. "After you, ma'am."

She clucked her tongue. "Always the perfect gentleman." She tipped her head, her emerald-gold eyes sparkling with mischief. "You know I never could resist that Bama boy charm," she quipped, traipsing out.

He stood there for a moment, befuddled. Watching her move was fascinating. The confident bounce in her step. The graceful lines of her lithe body with just the right amount of curves. Her rich chocolate hair bouncing jauntily on her shoulders. Was Addie flirting with him? Or toying with him? *Geez.* How in the heck was he supposed to remain unaffected by a woman like her? She was playing him like a fiddle.

"You coming, hotshot?" she called over her shoulder.

"You don't have to ask me twice," he uttered, feeling like a gullible moth going helplessly to the flame.

8

Despite the circumstance, being here with Maddox was exhilarating. Addie glanced at his rugged profile, his unruly curls, the determined set of his chin. His penetrating eyes, framed by dark lashes, were a deep ocean blue. He caught her gaze and smiled, displaying his splendid dimples. A goofy grin spilled over her lips, and she felt like she was sixteen again. The prudent thing to do was to remain guarded around Maddox, but the brush with danger had pickled her brain and made her reckless.

Breaking up with Maddox was the biggest mistake of Addie's life. When she believed him dead, her heart had shattered to pieces. She realized then that not having Maddox in her life was far worse than living with the fear of something terrible happening to him. Then, she learned he was still alive. Oh, how she'd wanted to run to him, beg him to take her back. Then her stubbornness had set in. She hoped he would contact her, but nothing. Well, until today, that is, when he waltzed into the diner. *And saved your life*, her mind added. She owed him some latitude for that.

While it was tempting to just pick up where they were before the break-up, she had to keep reminding herself that Maddox was here because of his loyalty to Corbin. She knew he still cared about her on some level, she could see it in his eyes. Obviously, he hadn't loved her as deeply as she had him, or he would have contacted her. There never would have been a Felicity. What kind of woman was this Felicity?

"Is everything okay? You have a strange expression on your face."

She forced a smile. "Yep." A dry laugh rumbled in her throat, her voice going high-pitched. "Well, aside from the fact that my house was ransacked and someone tried to kidnap me, I'm peachy."

He frowned. "You're acting strange."

"Am I?" She chuckled. "Well, chock it up to the day."

"Yeah, I guess you have a good excuse, for sure."

They were sitting side-by-side on the couch. Maddox angled to face her. "Okay, let's start at the beginning. I want to hear every detail, starting with when Jordan came to the resort."

She let out a long breath, gathering her thoughts. How stupid of her to fret about Maddox's girlfriend when she should be trying to unravel the mystery before them. Her life could be at stake, and she was thinking about Maddox! *Stupid, stupid, woman!*

"Maybe you should start by telling me how you met Jordan."

"Gram and Jordan's mother were at the same care center, both had Alzheimer's. Jordan and I struck up a friendship." She paused, the awkwardness of the conversation hitting her. Discussing her romantic relationship with Jordan wasn't something she wanted to do with Maddox. "The two of us dated for a while." Maddox's features tightened. *Interesting.*

"Why did you break up?"

She cleared her throat, shifting in her seat. "We broke up because ..." heat flamed her cheeks "...well, things just didn't work out." She picked at her fingernails.

Frustration tinged his handsome features. "If I'm going to help, you need to be open with me." He probed her with fierce eyes. "Why did you break up?"

She squared her chin. "Are you sure this is about Jordan?"

He didn't back down an inch. "What else would it be about?"

His expression was unreadable. "You," she blurted. "I broke up with him because I met you."

Maddox blinked in surprise. She couldn't be sure, but thought he looked pleased. Then the expression vanished, and he was the consummate professional once more. "Continue."

"Jordan and I remained close friends. I introduced him to Piper."

"I remember you mentioning her."

She nodded. "Piper and I met at a support group for caregivers of Alzheimer's patients. Piper's mother had Alzheimer's. Her father Hamilton is a world-renown surgeon, turned researcher. I knew Piper and Jordan would have lots in common. Sure enough, they hit it off and got married. Later, they formed their drug research company."

"Where Jordan developed PZT."

"Yes."

"Does Piper live nearby?"

"She and her dad have a family estate in Liberty Falls, the next town over, about twenty-five miles from here. Their research facility is in New Jersey. They go back and forth between New Jersey and Liberty Falls."

"Corbin said Jordan and Piper were having marital problems."

It was crazy how fast irritation spiked through her. "Corbin's wrong," she shot back. "Jordan and Piper were going on a cruise together. In fact, he stopped by to ask if he could pick up some jewelry I had in my possession. He wanted to give the pieces to Piper."

Maddox leaned forward. "What kind of jewelry?"

"Earrings and a bracelet. They belonged to Jordan's mom. He gave the pieces to me when we were dating."

Maddox lifted an eyebrow. "And you kept them even after Jordan and Piper got married?"

Heat crawled up her neck. "Yes, I tried to give them back, but Jordan wanted me to have them. I was close to his mother."

"I see."

"See what?" she fired back.

"Jordan still had feelings for you."

Her throat tightened. "That's ridiculous!" she squeaked. "He loved Piper. I was just a friend."

"Do you still have the jewelry?"

"Yes, it's in my room. None of it was taken during the break-in."

He rubbed his chin, a look of intense concentration settling over his features. "Tell me everything Jordan said to you."

She repeated the conversation.

He looked thoughtful. "Okay, from what you said, here are the points of interest: 'Piper's a good woman, but she doesn't understand. You're the only one I can trust.' Then, he asked you to forgive him."

She wrinkled her nose, more confused than ever. "None of it makes any sense. I'm hoping to get more information, tomorrow, when I meet with Piper."

"Good." He tipped his head. "Corbin said Jordan was meeting with a divorce attorney. It seems strange that he and Piper were leaving on a cruise the following day if they were having severe problems."

"Exactly." She folded her arms over her chest.

"Did Jordan give you anything the day he stopped by?"

"No."

He let out a breath. "Tell me again everything that happened, leaving out no details."

"Seriously? How many times do we have to go through this?"

"As many times as it takes to get to the truth."

She told him again, right down to the part about Jordan helping her collect the items in her purse. "I got the feeling that he'd seen someone or something that frightened him. I tried to see what he was looking at, but the terrace was filled with people eating lunch." She spread her hands. "People come and go all the time at the resort. I have no idea who Jordan was looking at."

His brows furrowed. "Maybe, the guy who tried to kidnap you?"

"Yeah, maybe."

"Someone must think that Jordan either told you something, or gave you something."

She threw up her hands. "Assuming this is even about Jordan."

He rubbed his chin. "From where I'm sitting, I'll bet this is about PZT. A drug with the potential to cure Alzheimer's could be worth billions."

"That's what Corbin said."

A new light came into Maddox's eyes. "Let me see your purse."

"Huh?"

"You said you tipped over your purse and Jordan helped you put the contents back."

"Yes," she said, not sure where this was going.

"Is it possible that Jordan slipped something into your purse without your knowledge?"

"Yeah, I guess. Anything's possible, I suppose." She scrunched her eyebrows. "Why would he do that?"

Maddox gave her a checkmate look. "Because you're the only one he could trust, remember?"

She stood. "I guess there's only one way to find out, right?"

"Right."

She retrieved her purse and sat back down beside him.

"Dump it out on the coffee table," Maddox instructed.

Great! Now Maddox would see the tampon, just as Jordan had. Oh, well. It was a fact of life. She turned over her purse, the contents falling onto the table.

"Does anything look amiss?"

Her mind clicked through the familiar items—her wallet, keys, phone, gum, the tampon, bits of scrap paper, loose change, a silver key. Wait a minute! She reached for the key, her heart picking up its beat. "This." She held it up. "I don't know where it came from."

Maddox reached for it, his hand touching hers. She felt a jolt of attraction and wondered if he felt it too. He held up the key, examining it. "It looks like it might go to some sort of storage facility or locker. Do you know of any place that rents lockers in Birchwood Springs? Was Jordan from Birchwood Springs or Liberty Falls?"

"He was from here. I don't know of any place that rents lockers, per se, but there are several storage facilities in the area." The key was plain Jane, like thousands of other keys. Her heart sank. Had they reached a dead end?

"Maybe your friend Piper will know what the key goes to."

"Yes, we can ask her tomorrow." She saw the skeptical look on Maddox's face. "What?"

"Do you think Piper can be trusted?"

She rocked back. "Of course," she said sharply. She didn't like the direction this conversation was taking.

He looked doubtful. "I dunno. You said Piper never told you that she and Jordan were having problems, and yet, he'd spoken to a divorce lawyer. Jordan said you were the only one he could trust."

Her voice rose. "He also asked me to forgive him, which makes no sense. Jordan never did a thing to me!" She gulped in a breath, trying to rein in her emotions. "Piper's my best friend. I trust her as much as I trust you ... as much as I trust myself."

He held up a hand. "Okay. Just making sure. What about her dad?"

"Hamilton Gentry."

He nodded.

"He's quiet. Standoffish. Has a brilliant reputation as a surgeon. I know he was fiercely devoted to his wife. He went into a deep depression when she passed away."

"According to the intel, he's the one who secured the financial backing for the business."

"Yes."

Maddox gave her a meaningful look. "If anything were to go awry with PZT, Hamilton could have a lot to lose."

She bit her lower lip. "I suppose." It was strange to think of Hamilton Gentry this way. She didn't like having to scrutinize Jordan or Piper, didn't like thinking that nothing was as she thought. She also didn't like having her home broken into or almost getting kidnapped. A feeling of gloom settled over her. She just wanted this to be over.

"I'd like to look at that jewelry."

She stood. "Sure." Addie was weary, a headache streaking over her forehead. She wanted to fall into bed and sleep a thousand years. First though, she had to call Sadie to make sure everything had gone okay with the conference. Another thought occurred to her, quickening her blood. Maddox vowed to stay by her side. Did that mean he'd sleep in the same room? An unexpected ripple of desire surged through her. How was she supposed to get any sleep with him there? She had the unreasonable urge to throw her arms around his neck and kiss him. Was she losing her freaking mind? How could she be thinking such thoughts right now when danger was pressing down on her? *Felicity!* She repeated the word over and over like it was a talisman. Yes, she'd loved Maddox, but it was too late for them. Besides, if he'd been the guy she thought he was, he wouldn't have found someone else so quickly.

The loud knocking at the door nearly caused her to jump out of her skin. Her knees went weak as she looked at Maddox, her heart thundering against her ribcage.

Maddox's muscles pulled taut like a panther ready to spring. "It's probably Sutton's guys," he said quietly. "Stay there," he ordered, holding out his hand.

Addie held her breath as he stole to the door.

"Who is it?" he asked, the muscles in his jaw twitching. He looked every bit the retired SEAL with his chiseled body and fierce expression.

"Sutton sent us."

Addie let out a relieved breath. She was surprised, however, at Maddox's next question. "What do we do?"

"Adapt and overcome."

"How much adapting?"

"As much as it takes."

His shoulders relaxed as he opened the door and shook hands with the two men. "Thanks for coming."

They stepped inside. Maddox closed and locked the door behind them. Both men were dressed in black shirts and slacks. They had stoic expressions and closely cropped hair, like they used the same barber. One was short with a barrel chest and thick biceps, the other tall with lean muscles like Maddox.

"Where's the package?" the short man asked, his hawk eyes scoping the room.

Maddox jutted his thumb. "In the bedroom."

A wave of nausea assaulted Addie. *Package?* Not a package, but a human being. Her attacker! What world had she inadvertently stepped into? She looked at Maddox who seemed perfectly at ease now that the identities of the men were assured. It went through her mind that even if there were no Felicity, it was doubtful Addie could survive in Maddox's world. How did Delaney do it? She was having a baby, for goodness sake! There was no guarantee that when Corbin walked out the door every morning that he'd come back in the evening. A shiver ran through Addie. She couldn't live like that! It was better that things had cooled with Maddox. She needed to keep reminding herself of that and not let the all-consuming attraction she felt for him trip her up. As much as it hurt, she'd made the only decision she could—to break it off to protect her heart. Maybe it was one of those situations where, if you had to go back and do it all over again, you'd make the exact same painful decision you did to start with.

Maddox motioned. "This way." The men walked by first, followed by Maddox. As he passed Addie, he touched her arm. His concerned look told her that her feelings were being broadcast on her face. "I'll be right back," he reassured her.

She nodded.

He paused and turned back. "Oh, could you get that jewelry for me? I want to look at it and then send it with these guys, so Sutton can run a check on it."

"Sure. Oh, I forgot to tell you. The bracelet clasp broke so I took it to a jewelry shop to have it repaired." She never had gotten around to calling Mr. Steinway about the bracelet. It had completely slipped her mind.

"We need to get that piece too."

"Okay, I'll call about it tomorrow."

He nodded. His perceptive eyes raked over her, making her feel like she was an open book. "Are you okay?"

The tenderness in his gaze caused a lump to form in her throat. No, she wasn't okay. Nothing about this whole thing was okay. "I'm fine."

He gave her a doubtful look.

"Really." She wrapped a plastic smile around her lips. "Go on in there. The men are waiting for their package." Irony hung heavy in her voice. "I'll get the jewelry."

"What's wrong?" he pressed.

Tears misted her eyes. "I said I'm fine," she growled. "Go!"

9

Nights were the hardest, the time when the terrors of the past rose like mountainous shadows, blocking out even the tiniest sliver of light. In his dreams, the dank scent of the jungle filled his nostrils and caused sweat to boil over his nose. His heart pounded out a haphazard beat as he clutched the sheet with his fist, trying to regulate his breathing. He'd dreamt of his captivity in Syria, suffered the hollow gnawing of his empty stomach, choked on the rancid water, felt the sinking desperation of fear that he wouldn't make it out of there alive.

His only consolation had been the camaraderie of his fellow SEALs. He was grateful his buddies were part of Sutton's private security team. The offer had been a package deal, all of them or none. Maddox was grateful for this new chapter in his life. He just wished he could lick this infernal PTSD. While it was his greatest desire to move forward and leave the past behind, his mind couldn't seem to get the memo.

Maddox took in a breath, willing his body to relax. *In through the nose, out through the mouth.* Why had the PTSD hit him tonight? Maybe it was because he was worried that he wouldn't be able to protect Addie from whatever was coming. A shiver slithered down his spine, causing the sweat on his brow to run cold. Today had been a close call. Had he arrived a few minutes later, Addie would've been gone. He had to remain vigilant and not let his personal feelings for Addie prevent him from protecting her.

He was on a pallet beside Addie's bed. He'd lain awake long after she'd fallen asleep, thinking about her. Something had shifted when Sutton's men came to get the attacker. Addie had become withdrawn, cool. He knew she was fighting her own demons about Jordan and Piper, but he got the feeling that her change in attitude had something to do with him. Addie was a hard woman to figure out. One minute he felt like they were getting closer and the next, there was a skyscraper-sized barrier between them.

He propped his arms behind his head, noting with satisfaction that his breathing had returned to normal. Relaxation techniques helped tremendously. And it didn't hurt to have something other than his own past to focus on. He grinned thinking how he didn't mind shifting his thoughts to Addie. He cocked his ears to listen for her breathing.

Silence.

Panic seized him as he sat up. He glanced toward the window and saw a flash of lightning. A second later, a loud clap of thunder sounded.

"Hey," Addie said, sleep coating her voice. "It's stormy."

"Yeah." The wind picked up, sending rain splattering against the window. He angled to face her bed. Another flash of lightning lit the room. He caught the outline of her face and realized she'd scooted to the edge of the bed and was lying on her side, looking down at him. A deep ache trickled through his body. It was torture being this close to the woman he loved when he couldn't take her in his arms. "How long have you been awake?"

"Long enough to hear you mumbling in your sleep. What language were you speaking?"

Crap! There was no telling what he'd said. Often the dreams were so terrible that he woke up screaming. "Arabic."

"I'll bet it was terrible over there."

"Yes," he admitted.

"How did you survive?"

He let out a long breath. "The only way I could—one day at a time." She'd probably laugh him to scorn if she realized how often he'd thought of her while he was in captivity. It was his favorite area of refuge that his brain could go to.

Thunder boomed, shaking the cabin. Rain poured onto the roof, sounding like endless nails pinging the shingles.

"I love the sound of the rain." Her voice had an ethereal quality like she was still partway in a dream.

He punched his pillow to adjust it and lay back down, trying to find a comfortable spot. "I remember."

"Really?"

"Yeah, I remember everything about you."

"Such as?"

He smiled at the note of interest in her voice. "You have an insatiable appetite for salty fries and mint chocolate chip ice cream."

"Speaking of which, that sounds really good right now."

He chuckled. "I don't know about the fries, but I could go for some ice cream."

"We'll have to pick some up tomorrow."

"Good idea."

"What else?" she prompted.

"Your level-head and forthright personality make you an excellent manager."

"Thanks," she said with gusto, and he got the feeling she was smiling.

He laughed to himself knowing this next one would set her off. Teasing Addie was immensely rewarding because she always rose to the bait. "You couldn't be on time if your life depended on it."

"Hey," she countered, "that's not true."

He suspected her lower lip was thrust out in a pout. "Uh, huh," he drawled. "You know it is."

She grunted. "For your information, I've been trying to do better about that. Moron," she added in a sulky tone.

"Touché," he laughed.

"What else?" she demanded, a definite edge to her voice.

He grinned. "Let's put it this way ... if you looked up stubborn in the dictionary, your picture would be right next to it."

"Am not!"

"Are too."

"Am not!" she huffed. "Take it back!"

"What's wrong, Addie?" he goaded. "You can't stand to hear the truth?"

"The truth is that you're a big, fat jerk wad!" He heard a flurry of movement, realized she'd sat up. A second later, she was flogging him with her pillow.

Laughter rose in his throat. "Hey, now." He raised his hands to shield his head. A second later, he grabbed the pillow.

"Give it back," she ordered.

"Not on your life." He put it under his head, stacked on top of his other pillow. "Yeah, that's much better," he drawled. "The other pillow you gave me was flatter than roadkill under a semi-truck."

She sniggered, then burst out laughing. "You're such a moron," she said in a singsong voice. "Can I have my pillow back?" she asked sweetly.

"I don't think so, sugar lips."

She groaned. "Sugar lips? Seriously? What else do you remember about me?"

"No matter how often you watch those silly Christmas movies on the Hallmark channel, you cry at the end."

"True," she conceded, "but who doesn't?"

"I don't."

She smirked. "Yeah, because you're a hardened Navy SEAL."

"Ex-Navy SEAL," he corrected.

"The name may've changed, but the job's still the same."

The tone of the conversation had shifted faster than the government in a third world country. He cringed at the bite in Addie's voice. There it was—the one thing they could never get beyond, his profession.

"Superman has to save the world," she said dourly.

He stiffened. "As Irish philosopher Edmund Burke said, 'The only thing necessary for the triumph of evil is for good men to do nothing.'" This was met with a stony silence that crawled over him like a dozen hornets. "I'll have you know that I'm doing a lot of good."

"Yeah, you're humble about it too," she shot back. "You sure you're not on some thrill-seeking ride? Running from real-life responsibility?"

The game was afoot now, each of them volleying to get their point across. "Not everyone who joins the SEALs is running from something. Some are running to something."

"Or using it as penance."

The comment was a knife in the gut. Addie knew him too well, knew how to hit him where it hurt the most. His eyes narrowed. "You sound just like my mama."

"How's your mama, by the way?" she said lightly. "Is she still the belle of the country club?"

He grunted. "More like the queen."

Addie laughed. "Yep, she rules the roost, for sure."

"Like somebody else I know," he muttered under his breath.

"I love your mama. She's a hoot."

"She loves you too." Even though Maddox and Addie had never spoken of marriage, his mama was already picking out invitations and planning the wedding when Addie dumped him. His mama was almost as devastated about the breakup as he was. Not really, but she was crazy about Addie.

"Is your daddy still trying to get you to become an attorney and join his firm?"

"No, he gave up on that years ago," he said mechanically, still smarting over Addie's jab. Darkness cocooned around him, making it easier to open a conversation about sensitive issues. "You know, you shouldn't keep blaming me for Corbin's mistakes. He's the one who ran out on you. I didn't." He was tempted to add that Addie was the one who gave up on them, not the other way around.

"And you shouldn't spend the rest of your life feeling guilty about B. J.'s death. Time to move on," she snipped.

He flinched. "Had I known you were gonna keep throwing B. J. in my face, I never would've told you about him."

"Yeah, well, the same goes for Corbin."

The chasm between them expanded larger than the ocean as they lay there like defiant warriors, refusing to give up their ground. His thoughts went to B. J. In his high school days, Maddox was an extreme sports fanatic and dreamed of one day making it to the X Games. That all changed the day B. J. was killed in a dirt biking accident. Maddox and B. J. were determined to prove which of them was the toughest. They started out jumping makeshift ramps and hills. As the day wore on, the challenges got greater until finally Maddox dared B. J. to jump a creek. Maddox went first and cleared it without issue. B. J., however, wasn't as lucky. He fell short of the goal and his bike took a nose-dive. B. J. was thrown off his bike. He was rushed to the hospital where he died a few days later.

Maddox had opened up to Addie, sharing his anguish and guilt over B. J.'s death. He drifted aimlessly for the next few years, became a menace, in and out of trouble with the law. His dad had to bail him out of jail a few times. Eventually, Maddox got himself straightened out and traveled the world, taking on freelance writing and photography projects. It was easier to wander strange lands and learn about other cultures than it was to stay in Alabama and worry about his own problems. When that ran its course and he could no longer find any fulfillment in it, Maddox joined the Navy. Yeah, maybe his entry into the SEALs was at first fueled by a desire for penance, but as a SEAL, he'd found his life's purpose. Now, that purpose continued as he worked for Sutton's security company.

Two weeks ago, on his first assignment, Maddox and his former SEALs saved the life of a young daughter of a diplomat who'd been kidnapped for ransom. He clenched his jaw. As much as he loved Addie, he couldn't give up who he was for her. Doing that would mean running the risk of losing himself and his newfound purpose. The problem was, he still hadn't figured out how to live without

Addie. She consumed his thoughts every day. Now that he was here with her, the longing intensified to the point where he could hardly stand it. He wanted both—his profession and Addie. Was that too much to ask for?

He turned over so his back was to her. A good night's sleep was what he needed more than anything. Nights were the hardest. It would all look better in the morning.

"I'm sorry I brought up B. J." Her voice was melancholy, ponderous.

He grunted in surprise. The sincerity of her words circled around him, and he felt himself soften. He let out a sigh. No sense in harboring grudges. "It's all right. I'm sorry I brought up Corbin." Even though Addie had forgiven Corbin for leaving home when her grandmother got sick, she still carried the scars.

"No problem." She paused long enough for him to wonder if she'd say anything else. "For what's it's worth, I'm sorry," she added, her voice cracking.

He turned to face her. "Sorry for what?" Thunder rattled the window.

"I'm sorry I can't be more like Felicity."

It was all he could do to halt the incredulous laugh before it escaped his mouth. "What?"

"I'm sorry I wasn't brave enough to be there for you through thick and thin."

He swallowed, processing what she'd said. His heart clutched as emotion lodged thick in his throat. A single tear trickled down his cheek. "Adelaide Spencer, you're the bravest woman I've ever met."

Her voice grew strangled. "If that were true, we'd still be together now."

"It's not too late," he said quietly. He held his breath, waiting for her to respond, feeling as though everything were hanging in the balance. One second crawled by ... two ...

"Goodnight," she croaked.

He swallowed his disappointment. "Goodnight," he clipped,

hoping the monotony of the falling rain would help him go back to sleep.

10

The next morning, Maddox awoke to the tantalizing smell of bacon. He sat up and rubbed his aching shoulders. No wonder he'd had a nightmare about his captivity in Syria. Sleeping on this pallet was only a few steps up from sleeping on the hard floor of his cell. He felt like he'd been rolled over by a bulldozer. He guessed it was around three a.m. when he finally drifted off to sleep. Thankfully, there were no further nightmares.

His gaze went to Addie's bed. It was empty. He sprang into action, getting to his feet. The bacon smelled amazing, causing his mouth to water. It dinged in his brain that Addie was cooking breakfast. What kind of second-rate protector was he? He couldn't afford to sleep in. How long had she been up? Alone in the kitchen? A moving target. He reached for his phone. His heart sank when he realized it was eight thirty. He couldn't remember the last time he'd slept this long.

He pushed a hand through his hair. He was grungy, in desperate need of a shower. First though, he needed to check on Addie to see if she was okay. Not bothering to get dressed, he lumbered downstairs in the t-shirt and boxer shorts he'd slept in. He paused for a second at the sound of Addie's voice, filling the air.

She was standing in front of the stove, stirring something in a skillet. A grin tugged at his lips as he watched her dance to the upbeat tune of the pop song she was singing. He loved how Addie was so impulsive and in-the-moment, not giving a rip what anyone thought of her. In his parents' world of old Southern money, image was everything. Every word and action was carefully measured to make the right impression in high society.

Desire simmered in Maddox's stomach as his gaze flickered over Addie's thin waist, the gentle swaying of her hips, her curls swishing happily on her shoulders. Even in jeans and a simple sweater, she was the most captivating woman he'd ever lain eyes on. He surveyed the kitchen and combination living room. Everything was put back together and cleaned up, spic and span. Addie had been busy.

"Good morning."

She jumped, her free hand going over her chest. "Oh, my gosh! You scared me." She whirled around, her cheeks going rosy like sun kissed apples. "You caught me singing, I'm afraid."

"You have a beautiful voice."

A nervous laugh rumbled from her lips. "Well, I'm no Delaney Mitchell."

The distance between them shrank as his eyes held hers. "No, you're one hundred percent Addie Spencer," he murmured appreciatively.

Her eyes rounded as she cleared her throat.

So dang frustrating! In the next instant, the skyscraper barrier rose between them. He could literally see Addie withdrawing from him.

"You should've woken me up."

Her voice had a forced cheerfulness. "Nah, you needed the sleep. Besides, you looked so cute this morning all curled up in a ball." Her eyes bubbled with laughter. "Snoring like a foghorn, I might add."

Heat crawled up his neck. "I don't snore."

"Do too," she winked, her hand going to her hip as she waved the spatula out beside her. She made a point of looking him up and down. "Why don't you get a shower, while I finish up breakfast?"

He frowned, his feet staying rooted to the floor. "I don't like the idea of leaving you down here alone. Not when there's no alarm system."

"What time are the guys coming?"

"Ten."

"What time are we going to visit with your friend Piper?"

"One o'clock."

Maddox caught the shadow that crossed her features. Despite her carefree appearance when he first entered the room, Addie was apprehensive about visiting Piper. He didn't blame her. It was sure to be an emotional encounter. He suspected that it might also be tense. While Addie was holding to the notion that Piper and Jordan had a good marriage, the facts spoke otherwise.

Addie offered a smile, dispelling the gloom, before turning back to the stove. He bridged the distance between them and stood beside her.

"What ya makin'?" He looked at what she was stirring, pointing. At first, he thought his eyes were deceiving him. "Is that sausage gravy?"

"Sure is." A proud smile tipped her lips.

His voice rose. "Are you kidding me? I love biscuits and gravy!"

"See, you're not the only one who remembers." She wiggled her eyebrows.

"Did you make biscuits too?"

She pointed. "Baking in the oven."

"H—how in the heck did you learn how to make biscuits and gravy?" he sputtered

She laughed. "Delaney taught me."

He was at loss for words. The woman of his dreams was standing beside him and she'd made his favorite meal. "Wait a minute." He grabbed her arm, his expression dead-pan.

"What?"

"I've gotta pinch myself to make sure I'm not still sleeping. This is too good to be true."

"Hey, now." She lightly shoved him. "Go take a shower." She wrinkled her nose. "You stink." She lifted her chin. "I'm not having a stinky person at the table."

"I don't stink," he countered, feeling offended, even though he knew she was mostly joking. He had to fight the urge to sniff under his arm.

She giggled. "Go. I'll be fine down here."

"I dunno." He glanced around the cabin, thinking how easy it would be for someone to break in.

"I've been up for three hours already, and I've been perfectly fine. A few more minutes won't kill me." She lifted an eyebrow. "I say a few minutes, but I guess that depends on how long it takes you to shower." She cocked her head, a teasing light flickering in her eyes, picking up the gold flecks. "From the looks of that unsightly frizz, it might take a while to tame that hair."

He was glad she was loosening up towards him. He touched his curls. "Sheesh. I've only been up a short while and already I'm getting ripped by that lethal tongue." He grinned, loving every minute of it. "All right. I'll shower." He reached to grab a piece of bacon from the plate beside the stove, but she slapped his hand.

"No eating until breakfast."

He let out a long breath, his shoulders sagging. "All right. What are you? The bacon Nazi?"

"Yep." She lifted her chin, looking stern. When she turned her attention back to the gravy, he snagged a piece.

Her mouth fell, making her look like a disgruntled kid. "Maddox!" she growled. "You're supposed to wait."

He grinned, loving how easy it was to get a rise out of her. "This is the appetizer."

She brought her lips together in a tight line. "Fine," she pouted. She pointed with the spatula. "Go. Chop, chop. And hurry. Biscuits aren't good cold."

He saluted. "Yes, ma'am."

MADDOX ATE until he thought his stomach would pop. "That was fantastic."

"Really?" Her eyes filled with cautious hope.

"Really. Some of the lightest biscuits I've ever had."

Her lips curved with pleasure as she sat back in her seat. "Thank you."

A current of desire buzzed through Maddox. Everything he'd ever wanted was sitting right there in front of him. All he had to do was stand up and pull Addie into his arms. Well, he could go that route ... if he were a glutton for punishment. In two-seconds flat, Addie would slap him—no punch him—and order him out of her house. Then she'd be left alone to face this threat. He decided then and there that someone upstairs must have a sense of humor. Otherwise, why in the heck would he be in this situation? He'd better school his feelings before he made a complete idiot of himself. "Despite all the turmoil ... it was good to see you singing this morning."

Color seeped into her cheeks as she gave him a nervous laugh. "I was feeling pretty down this morning when I first got up. Singing helped take my mind off everything." She hugged her arms, her eyes turning to dark pools of green. "Too much alone time's not good. I start thinking about everything." Her voice faltered. "Jordan's death. How Piper's now a widow. My almost kidnapping." She shook her head, her features tightening. "The crazy part is that we still don't have any answers."

He rubbed his jaw, mentally running through the plan. "I should hear back from Sutton today. Hopefully, he'll be able to shed some light on the kidnapper, find out why he targeted you and if he's the one who killed Jordan."

"Yes," she said despondently, "and I hope Piper will be able to tell us what was going on with Jordan."

He gave her a meaningful look. "Including why Jordan met with a divorce attorney." It took half a second for the air between them to grow tense. "We have to press Piper on the state of her marriage, even if it's uncomfortable," he added.

She threw up a hand. "Geez. Why does it matter what kind of relationship they had? Jordan's gone."

He heard the tremor in her voice, felt a wave of sympathy for the loss of her friend. It was all he could do to keep from reaching over and taking her hand. "It might not matter, but we have to turn over every stone. That's the only way we'll find out the truth." He eyed her, knowing his next comment would set her off. Nevertheless, it needed to be said. "I've been thinking about the key Jordan gave you."

She straightened in her seat, interest flickering in her eyes. "Have you had some ideas about what it goes to?"

"A few." He waved a hand. "But that's not what I want to talk about."

She cocked her head, looking thoughtful. "Then what?"

"Jordan gave the key to you, not to Piper, his wife. Does that not strike you as odd?"

Her forehead raised. "I dunno. Not necessarily. We were good friends, and I happened to be in the same location where he was."

"You didn't *happen* to be there." He made air quotes. "Jordan came to see you."

She frowned, wariness seeping into her voice. "To get the jewelry for Piper."

"Yeah, that's what he said."

She gave him a hard look, spitting out the words. "I have no reason to doubt that Jordan came to see me to get the jewelry."

"And yet he happened to drop a key into your purse. Now someone's out to get you." He fought the urge to roll his eyes. "Do you not see a pattern here?"

"You don't have to get smart about it." Her jaw tightened. "I don't understand why you're so determined to throw Piper under the bus."

It took effort to keep from raising his voice. "I'm not trying to throw anyone under the bus. Jordan said you were the only one he could trust, meaning that he might not have trusted Piper. That's all I'm saying."

"That's absurd!" she scoffed, her face turning red. "Of course he trusted Piper."

He held up a hand. "You've got to remove your emotions from this, look at it analytically."

She shook her head, her voice cracking with emotion. "I just lost one of my closest friends. My best friend lost her husband." Her nostrils flared, the words falling like concrete blocks from her lips as she balled her fist. "Forgive me if I'm a little emotional."

The conversation was spiraling out of control. He had to rein it back in. "I get it. What you're going through is tough, but I'm not the enemy here."

"Then stop acting like it," she shot back.

They sat eyeing one another until Maddox spoke. "All I'm saying is that it might not be wise to let Piper know we have a key."

She gave him an incredulous look, throwing her hands in the air. "How many times do I have to tell you that you're wrong about Piper?" Her eyes misted. "She loved Jordan, and he loved her."

He gave her a measured look. "How much do you trust Piper?"

"Implicitly." Her green eyes flashed, chin tilting up in defiance, ready to take him on. She was stunningly beautiful and so dang stubborn.

He drummed his fingers on the table, thinking aloud. "So, you think we should tell Piper about the key?"

She flicked her wrist. "Absolutely. If there's even the slightest chance that Piper knows what it could go to, then it would save us time."

"True," he conceded.

She sat there glaring like he was public enemy number one. "From the way you're going after Piper, I'm beginning to think you have a chip on your shoulder about women."

He laughed in surprise. "Nope. Not all women." He gave her an appreciative look, his gaze lingering on her long enough to evoke a deep flush over her cheeks. "Just one headstrong beauty with corkscrew curls and a sharp tongue that could lacerate metal."

She fast-blinked a couple of times, then let out a nervous laugh. "All right, Bama boy. You're putting on the charm a little thick," she blustered, touching her hair.

He couldn't stop the grin that stole over his lips. "Nope. Even I'm not that charming." He winked. "Just telling the truth."

Her face blared like a beacon, her mouth moving jerkily like she was at a loss for words.

"The more things change, the more they stay the same," he mused.

"What does that mean?" she demanded.

"You don't have to fight me at every turn."

Her eyes widened. "You're such a moron," she muttered.

"Takes one to know one," he taunted. The fight in her was thrilling.

She blew out a long, frustrated breath, but a hint of a smile touched her eyes. Like him, she was invigorated by the verbal sparring.

He put on his best fearful expression. "You know, sometimes you can be a little scary."

She pulled a face. "Huh?"

He motioned at her with his hand. "Not just you, but all women."

"Oh, no. Here we go." She rolled her eyes as she pushed back her chair and stood. She reached for her empty plate and glass, taking them to the sink.

He also stood, grabbing his plate. As tempting as it was to launch into his explanation right off the bat, it was better to remain quiet, whet her appetite to capture her attention.

She sighed, turning to him. "Okay, let's hear it." She rinsed off her plate and fork and placed them in the dishwater. Next, she took his plate from his hand. Their skin brushed, causing a tingle to rush through him. He could tell from her startled expression that she felt it too. Didn't Addie get it? What they had together came along only once in a lifetime, to those who were lucky. The time he'd spent with Addie was the best of his life, like walking in the sun 24/7. Without her, life was drab and gloomy.

He pointed at the cookie sheet. "Do you have something to put the biscuits in?"

"Yes, in the upper cabinet, to the left of the fridge. Over there."

He opened the cupboard and reached for a container and lid. A smile played on his lips. "I still can't believe you made me biscuits and gravy." He gave her a sideways look. "No Southern boy living and breathing can resist a woman who knows how to cook." His voice was light, but he could tell from the way she stiffened that she caught the serious undertone of his statement.

"So?" she said offhandedly. "Can Felicity cook?"

Wow. This Felicity thing had taken a life of its own. Did he dare tell Addie that the whole thing was a ruse? Nah, it was kind of fun seeing Addie squirm a little. "Oh, yeah. She's an amazing cook."

A dark thundercloud puffed over her face. "How fortunate for you," she said tartly. Long pause. "You never did finish your story, about why women scare you."

"Oh, yeah." Addie was getting bent-out-of-shape about Felicity. Did that mean she still cared about him? The notion sent his heart pumping a little faster. *Down, boy*, he cautioned himself. Even if Addie did care, there was still the enormous obstacle of his profession looming over them. Neither of them knew how to get past that. He leaned against the counter, folding his arms. "Okay, it all started with Adam and Eve."

She snorted out a laugh. "Seriously?"

"Just hear me out. Eve partook of the fruit, leaving poor Adam no choice but to also partake."

"Original sin, huh." She shook her head. "Blame it all on poor Eve."

"Okay, you want another example from the Bible? Take Sampson and Delilah. The guy got his mind all wrapped up in a woman and she tricked him into cutting his hair."

"All right. I'll play along." Her eyes sparkled with interest. "What else you got?"

"David and Bathsheba," he said, his tongue hanging on the word *bath*.

She laughed. "I don't think her name is pronounced that way. It's more like Basheba, with the T being silent."

"It's Bath Sheba. After all, her bath was what started all the trouble."

"Oh, no. Don't go blaming David's treachery on Bathsheba. The poor woman was simply taking a bath. It wasn't her fault David was a Peeping Tom."

"She was bathing on a rooftop. If you ask me, she was begging for trouble."

Her eyebrows shot up. "Actually, if you go back and read the Bible reference, it doesn't say specifically where Bathsheba was. David was on the rooftop when he saw her taking a bath—something she was doing not only for hygiene purposes but also for a ritual ceremony required by the Law of Moses. The fault lay clearly with David. Think of the beginning, how the story was framed, 'In a time when all kings went to war, David stayed back.'" She wagged a finger, giving him a victorious look. "An idle mind is the devil's workshop."

He let out a low whistle. "Wow, you know your Bible references."

"I've taken a few classes on the subject," she quipped.

Addie was wicked smart. Her appetite for continuous learning was one of the things that first attracted Maddox to her. Like him, she loved traveling to new places. They used to talk for hours about the places they'd like to one day visit together. It cut to know that would never happen.

"Putting the blame on Bathsheba's par for the course. A typical male perspective," she huffed.

He winced. "Ouch. That hurt."

She rolled her eyes. "Is that all you've got, Bama boy?"

"What about Jacob? The poor sucker worked seven years for the love of his life and ended up with the sister. Need I say more?"

Her eyebrow shot up. "The women didn't do that. It was their father."

He blew out a long breath. "Okay, I'll give you that one…if we're splitting hairs."

She shot him an incredulous look. "Give me that one? Really? All right, mister. What about Queen Esther? Her valor saved an entire nation."

"All right," he drawled. "You've got me there."

She looked back at the table. "Would you hand me those glasses?"

"Sure." As he handed them to her, something hanging on the side of the refrigerator caught his eye. He peered, getting a closer look. It was a card with scraggly edges like it had been crafted by a child. There was a tree and a smiley-faced heart drawn in crayon with two words—Be Happy. It looked like something a student would give a teacher. To Maddox's knowledge, Addie had little interaction with children. "What's that?"

She followed his eyes. "What?"

"The card on the refrigerator. What's the story behind that?"

She looked thoughtful. For a second, he thought she was going to tell him, but a cryptic smile curved her lips. "A story for another time."

"Now you have me intrigued. Come on," he urged. "Tell me."

She wiggled her eyebrows. "Nope. Don't think so," she chimed. Their eyes met, sending a burst of exhilaration shooting through him. Being here with Addie felt right—more right than anything had felt in a long time.

He moved closer, the air between them crackling with unleashed energy. "But I'll be so disappointed," he murmured, his gaze tracing down the line of her delectable neck, begging to be kissed.

"I guess you'll have to get used to disappointment," she uttered, her voice going husky. He caught the flicker of desire in her eyes igniting a fire in him. His fingers itched to touch her hair. "What if I tickle it out of you?" he teased.

Her eyes widened as she rocked back. "You wouldn't dare!"

"Oh, yes, I would," he grinned, reaching for her.

She squealed and jumped as he started tickling her. "Stop," she protested, laughing.

"Okay, if I must, I must." He blew out a long, dramatic breath.

Her lips curved into an unencumbered smile. For an instant, the problems seemed to vanish like morning mist over a lake, giving way to the rising sun. This is what contentment was—being with the woman he loved, doing simple things like cleaning the kitchen. He realized she was studying him with a bold, reckless glint in her vivid green eyes like she was challenging him to kiss her. Blast it! The wise thing to do would be to walk away to protect his heart.

Walk away! the voice in his head commanded. But Maddox had never been one to walk away from a challenge. A silent exchange passed between them, making him ultra-aware that they were alone. He stepped closer, his finger trailing lightly down the curve of her jaw. The intimacy of the moment enveloped them like a silken parachute. "You know, it's not fair," he said softly. Yes, he might be jumping out of a plane, but he had a parachute, right?

She cocked an eyebrow, moving so close he could feel her warm breath on his face. "What's not fair?"

His heart slammed against his ribcage like an out-of-control drummer. Somehow, he managed to keep his voice light. "The way to a man's heart is through his stomach."

"That's what I hear." A sensuous smile curved her lips. Like him, Addie never did anything halfway. She fought hard and loved hard. His kind of woman from the word *go*.

"You made me biscuits and gravy." He wound a tendril of her hair around his finger. "How's a man supposed to resist that?" he uttered, sliding his arm around her waist. His eyes traced the outline of her soft, full lips. "I could kiss you right now."

"Not if I kiss you first," she said fiercely. She closed the distance between them and pressed her lips to his. For a second, he let her lead, her lips moving coaxingly with tantalizing persuasion, sending a tender ache stirring through him. Then the need for her grew as his mouth took hers. Fire and brilliance cut a path through him, a dozen volcanoes erupting at once. Instinctively, he ran his hands up her back and threaded his fingers through her thick mane of glorious curls. Both gave as much as they got, passion running a swift river through his blood.

Torment and exquisite joy warred within him as he pulled back, his gaze caressing the lines of her extraordinary face. The admission of his traitorous heart tumbled from his mouth like the haggard confession of a war prisoner tortured to the brink of breaking. "Addie, I—" *Love you*, he was about to say, but she patted his cheek.

"Do me a favor." A playful grin swirled over her lips.

"Sure," came his dazed reply. He'd cross a dozen deserts, climb Mt. Everest, anything she wanted.

"Give my regards to Felicity."

While he was standing there, jaw dropped to the floor, trying to figure out how to answer, she sauntered away. When she reached the door, she glanced back over her shoulder. "Finish cleaning up, would ya? I need to get ready before the alarm guys come. Then we can head to Piper's. Afterwards, I need to stop by the resort to check on the water filter conference."

"Sure." He rubbed his neck, wondering what in the heck had just happened.

One step forward, ten steps back. The story of his life, he thought glumly as he reached in the cupboard to grab a container for the gravy.

11

Addie's nerves were jumping like a frog on caffeine when she drove her Jetta through the large, stately gates of the Gentry Estate. As the splendor of the tall evergreens, standing like sentinels on each side of the driveway, gave way to the magnificent, brick, Tudor mansion, she glanced at Maddox, who was sitting in the passenger seat, to get his reaction. His chiseled jaw was set firm, his keen eyes taking in everything. She tightened her grip on the steering wheel, mentally preparing herself for the encounter with Piper. Even though Addie had adamantly defended her best friend, a part of her wondered if Piper and Jordan really were having marital problems. If that were the case, why did they keep it from her?

She turned off the engine and was about to open the door when Maddox touched her arm, sending a rush of tingles through her.

"Are you okay?"

"I'm fine. Why?" She forced a smile.

"You seem like you're on edge."

She had to fight the urge to laugh in his face. "Yeah, I guess I am a little nervous, but that's to be expected, right?" Emotion rose in her throat. "I'm seeing my friend for the first time after she lost her husband to a senseless, violent act." The all-too-familiar anger blistered over her at the injustice of it all.

He nodded. "I'll be right by your side the entire time."

"Thanks." She was touched by the concern on his handsome face. She offered an appreciative smile as her thoughts involuntarily went back to the kiss. Heat blasted up her neck. That was one for the books. Wow! No guy had ever made her feel the way Maddox did. After this morning, she knew beyond a shadow of a doubt that she was still crazy about him. Her chest tightened. Felicity! Even though she knew nothing about the woman, she was starting to detest her.

He cleared his throat. "About what happened earlier."

A hard amusement rose in her chest. "Are you talking about the kiss?"

He blinked in surprise, a quirky grin ruffling his lips. "Well, yeah."

Panic fluttered in her stomach. Was he trying to tell her it was a mistake? That he never should've kissed her because there was someone else in the picture? She couldn't deal with that right now! She opened the door.

"Hey," he said, his brows wrinkling with frustration. "We were in the middle of a conversation."

Her back went stiff as she gave him a sideways glance. "If you're expecting me to apologize for the kiss, you can save your breath." A tight smile stretched over her lips. "You were mine long before you were ever hers."

He flinched then burst out laughing.

Her eyes narrowed. "Really? You think this is funny?" She got out of the car and slammed the door behind her. The nerve of him! He jumped out and rushed to catch up to her as she bounded up the stairs.

"What's going on with us?" A cocky grin wormed over his lips. "You're jealous of Felicity."

"Hah! I don't even know Felicity. If anything, I feel sorry for her."

"What's that supposed to mean?"

"Never mind," she grumbled, punching the doorbell.

"No, you started it. I wanna know what you meant by that."

She clenched her teeth. "Can we not do this now?" She pulled at her sweater, trying to clear her head, which was dang near impossible considering the source of her anxiety was standing right next to her. It didn't help matters that he smelled fantastic—musk, clean water, and mint. The combination was one hundred percent Navy SEAL male. She clenched her fist. She couldn't think about Maddox right now, not when there was so much at stake. She had to focus on questioning Piper. The sooner they could get to the bottom of the mystery, the sooner Maddox could go his merry way and she could get on with her life.

Her heart about stopped when he slid an arm around her shoulders and pulled her close.

"What're you doing?" she demanded.

"You're just hoping there's another round of kissing," he murmured in her ear.

A wave of desire overpowered her before she could crowd it out. "Moron," she grumbled, pulling away from him, but he only laughed. She might've slugged him in the gut, but the door opened.

Tears rushed to Addie's eyes. "Hey."

"Hey," Piper responded. Her thin face caved as a sob rose in her throat.

Addie threw her arms around Piper and pulled her into a tight hug. Piper's shoulders shook as she wept. Tears streamed down Addie's face. Her heart felt like it would break in two. "I'm so sorry," she uttered a few minutes later when they pulled apart.

Piper nodded, bringing a hand to her mouth, stifling a hiccup in her throat. Self-consciously she mopped her eyes and touched her hair. It was then that Addie realized she'd not formally introduced Maddox. Piper had heard about him often enough, but she'd never actually met him. She motioned. "This is Maddox. My ..." She scrambled to come up with the right words to describe him, not for Piper's sake but for Maddox's.

"Her friend," he inserted, a hint of amusement in his ocean blue eyes.

Recognition touched Piper's expression. "Of course. You're Addie's

Navy SEAL." She frowned, glancing at Addie. "I didn't realize the two of you were back together." Before Addie could articulate a response, Piper continued. "It's a good thing. Addie was devastated when she thought you were dead." She gave Maddox a brief smile. "I'm glad things are working out for the two of you."

There was no guile in Piper's tone, merely a statement of fact. Somehow, that made it worse. Heat stung Addie's cheeks, and she didn't dare make eye contact with Maddox.

"It's nice to finally meet you in person," Piper said mechanically. "Please. Come in." She led them past the formal living room into the family room off the kitchen. Addie sat down on the sofa. Maddox sat down dangerously close to her with Piper choosing one of the over-stuffed chairs across from them.

The last time Addie had seen Piper, she'd been on top of the world, excited about the upcoming release of PZT. The woman sitting before them was a shadow of her normal self. Petite with short, dark hair and lively, dark eyes, Piper was stylishly attractive. Today, however, her eyes were bloodshot and sunken around the edges like over-ripe fruit. Her tear-stained cheeks were so pale, they looked almost gray. Piper reminded Addie of a fragile twig that could break under the slightest amount of pressure.

Addie's heart ached for her friend. No words were sufficient to express the sympathy and concern she felt. "I'm so sorry you're going through this," she uttered.

Piper's lips pulled into a taut line. "I still can't believe Jordan's gone," she said quietly, clasping her hands in her lap.

"Me either."

Piper gave her a direct look. The haunted expression in Piper's eyes battered Addie like a wrecking ball. "Did you know Jordan was coming to see you at the resort?"

"No, he just showed up. I was running out the door to pick up last-minute items for a conference and had planned to grab lunch while I was out. Since Jordan showed up, I asked my assistant to get the items for me and suggested that Jordan and I grab something at the café.

We sat out on the terrace and talked." Her voice faltered. "He was hit as he walked out the front of the resort."

"Why did Jordan come to see you?"

"He stopped by to pick up some jewelry I was holding for him— earrings and a bracelet. He wanted to give them to you on your cruise." Her heart hurt thinking how Jordan's last actions had been an attempt to do something nice for his wife. Hopefully, eventually, that would be a healing balm to Piper to know Jordan was thinking of her until the very end.

Piper looked surprised. "Did you tell me that already?"

"So much has happened. I can't remember." Addie wanted to forget that horrific phone call where she'd informed Piper that her husband was killed. Maddox shifted in his seat. Addie could feel his impatience, knew he wanted her to question Piper about her marriage, PZT, and the key. Also, she needed to know why someone was targeting her. She glanced his direction, her eyes telling him to take a chill pill. Piper's feelings were at stake here. She had to ease into the hard topics.

"Do you still have the jewelry?" Piper asked. "I'd like to get it, if you don't mind." Her mouth worked like she was trying to control her emotion. "It would be nice to have that as a final memory."

"Um, about that ..." Addie had called Steinway's this morning, only to learn that he'd been unable to repair the clasp on the bracelet. He sent it to his nephew in Brooklyn who specializes in fixing hard-to-repair jewelry. Mr. Steinway assured her he'd contact his nephew today to find out the status.

Piper leaned forward. "What's going on?"

Addie looked to Maddox for help.

"Currently, the jewelry's being examined," Maddox said.

Piper's brows slanted down in a V as she looked back and forth between Addie and Maddox. "Examined? I don't understand."

"The same day Jordan was killed, my cabin was broken into," Addie blurted.

"What?" Piper's face drained as she clutched the arms of the chair.

She looked so weak and vulnerable that Addie feared she might pass out.

"Yesterday, Addie was almost kidnapped," Maddox added.

Tears rose in Piper's eyes as she put a hand to her mouth. She shook her head. "Why?" she uttered.

Maddox leaned forward, clasping his hands together in his lap. "That's partly why we came here today, in the hope that you can shed some light on the situation."

"And to check on you," Addie inserted, shooting Maddox a dark look.

Maddox's voice became businesslike. "We believe that Jordan's death and the attacks on Addie are linked to PZT, the Alzheimer's drug you and Jordan have been developing."

Addie halfway expected Piper to jump up and lash out, but she just sat there. When she spoke, Addie never could've imagined the words that would come out of her mouth.

"I'm so sorry that Jordan involved you in this," Piper said.

The blood left Addie's head, making her feel dizzy. "What?" A river of heat flushed through her body when she saw Piper's guilty expression. "What're you talking about?" Her back went ramrod straight as she leaned forward. "Were you and Jordan having marital problems?"

Piper folded her arms tightly over her chest. "Yes," she finally admitted.

The word hit Addie like a slap in the face. She looked at Maddox, expecting to see an *I-told-you-so* expression on his face, but she saw only sympathy. "Why didn't you tell me?" she asked, turning her attention back to Piper.

A single tear dribbled down Piper's cheek. "I dunno." She let out a half-laugh, swiping her runny nose. "I was embarrassed, humiliated." She rubbed her hands on her jeans. "Jordan was having an affair."

The breath whooshed out of Addie's lungs. "What? No, Jordan wouldn't do that to you."

Piper's eyes hardened. "Unfortunately, he did."

Addie tried to process what she was hearing, but her mind buzzed like an overcrowded beehive. "I don't understand. He loved you."

Maddox touched her arm, giving her a quick, reassuring smile before turning his attention to Piper. "Maybe you should start from the beginning and tell us everything."

Piper nodded. "A little over six months ago, Jordan started acting strange—keeping late hours, making impromptu trips, becoming secretive."

"Like how he came to see me unannounced on the day of his death and didn't tell you where he was going." Addie didn't realize she'd spoken the words out loud until Piper answered.

"Yes. At first, I attributed Jordan's erratic behavior to stress. PZT is in the final testing phase, and we're getting ready to submit our drug application to the FDA."

Addie nodded. "Jordan mentioned that."

Piper's features tightened. "Did Jordan also tell you that he planned to sell the formula to our competitor, Barrett Medical?"

Addie's throat constricted to the point where she felt it might swallow her tongue. Her words came out breathless. "Jordan was a good person. He loved you. He was honest." She clenched her hands. "He wouldn't do that to you." The words sounded small and insignificant in her own ears, like she was shouting against the wind. "Above all, Jordan wanted to help cure Alzheimer's." Her voice quivered with intensity. "He wanted to protect families from suffering the same fate we did. Jordan's mother, your mother ... Gram."

Piper's eyes were a curious mixture of pity and anger. "I know it's hard to believe." She grunted out a laugh. "I could hardly believe it myself, at first." Her voice took on a faraway quality as she stared past Addie into space. "My dad came to me. Told me his suspicions. There were rumors that Jordan was working a secret deal with Blanche Richey the VP of Barrett Medical." Her jaw hardened. "Eventually, I hired a detective and discovered that the rumors were true." Her eyes streaked with pain. "Further, I learned that Jordan and Blanche were having an affair."

The current was rushing so swiftly that Addie could hardly keep her head above water. "The two of you planned to go on a cruise the following day. You told me so yourself." She eyed Piper, daring her to deny it. "Why would you do that if your marriage was on the rocks?"

Piper crossed her legs and wrapped her hands around her knees. "Jordan had a falling out with Blanche. He realized she was in cahoots with another man and only using him to get the formula for PZT. Jordan severed all communications with Blanche. He and I started seeing a counselor." Her voice broke. "I thought everything was fine."

"Why didn't you tell me any of this was happening?" Rocks knocked together in Addie's stomach. She and Piper shared every-thing...or so she'd thought.

"You don't know how much I wanted to." Piper gave her a pleading look. "Jordan was embarrassed over his actions, and I wanted to just move on."

Maddox interrupted the conversation. "There's something I'm not getting." He tilted his head. "You said PZT is in the final testing phase and that a drug application will be filed with the FDA in the near future."

Piper nodded. "Correct."

"Jordan was part owner of your drug company, right?"

"Yes, he and I were partners in Therapia," Piper answered. Her expression was one of annoyance, like she didn't understand why he was interjecting himself into the conversation.

"After my cabin was ransacked, Maddox came into town to protect me," Addie explained. "He's trying to get to the bottom of why someone's targeting me."

Understanding registered on her features. "I see." Piper looked at Maddox, the lines on her face smoothing. "You were saying?"

Maddox scooted to the edge of the sofa. "Once PZT hits the market, it will potentially be worth billions of dollars, correct?"

Piper spread her hands. "That's the hope."

"Assuming the drug works," Maddox added.

"Oh, I assure you. It works," Piper countered, lifting her chin.

"Okay, so you have a revolutionary drug—that works—about to

hit the market." Maddox's tone grew musing. "Jordan is half owner of the company that developed it. He's in the driver's seat. Why would he want to sell it?"

Addie frowned. An excellent point. She looked at Piper, awaiting her explanation.

Piper let out a long breath. "Getting a drug on the market is a long, painstaking process. It can take years to complete the process. Jordan grew impatient with the red tape. He wanted to cut to the chase and release the drug ASAP to get it to as many people as possible. Barrett Medical has a history of circumventing the system. I'm sure Blanche promised Jordan the Moon," she added bitterly, "told him everything he wanted to hear." Piper's expression grew grim as her eyes met Addie's. "Even though I didn't agree with Jordan's reasoning, I understood where he was coming from. Think of what it would've meant to my mom and your grandmother if they'd had access to PZT."

Tears rushed to Addie's eyes. Had Jordan developed PZT sooner, it might've cured Gram's Alzheimer's. Still, it wouldn't have saved her from developing brain cancer. She was surprised when Maddox reached for her hand, giving it a comforting squeeze. He gave her an empathetic smile, showcasing his left dimple. An unexpected warmth settled over Addie. In that moment, she realized how grateful she was to have Maddox by her side.

Maddox frowned. "None of this explains why Jordan was killed."

"I have my suspicions," Piper said darkly. "Brent Barrett the CEO and founder of Barrett Medical and his lackey, Blanche Richey, thought they had the greatest discovery of this century in the bag. Then, Jordan foiled their plans. The two of them would stop at nothing to get their hands on the formula for PZT."

What Piper said made sense. Addie turned to Maddox to get his reaction. She could almost see the wheels turning in his head.

Maddox stroked his chin. "I'm assuming you keep the formula for PZT under lock and key?"

"Industrial espionage is the plague of drug research and development. We have a single computer that we keep locked in a vault. The formula for PZT is on that computer." Piper held up a finger. "However, we suspect that Jordan kept a personal copy."

"Your entire theory hinges on the idea that PZT actually works," Maddox said.

Piper lifted an eyebrow. "I assure you, it works."

The tension in the room grew palpable. A second later, Piper's father entered. Maddox and Addie moved to stand.

Hamilton held out a hand. "Don't get up." He sat down in the chair next to Piper. She did the introductions. "Maddox, this is my dad, Hamilton Gentry. Maddox is a close friend of Addie's."

"Hello," Hamilton said cordially as he touched his glasses and nodded. He offered a polite smile to Addie. "Nice to see you."

"You too." As close as Addie was to Piper, she hardly knew Hamilton. To her, he would always be Dr. Hamilton Gentry, the renowned surgeon, who was a little uptight for her taste. Mid-height, Hamilton was wiry with dusty-blonde hair going silver around his temples and thinning on top. In other words, he was the quintessential picture of a successful doctor. He turned to Piper, a brief smile touching his lips. "What did I miss? I was in my office on a phone call," he explained.

"Maddox was questioning the effectiveness of PZT," Piper said.

Piper's tone was neutral, but Addie could tell from the tight pull of her jaw that she didn't like Maddox calling her work into question. Addie didn't blame her. In Maddox's defense, however, he was turning over every stone to discover the truth.

"I told Addie and Maddox that I believe Brent Barrett or someone at Barrett Medical is responsible for Jordan's death, that they were trying to steal the formula for PZT. Maddox asserted that my theory hinges on the validity of PZT."

Addie leaned forward. "Even if that's true, it still doesn't explain why someone would be after me."

Hamilton's brows darted together, concern seeping into his eyes. "What?"

"Someone broke into my cabin and tried to kidnap me." A shiver ran down Addie's spine as she hugged her arms.

A stricken look came over Hamilton. "Are you serious?"

"Unfortunately, yes," Maddox answered.

Piper gave Addie a probing look. "Did Jordan say anything to you? Give you the formula? Obviously, someone thinks he did, or you wouldn't be a target."

Addie had never been blessed with a poker face. She knew the answer was broadcast in her expression.

Piper leaned forward, eyeing her. "Addie?"

Rather than answering, Addie turned to Maddox. She'd been fully prepared to tell Piper about the key this morning. Now, however, everything was muddled and confusing. Never in a million years would she have dreamt that Jordan and Piper would've kept so much from her. She couldn't help feeling betrayed by them both. Especially Jordan! How could he stoop to having an affair? Did loyalty mean nothing to him? Clearly, he was not the man she thought he was. So much for her ability to judge character. She gave Maddox a questioning look.

He nodded. "It's okay. Tell them."

"Tell us what?" Piper asked, an edge in her voice.

Addie tucked her hair behind her ears. "Right before Jordan left the terrace where we were having lunch, he dropped a key into my purse."

Piper frowned. "What sort of key?"

"Show her," Maddox prompted.

Addie bent over and reached for her purse, placing it in her lap. She retrieved the silver key and held it up. "This."

"What does it go to?" Piper asked.

"We were hoping you could tell us," Maddox inserted.

Addie handed Piper the key. She examined it. "It could go to almost anything." Disappointment sounded in her voice.

"Did Jordan have a gym membership? Or storage facility?"

"Not that I know of." Piper looked to her dad for help.

"I have no idea." Hamilton shook his head regretfully. "Jordan's behavior was so strange at the end. Who knows what was going through his head."

Addie caught the note of bitterness in Hamilton's voice. His distaste for Jordan was twofold—he'd been unfaithful to his only daughter, and he was sabotaging the company Hamilton helped him create.

"Wait a minute." Piper's voice grew animated. "When Jordan's mother passed, he put her things in a rented storage unit until he and his siblings could sort through her will. I assumed after everything was taken care of, Jordan would have no further use for a storage unit." She paused, tilting her head. "I wonder if, maybe, he still had it."

"There can't be that many storage facilities in Birchwood Springs," Maddox said. "Let's start by calling those."

Piper frowned, a hint of accusation in her eyes, as she looked at Addie. "Why did he give you a key? We were working things out. I thought Jordan and I were building trust." Her voice hitched. "And yet, he went to see you without my knowledge."

Addie grunted, hating feeling guilty for something over which she had no control. "I wish I knew."

"Someone—presumably from Barrett Medical—must think you have the only other copy of the formula for PZT," Hamilton said. "They think it's easier to get to you than to break into a secure vault."

Fear lurked in Addie's throat. "Well, I don't have it," she spat.

Piper's eyes held hers. "Did Jordan give you a hint about what the key could go to? What did the two of you talk about during lunch?"

"Just chit-chat mostly, but I could tell Jordan was on edge." No way was Addie going to tell Piper that Jordan said she was the only one he could trust. He'd also said Piper didn't understand. What didn't she understand?

Piper gave her a perceptive look. "There's more. I can tell."

The words seemed to tumble out of Addie's mouth of their own accord. "Jordan said you were a good woman but that you didn't understand." She cringed at Piper's wounded expression. "I'm sorry, but those were his words."

Piper leaned back in her seat, looking deflated. Hamilton put an arm around her shoulders. "Are you okay?" he asked, his voice surprisingly gentle. There was obviously another side to him that Addie hadn't seen. Clearly, he had a soft spot for his only daughter.

"Yeah." Piper offered a weak smile. "I'm sorry. This is just so... hard. I'm sure Jordan meant that I didn't understand his need to fast-track PZT to market."

"Makes sense," Maddox said.

There was something else Addie needed to add to the conversation—Jordan's strange words at the end. "Just before Jordan died, he asked me to forgive him."

Piper let out an audible gasp.

"What do you think Jordan meant by that?" Addie continued.

Piper looked at her dad as a silent exchange passed between them. Finally, Hamilton spoke. "Show them the video."

Piper's eyebrow lifted. "Do you think that's wise?"

A grim determination set over Hamilton's features. "At this point, it seems to be the best option."

"What you're about to see is highly confidential and could cause us grief if word of it ever got out." Piper eyed Addie and Maddox. "I need your promise that you will keep this to yourselves," she added when they remained quiet.

"Okay," Addie agreed, her gut churning with uncertainty.

Maddox squared his jaw. "Sorry, can't make any promises until I know what we're dealing with."

The air held its breath as Piper looked at Hamilton. Finally, he gave her the okay to continue. She held up the remote and pressed a button.

A picture came on the screen. Addie instantly recognized the elderly woman. "That's Priscilla Roseman." She and Jordan were in an office, sitting across from one another.

Maddox turned to face Addie. "Do you know her?"

"She was an Alzheimer's patient at the same care center with my grandmother and Jordan's mom."

Jordan peered into the camera and announced the date of the interview, a little over a year ago. "State your name," Jordan said.

"Priscilla Marie Roseman."

"Your birthdate."

"November 3, 1945."

"How many children do you have?"

"Four. Two boys and two girls."

"How many grandchildren?"

Priscilla smiled. "Sixteen and one on the way."

As the interview progressed, Addie was utterly amazed ... floored. The last time she'd seen Priscilla, the poor woman was wearing a hospital gown, being spoon-fed applesauce. The Priscilla on the interview was nicely dressed, well spoken, completely lucid. She spoke of her career as a nurse, how much she missed her late husband, how she was looking forward to leaving the care center and going back to her home, where she planned to take up gardening. Addie looked down and realized she was still holding Maddox's hand, squeezing it for all it was worth. "Sorry," she stammered, releasing it. She looked at Piper. "H-how?"

Piper clicked the remote, turning off the TV. Her face had regained some of its color, her eyes shining with pride. "PZT."

"Jordan gave this woman PZT?" Maddox asked.

"Yes," Piper answered.

Disapproval sounded in Maddox's voice. "But the drug hasn't been submitted to the FDA, much less approved."

Hamilton touched his glasses. "Hence the risk in showing you the video."

Piper's face glowed with an inner light. "Jordan knew what PZT could do. He knew the lives that could be changed by it. He felt like it was an atrocity to sit back and watch people waste away when the cure was right there."

"So, he tested it on the patients at the care center," Maddox inserted.

"Not all the patients," Piper said, a touch of impatience in her voice. "Just those he felt would be good candidates." Her voice grew tremulous. "I only wish he'd developed PZT in time to save my mother." Her eyes locked with Addie's. "Or your grandmother."

A rush of emotion rose in Addie's chest. How many times had she prayed that Gram would be healed? To think that the cure was just around the corner. Sadly, not in time to help Gram. The irony carved through her like a scalding knife. Even though Gram's life had been taken by cancer, it would have been miraculous if she could've known her family in the end. If she could've known how much she was loved.

Regret sounded in Piper's voice. "To answer your question, I think Jordan asked you to forgive him because he wasn't able to save your grandmother."

Tears sprang to Addie's eyes, and she was unable to stop them from spilling down her cheeks. Understanding flowed between her and Piper. Just like that, Addie realized what was driving Jordan— why he refused to wait until PZT could be put on the market. Even if one life could be saved, it was worth the risk.

"While I don't agree with Jordan's methods of trying to bypass the system," Piper continued, "I also know the good PZT can do. That's why I'm pushing so hard to get it on the market, so that it'll be available to all people who suffer from this terrible disease." She looked at Addie. "I'm just sorry that you got caught in the crossfire."

Maddox let out a breath. "All right. That helps answer a lot of questions. We need to find what the key goes to, so we can put an end to this thing once and for all." He held out his hand. "The key please."

Addie realized then that she'd handed the key over to Piper for examination and hadn't gotten it back.

"I'll hold onto it for safe keeping," he added.

For a second, Piper looked like she might argue but instead gave him a strained smile. "Of course." She handed it over. Addie could tell it was hard for Piper to trust Maddox, which was understandable considering they'd only just met.

"Maddox may look like your everyday piece of eye candy," Addie joked, "but I can assure you, he's very capable and can be trusted implicitly."

Maddox jerked, a surprised smile creeping over his lips. "Wow, I don't believe it. Addie Spencer just gave me a compliment."

Addie laughed. "Don't let it go to your head." She saw the startled look on Hamilton's face, which made the situation even funnier. His brows shot down like he was about to reprimand Addie for telling a joke. She had the ridiculous urge to burst out laughing. She looked sideways at Maddox. Amusement lit his eyes as they shared the moment.

Hamilton stood, offering a stiff bow. "If you'll excuse me, I have a meeting with the funeral director in an hour." He looked at Addie and Maddox. "I trust you'll be attending Jordan's funeral next Wednesday?"

"We wouldn't miss it," Addie said speaking for them both.

"Very well. Good day." He turned on his heel and strode out of the room.

Addie felt sorry for him. He was so robotic and socially awkward.

Maddox brought his hands together, his tone becoming all business. "Okay, we need to find out what the key goes to."

"I'll get my computer," Piper said, "and look up storage locations."

His lips pressed together in a determined line. "All right. No time like the present."

MADDOX LOOKED out the car window at the passing trees ablaze with the crisp, tawny colors of fall. His gaze traveled up to the clear blue sky touched with tufts of stringy white clouds. The storm the night before had left everything fresh and clean.

Addie chuckled. "Look at you ... salivating over the landscape. I'll bet you wish you had your camera right now."

"It would be nice," he agreed, "under a different set of circumstances."

"Yeah, if we weren't on some wild goose chase to find out what the key goes to. Or if someone weren't trying to kidnap me ... or worse." She shuddered.

He touched her arm, the familiar zing racing through him when their skin touched. "Don't worry. I won't leave your side until this is over. Promise."

Addie gave him an appreciative smile before turning her full attention back to the road. She tightened her hold on the steering wheel. "Do you really think it could be that simple? That the key goes to Jordan's storage facility?"

"We can only hope." His thoughts went back to the conversation with Piper and Hamilton. "What's your take on the things Piper said about Jordan?"

"Which part?"

"The part where she said he was trying to sell the drug formula to Barrett Medical?" His question was met with silence, making him wonder if she was going to answer.

"To tell you the truth, I'm not sure what to think. Does it sound like the Jordan I knew? No, not in the least." Her voice hardened. "Then again, my two closest friends were having major marital problems, and neither of them breathed a word of it. What do I know?" She glanced at him. "What's your take?"

"Everything Piper and her father said sounded plausible. It corroborates what we know about Jordan—that he'd been to a divorce attorney."

"It fits with the things Jordan said, how Piper didn't understand and why Jordan asked for my forgiveness." There was a glum note in her voice.

"I'm sorry about your grandmother. I can only imagine how hard it must've been to see that video of the Alzheimer's patient—to think your grandmother could've been cured."

She gave him a sad smile. "Yes, it was hard." She let out a half-laugh. "Crazy, but I found myself feeling jealous of Priscilla Roseman when I watched that video." Her voice hitched. "At the end of the day though, I'm happy for her. She has her life back, knows who she is, knows her children and grandchildren." She let out a heavy breath. "Regardless of what shortcomings Jordan had in his personal life, I'm grateful that he developed PZT."

"Interesting, how all three of your lives were brought together by Alzheimer's."

"Yes, it is."

"And, all of the people who had Alzheimer's died before they could take PZT."

"Yeah. Sad." Silence settled between them.

"A penny for your thoughts?"

She gave him a slight smile. "I was thinking about the card on my refrigerator. The one you asked about."

His interest piqued. "Yes?"

"I was at the care center, visiting Gram." She paused and took in a shaky breath. "I had just learned that she had cancer and that the prognosis wasn't good."

"I can't begin to imagine what you've been through," he uttered, feeling the urge to put his arms around her and pull her close.

"Thanks," she said mechanically, resuming her narrative. "Gram was lying in her bed. I was sitting beside her, praying and shedding a few tears, when I felt a tug on my arm." She laughed softly. "I looked, surprised to see a little girl standing in front of me. She had these big brown eyes that seemed like they could see into your soul, her hair in braids. She never said a word, simply smiled and handed me the card before bounding out of the room. I looked down and read the message —Be Happy." Her voice caught. "I knew in some inexplicable way that my prayer had been answered by that little girl. Later, I found out the girl was there with her mother. Priscilla Roseman is her grandmother."

A tear slipped down Addie's cheek. She wiped it with the palm of her hand, a self-conscious laugh issuing from her throat. "I'm glad that Priscilla now knows what a wonderful granddaughter she has." Addie took in a deep breath and shot Maddox a brief smile, shrugging her shoulders. "Now you know the rest of the story."

"Thank you for sharing that," he said quietly. Addie was truly one in a million. No wonder he'd fallen so hard, so fast for her. There was so much he wanted to say to her right now. He wanted to take her by the arms and shake some sense into her—make her realize that the two of them were meant for one another. Make her realize that he still loved her, had never stopped loving her. That she consumed nearly his every thought. "Hey, I want you to know that regardless of what happened between us in the past, I'm glad I'm here with you."

Her expression was unreadable as she stared at the road ahead of them. "Thanks."

He got the feeling that his words had fallen flat.

She drew in a deep breath as if trying to bottle up her emotion. He'd gotten a glimpse into her soul and now the dark curtains had been pulled over the window. She was once again the tough, capable, take-crap-off-no-one girl. Heck, he loved that aspect of Addie too. She looked in the rearview mirror at Piper who was following them. Maddox glanced in the side mirror to make sure no one was tailing Piper. All seemed to be okay...for now. After Piper got out her laptop, it had taken less than fifteen minutes to track down the unit. There were several storage locations near Birchwood Springs. Putting the phone on speaker, Piper called all of them saying that she'd received an invoice for Jordan Phelps and was calling to question the balance. The first three people had no record of Jordan Phelps. On the fourth call, however, they hit pay dirt. The lady on the other end of the phone found Jordan in her system.

"I'm showing that a payment was made a week ago. The account is current."

"Then why did I get an outstanding invoice?" Piper questioned. "What unit number are you showing in your system?"

"Twenty-seven."

"Ah, this invoice is for forty-three. It must've been sent to me in error. I'll just shred it. Thanks," she clipped, ending the call.

Feeling his gaze, Addie looked his direction. "What?"

The mood between them was way too somber. Maddox had to do something to lighten it. "I was just thinking, it was around the same time last year when we traveled down this very road to the trailhead where we hiked. Remember?"

"How could I forget?" She chuckled. "Hiking is a loose term

though. We mostly walked, while you snapped pictures of the landscape and every animal that moved."

He laughed. "If I'm remembering correctly, we also made time for a few other things," he said in a low, husky tone. "We gathered around that cozy fire, sitting so close you couldn't wedge a sheet of paper between us. Quite similar to what occurred this morning, actually." A grin tugged at his lips. "You were the first to kiss me then too."

Color fanned her cheeks. "No, you've got it wrong. I distinctly remember you kissing me first," she grumbled. "At any rate, I thought Southern gentlemen weren't supposed to call attention to those types of things."

He ignored her smart remark. "Of course, it was more than just kissing around the fire." He drank in her profile—dainty nose, chin set in iron determination, full rosy lips, tangles of brown ringlets spilling over her shoulders. Her slender hands were gripping the steering wheel with a vengeance, and the stormy look on her face told him it would only be a matter of seconds before her temper blew. "There was some hugging involved, a little necking ..."

"Stop!" She shoved him hard, the motion causing the car to weave onto the shoulder of the road, the warning hum of the textured asphalt reverberating loudly against the tires.

"Whoa, Nellie!" Maddox yelled, holding onto the dash.

Addie clutched the wheel, correcting her mistake, as she swerved back into their lane.

"Are you trying to kill us?"

"You started it," Addie sulked.

"I was just playing around. I didn't expect you to run us off the road."

"I didn't," she said tartly. "We barely went on the shoulder."

"Barely, huh? That's an understatement."

She grunted.

Maddox's phone buzzed. He fished it out of his pocket.

"Let me guess," Addie said, her voice loaded with irritation. "It's Felicity."

"Nope," he said pleasantly. "It's Sutton." He swiped to answer. "Hello."

In true Sutton form, his boss launched right into the conversation. "I have some information on the kidnapper."

Maddox glanced at Addie, could feel the interest radiating off her. "I'm all ears."

"All right. Thanks for the intel. Heart of a warrior," Maddox clipped after several minutes, ending the call.

Addie scrunched her nose. "Heart of a warrior?" Her voice had a teasing edge. "What was that about? Kind of has an Indiana Jones meets Braveheart feel to it."

"Just a phrase we say to each other, it helps us remember our purpose." Normally, he didn't mind Addie razzing him, but not about that.

She laughed. "O—kay." She switched gears. "What did Sutton say?"

"The attacker's name is John Wilson. He's from North Dakota, has a long rap sheet that includes burglary, attacking a police officer, and domestic violence. He was contacted on the dark web by an anonymous person who hired him to kidnap you."

"For what reason?"

"Wilson didn't know. He was to be given further instructions after he had you in his possession."

"Great! We're no closer to finding out who's behind this than we were before," Addie spouted.

"Not necessarily. While John Wilson didn't know the identity of the person who contacted him, he was paid half his fee up front. Get this, the payment was deposited electronically into his bank account."

"That was stupid. I thought most criminals demanded their money in cash, so it couldn't be traced."

He grunted a laugh. "Yeah, you'd think so. I guess Wilson never expected to get caught, and he certainly didn't anticipate being interrogated by Sutton's ..." he hesitated "... experts."

"You mean torture specialists," she said dourly.

"I don't know what kind of sordid picture you're conjuring up in your mind, but there are various ways to extract information other than torture, such as truth serum, emotional threats..." a smile tugged at the corners of his mouth "...being dropped in the middle of a foreign country with no money or ID."

She chuckled dryly. "Call it what you will, but it's still a version of torture."

"Hey, don't knock it. Sutton got us the info we need. Before it landed in Wilson's account, the money ran through a series of accounts, but Sutton's IT guys were able to track it to an offshore account owned by Barrett Medical."

She pursed her lips. "That fits with what Piper said."

"Yes, it does."

She flashed a chipper smile. "I told you Piper was on the up-and-up."

"So far."

She stuck out her tongue.

"Careful, or I might have to kiss you again," he murmured, quite pleased with himself when her face turned scarlet. He couldn't get that kiss they'd had this morning off his mind. After they got back to the cabin this evening, he hoped to finagle another one.

"You really are a moron," she muttered.

"But a very lovable moron, right?" He gave her a goofy grin.

She laughed and shook her head. "Yeah, sometimes."

"Okay, back to the serious stuff. The jewelry came up clean."

"I guess we can check that off the list." Addie lifted a finger from the steering wheel. "There's still the bracelet, but if the other jewelry came up clean—"

"Chances are the bracelet will too," Maddox finished.

"Exactly." She hesitated, her lips forming a grim line. "Now for the million-dollar-question. Did Wilson kill Jordan?"

"He claims he didn't."

"Does Sutton believe him?"

He tried to think of a way to respond delicately to her question.

"Sutton's interrogators are thorough. I think it's safe to say that we can bank on the information they gave us."

"All right," she finally said, but he could tell from her tight expression that the idea of interrogation didn't sit well with her. It didn't sit well with him either, but it was a hard fact of life. Better to interrogate the guilty than to let the innocent suffer.

"Sutton sent a team of investigators to New Jersey to check out Piper and Jordan's facility. They'll interview the employees, see if anything unusual turns up."

She frowned. "Do you really think that's necessary?"

"No stone unturned, remember?"

Disapproval coated her voice. "Need I remind you that Piper's my closest friend? I don't want her to think I'm checking up on her."

He tensed. "Need I remind you that my job is to protect you? To do that effectively, I need to know all the angles."

She thrust out her lower lip in a pout. "Fine. But would you mind telling Sutton to make sure his guys are stealthy about it? I've already lost one friend. I don't want to lose another."

"I think I can handle that." Man, she was a fireball, fighting him at every turn. There was another tidbit to his conversation with Sutton that he wasn't ready to tell Addie. Sutton suggested that it might be beneficial for Maddox to go to New Jersey and question Brent Barrett in person. That way, Maddox could gauge his reaction. Maddox was all for it, but no way was he leaving Addie's side. She'd have to go along too. He wasn't sure how she would feel about that. He decided to wait until tonight to broach the subject. First, he wanted to see where this key led.

She frowned. "You know, there's something about this whole thing I don't get."

"What's that?"

"What does Sutton get out of all this?"

A startled laugh broke through his throat. "Excuse me?"

She shot him an agitated look like she didn't appreciate him laughing at her question. "Corbin's my brother. Of course he would feel responsible for me. You're here because Corbin's one of your best friends and you want to help him."

"Yeah, that's partly true, but I also care about you." He caught her look of surprise.

"Thanks," she said, giving him a slow, soft smile that did funny things to his insides. She tightened her hold on the steering wheel. "So, what's Sutton's angle? Is Corbin paying him to help me?"

"I don't know the details of what Corbin worked out with Sutton, but I would venture to say that Sutton's helping because that's the type of person he is. Money's no object for Sutton. He's a multi-billionaire. Sutton would offer his resources to Corbin out of sheer loyalty." He could tell from her perplexed expression that she was trying to work that through her head.

A few beats stretched between them before she spoke. "You think a lot of Sutton."

His response was immediate. "Darn straight I do. It's a privilege for me and my former SEAL buddies to work for him."

"You love what you do."

The forlorn tone of her voice hit him like a truckload of bricks. "Yes," he finally said, "I do."

She gave him a resigned smile as she nodded. "I'm glad," she said softly. He could almost see her pushing him away. While he was trying to think of something he could say to break down the barrier she was erecting, the storage facility came into view.

"Here we are," Addie said turning onto the road leading to it. "Here's hoping the key goes to the unit."

"Indeed."

13

Addie held her breath as Maddox pushed the key into the lock on storage unit number twenty-seven. Anxiety clutched Addie's stomach as she looked at Piper. Her poor friend looked like she was barely holding it together. "Are you okay?"

Piper gave her a strained smile. "I'm hanging in there."

Addie stepped up beside Piper and took her arm, patting her hand for reassurance.

A second later, Maddox turned the key. Addie felt a burst of exultation when the lock opened. Maddox pulled up the metal door. At first, it was too dark to see anything. Then, the sunlight filtered in. Addie surveyed the unit with a quick glance. There were a couple of filing boxes on the floor, a tandem bicycle, and a shelving unit along the back wall. Otherwise, the unit was empty.

"The good news is that it shouldn't take long to look through these items," Maddox said.

By unspoken consent, Addie and Piper walked over to the boxes, while Maddox headed for the back shelves.

Addie turned on the flashlight on her phone. She lifted a lid and peered inside. The box contained pictures of Jordan's family. Addie recognized Jordan's younger brother and sister in the photos, along with his parents. They were taken at all different stages of their lives.

The other box was full of bank statements and bill stubs. She picked up a statement, inspecting it. Jordan's mother's name and address were listed on the top. It was dated ten years ago. She rifled through the bill stubs, all belonging to his mother. Her heart felt heavy in her chest. At first glance, there was nothing here but old pictures and outdated paperwork. Why did Jordan leave her the key? Maybe the clue was hidden in one of the boxes. They'd have to dump them out and sift through the contents piece by piece.

Piper leaned over and picked up a photo of Jordan as a teenager, his arm slung around his younger brother Steve. They were in a boat, smiling broadly for the camera, holding up open, soft drink cans. Addie heard a muffled sound and realized Piper was crying. She slid her arm around Piper's thin shoulders.

"I still can't believe he's gone," Piper stammered. "The two of us were going to change the world."

"You have. Once PZT hits the market, the world will know you two as heroes." A lump formed in Addie's throat. She hated that Piper was going through all this turmoil and loss. When Addie thought Maddox was dead, she'd nearly gone out of her mind with grief. Of course, Maddox came back, but Jordan wouldn't.

Gratitude simmered in Piper's luminous eyes. "Thank you. You're such a good friend."

Her voice cracked. "I'm so sorry you got caught in the middle of this."

"Me too," Addie sighed, "but it's not your fault."

"Hey guys. I think I found something," Maddox said.

For an instant, they looked wide-eyed at each other. Addie removed her arm from Piper's shoulder. Hurriedly, Piper wiped her eyes as they rushed back to Maddox. In one hand, he held a large padded envelope. In the other, a black rectangle box with a cord attached that Addie recognized as a computer accessory.

Piper frowned. "That looks like the external hard drives we have at Therapia."

Maddox turned it over in his hand as Addie shined her flashlight. On the back, was a small white label with two words: Therapia. PZT.

Addie's heart began to pound. "This has to be what Jordan wanted me to find." She looked back and forth between Maddox and Piper and could tell from their expressions that they agreed. "Do you think Jordan's copy of the formula is on it?" Addie asked, eagerness rising in her chest.

Piper nodded. "Probably so." Her tone grew speculative as she turned to Addie. "I'll bet Jordan realized someone was after him that day he had lunch with you. He probably dropped the key in your purse for safe keeping."

Addie thought back to the events that occurred. "Yep, I believe you're right."

Piper reached for the hard drive. "If I know Jordan, it's probably encrypted, but I can take it back to Therapia and have my tech team look at it."

Maddox held it out of her reach. "Not so fast. I'll hold onto this for now."

"But it's my property," Piper protested, her voice going an octave higher. "If that drive contains the formula, I can't risk it falling into the wrong hands." Her voice quivered with intensity. "It could undermine my business, everything Jordan and I worked so hard to achieve."

Maddox squared his jaw. "This could be the missing piece in all of this. I have no intention of relinquishing it until I get to the bottom of what's going on."

"You have no right," Piper fumed, her hand going to her hip. She turned to Addie. "Tell him."

Addie felt like a pebble caught between a car tire and the hard pavement—with Piper being the tire and Maddox the pavement.

"Please, Addie," Piper continued. "You know how important this is to me, how important it was to Jordan." Piper's gut-wrenching expression cut Addie to the core.

Addie homed in on Maddox. "Piper's right. Once that hard drive leaves your hands, you can't guarantee that the wrong person won't get ahold of it."

His eyes were as unyielding as stone. "I'm sending it to Sutton."

She lifted her chin. "And who will Sutton get to look at it? Someone you don't know."

"All right, I'll insist Sutton makes sure it goes to Logan Steele. He served with me in the SEALs. I trust him implicitly."

She leaned closer. "Uh, huh. You trust him because he's a close friend, right?"

"That's right," he snapped, wariness creeping into his eyes.

Triumph surged through her, and she knew she had him. "Well, Piper's my closest friend. I trust her implicitly."

Maddox's brows crinkled. "Don't turn this around."

The two of them going head-to-head wouldn't accomplish anything. Addie gave him a pleading look. "Would it hurt to give it to Piper? That way, we can make sure the formula won't fall into the wrong hands. Piper can keep us updated on what her tech team learns."

"You bet I will," Piper said quickly.

Maddox belted out an incredulous laugh. "Are you listening to yourself, Addie? Whatever's on this hard drive could've cost you your life. You're still in danger. No way am I handing it over to anyone—" he looked at Piper "—best friend or otherwise, until we find out what's on it." He stood there glaring. In another situation, Addie would've thought him magnificent with his tall stature, rock hard muscles, chiseled features and blazing eyes. He was every bit the diehard warrior.

"Come on, Maddox," she urged. "Piper's business is on the line. She lost her husband. Like Piper said, Jordan most likely dropped the key into my purse because of the situation. Had Piper been there, he would've given it to her instead."

"Maybe he would have, maybe he wouldn't." He blew out a breath, his eyes never leaving Addie's. "While I appreciate your loyalty to your friend, my job is to protect you, even if that means protecting you from your good intentions." His jaw clenched. "The hard drive stays with me."

Piper gave him a rigid look. "How do we know we can trust you?"

"I trust him," Addie countered. She was surprised that the admission had come blurting out. Even so, the truth of her words hit home. She trusted Maddox more than anyone outside her family, even more than she trusted Piper.

"This doesn't concern you," Piper argued, eyeing Maddox.

"Anything that concerns Addie, concerns me," he countered, locking gazes with Addie for one, long moment.

Addie felt the blood quickening through her veins, then came the wave of familiar desire. What she didn't expect, however, was the blanket of comfort that covered her. Addie was so very grateful to have Maddox in her corner. Maybe there was no hope of them ever getting back together. Maybe her stupid fear of his dangerous profession had pushed him into the arms of another woman. But here and now, she knew that a part of him still cared about her. Right now, that was enough. Time to step up to the plate, even if it meant ostracizing her best friend.

She turned to Piper. "You know, maybe Maddox is right. The man he works for is honorable. If the formula for PZT is on that hard drive, we'll make sure it stays safe. After it's checked out, we'll return it to you. You have my word."

Piper's jaw worked like she wanted to say more. Instead, she clamped her lips shut and waved a hand of dismissal as she turned to go.

Addie's gut tightened. "Wait! Don't leave upset." She was about to charge after Piper when she heard a series of loud pops.

"Get down!" Maddox shouted, lunging for her. They toppled to the cement floor, his body shielding hers. She became aware of the weight of his body and was appreciative of his protection. Her heart sank, however, as she looked up.

A masked man wearing all black had Piper in a choke hold, pointing a gun at her temple.

"Hand over the drive," the man ordered, "or the woman gets it!" He tightened his hold on her neck. Piper gurgled and coughed.

"P—please, don't hurt me," she stammered, her eyes wide with fear.

Addie felt Maddox move slightly. It occurred to her that he was reaching for his gun. Of course Maddox had a gun, but she'd not thought twice about it until now.

"Don't move!" the man growled in a raspy voice like he had a frog in his throat that he couldn't clear.

Maddox froze.

"Push the drive towards me," the man ordered. "Now!"

Addie realized that the drive was a foot to their left. Maddox must've let go of it when he rushed to protect her.

Piper's voice trembled as she spoke to the gunman. "You don't have to do this. Whatever someone's paying you, I can pay more."

"Shut up!" he screamed, clutching her in a vise grip. She yelped in pain.

Terror clawed down Addie's spine. "Do what he says," she said in a low tone to Maddox. She couldn't bear the thought of anything happening to Piper.

Time seemed to stop. Finally, Maddox cursed under his breath, pushing the drive forward.

The gunman released Piper. "Give it to me," he ordered.

Piper stumbled forward and reached for it with shaky hands. She turned and went back to the gunman. Addie expected him to jerk it from her hands, but he grabbed Piper instead.

Piper let out a cry, sobs bubbling from her throat.

Addie felt her own eyes mist. "You've got what you want. Let her go."

The gunman held Piper as a shield as he backed out of the storage unit.

Maddox sprang to his feet. "Stay here," he ordered, charging after the gunman with his gun drawn.

The next instant, shots were fired. Addie's heart nearly stopped. Had Piper been shot? Maddox? Shakes rippled through Addie's entire body as she stood. Not heeding Maddox's command to stay put, she rushed outside.

Piper was crumpled in a heap on the grass, her hand clutching her throat as she gulped for air, half-crying, half-choking. A stab of fear shot through Addie. Where was Maddox?

Her knees went weak when she saw him jogging toward them, a furious expression on his face. "He got away," he growled.

Numbly, Addie pushed her feet forward. When she reached Piper, she dropped to her knees. As she pulled Piper into a hug to comfort her, a tingle of thought pricked Addie's mind. The gunman's voice was raspy.

Strip that away and there was something familiar about it.

For the life of her, she couldn't place it though.

14

"What's your risk assessment? Is it safe to say the threat is over?"

Maddox pushed a hand through his hair as he considered Corbin's question. "It's possible, assuming the formula was on the hard drive." His gaze fell on Addie in the kitchen making dinner. Her movements were deft and graceful as she opened the fridge and pulled out a head of lettuce and tomatoes. Warm brown ringlets bounced softly on her shoulders as she moved.

"If it's not?" Corbin asked, his voice tense.

Maddox tightened his grip on his cellphone. "Then we're back to square one." Maybe it was paranoia due to his time in the SEALs, but he couldn't shake the feeling that they weren't out of the woods yet.

Addie pulled a knife from the drawer and began slicing a tomato. He could tell from the tilt of her head that she was listening to his conversation. "Is that Corbin?"

He pulled the phone away from his mouth. "Yes."

"Tell him I said hello," she said loudly.

"Did you hear that?" Maddox asked into the phone.

"Yep. Sure did. How does Addie feel about going to New Jersey?"

"We haven't had a chance to discuss it yet," Maddox said evasively.

Addie's ears perked up as she gave him a questioning look.

Corbin chortled out a chuckle. "You'd better get on the horn, dude. I talked to Sutton before I called you. He's sending a jet to pick you up in the next few hours."

Maddox let out a breath. "I'm planning on taking care of that next." The inquisitive look on Addie's face let him know that he'd be taking care of it immediately after he ended the call. "How are Delaney and the baby?" The pause on the other end of the line let Maddox know the answer to his question was not good.

"Delaney's hanging tough, but she had a rough day. She's been having a lot of lower back pain. The meds are starting to lose their effectiveness, and her blood pressure's rising." He paused, his voice sounding strained. "We just keep praying that all will go well."

You and me both. "I'm sorry, man." Maddox felt for Corbin, couldn't imagine the stress he must be under, not knowing if his wife and child would come through this.

"What's wrong?" Addie wanted to know, the corners of her mouth drooping. "Is Delaney okay?"

He held up a finger. "Hang on a sec and I'll tell you everything."

Reluctantly, she bit down on her lower lip, nodding.

"Keep us updated on your situation," Maddox said to Corbin.

"Will do. You do the same. Safe travels to New Jersey. Hopefully, you'll get some answers to put this thing to rest."

"I hope so. See ya," Maddox quipped, ending the call.

Addie gave him a steely look that said he'd better spill it right then and there. "All right. What's going on? Don't sugar-coat it," she warned.

"Delaney's hanging tough," he said, using Corbin's words.

Worry creased her features. "But?"

"But, she's having a hard time. The meds aren't working to keep her blood pressure down."

Her lips formed a grim line. "I was afraid of that." She rubbed a hand across her forehead, pushing back her bangs. "How did Corbin sound?"

He stood and walked towards her. "Stressed, haggard, but determined to move forward."

"Sounds like my brother." She tucked her hair behind both ears, looking thoughtful. "The Watermill conference ends tomorrow." She grimaced. "Although at this point, I've hardly even been there."

"At least you got a few hours in this afternoon."

"Yeah, at least I got that. If Sadie weren't holding down the fort, I'd be sunk." She wrinkled her nose. "Fine manager I am," she grumbled.

"Don't be too hard on yourself. You've had a lot to deal with."

She grunted. "That's an understatement."

A couple hours after the attack at the storage facility, Addie and Maddox went to the resort where Addie got caught up on work. Although, Maddox could tell that Addie's mind was mostly on Piper. Understandably, Addie was worried about the emotional state of her friend. Piper had been inconsolable, muttering that if the stolen hard drive contained the formula for PZT, she was ruined. Maddox felt sorry for Piper and all that she'd been through. He'd read somewhere that getting a new drug on the market cost in the neighborhood of $350 million dollars. The poor woman had a lot to lose in the deal. No wonder she was stressed.

Maddox's mind ran through the events that occurred earlier today. From what he could tell, the masked gunman was alone. He fired shots into the air before entering the storage unit. How did the gunman know where they were? Were he and Addie being tailed? Or was Piper the one being tailed?

"After the conference ends tomorrow, I'm thinking of heading to San Diego to see Corbin and Delaney. I can be back in time for the funeral next Wednesday." She stopped, eyeing him. "You're not listening to a thing I'm saying, are you?" She scrunched her brows. "I can tell you're a million miles away. I might as well have been talking to the wall."

A grin stole over his lips as he leaned forward. "I'm sorry. Did you say something?"

She rolled her eyes.

"Don't let me interrupt," he continued.

"What?" she asked dubiously.

"Your conversation with the wall."

She chuckled in half amusement, half annoyance. "All right. I guess I deserved that."

He lifted an eyebrow. "Just remember you said it, I didn't."

She gave him an irritated look, but a smile tugged at her lips. "Okay, enough of the chit chat. What're you thinking about?"

He leaned back against the counter, folding his arms over his chest. His eyes made a slow run over her, lingering on her collar bone and the delicate line of her slender neck. "I was wondering how you managed to become even more beautiful than the last time I saw you."

A rosy hue brushed her cheeks as she tipped a smile. "Nice try, Superman. Now tell me what you were really thinking about."

"Aside from you ..." He blew out a long breath. "If you must know, I was wondering why the gunman fired into the air instead of at us. The way we were positioned in the storage unit would've made us easy targets, like shooting fish in a barrel."

The change in her was instantaneous. Her face paled, lips drawing into a tight line. "That's a lovely thought," she said sarcastically.

"It's true," he shrugged. "Believe me, I'm glad he didn't. I was just wondering why though." He paused, collecting his thoughts. "Also, how did he know we were at the storage unit? That we'd found the hard drive?"

"Do you think he's been following us?" Her eyes widened with concern.

He pondered the question. "I don't think so. I make a point of being aware of my surroundings." His mind went through the checklist of his security routine. He'd swept the cabin for bugs a few times and checked the new alarm system. Also, he made a point of sweeping Addie's car for bugs every time they got in it. Everything was clear on their end. "I wonder if Piper and Hamilton's home is bugged."

"If someone were listening in on the conversation, he would've known where we were headed."

"Exactly."

"Should I call Piper and tell her?"

"That's probably a good idea." He paused. "Although at this point, I'd venture to say the damage has already been done."

A stricken look crossed her features as she looked around, lowering her voice. "Do you think the cabin is bugged?"

"No, I've been checking. We're in the clear."

She nodded in relief.

He motioned at the veggies she was chopping. "Whatcha making?"

She looked down. "A chef salad," she replied dully, picking up the knife and resuming her chopping.

He could tell her mind was still on Piper and the problems. "Sounds good."

"Well, you might not say that when you hear what kind of dressing we have." She tore the lettuce and placed it in a glass bowl.

He groaned. "Don't tell me. Blue cheese?"

A smile tipped her lips. "Yep."

"You know how much I hate blue cheese."

Her eyes sparkled with amusement. "I remember." She shrugged. "It's not like I knew you were coming. It's what I happen to have on hand. You'll like this kind though. It's mild and creamy, tastes more like ranch than blue cheese."

He quirked an eyebrow, talking with his hands. "That's like saying that you'll like this pile of manure better than this one because it's milder."

"What?" She burst out laughing. "That's the most ridiculous thing I've ever heard." She shook her head. "I can't believe you're comparing blue cheese dressing to manure."

He sighed in defeat. "You're right. I shouldn't be comparing it to manure."

"That's right." She flashed a victorious smile.

He pumped his eyebrows. "I should be comparing it to mold. That's what it is."

"Is not," she countered in annoyance.

"Sure, it is. Where do you think the blue veins come from? Mold." He pulled a face. "That's why it smells so gosh awful." His tone grew speculative. "You know, in Papua New Guinea, blue cheese is known as the cheese of the dead."

"You're making this up," she said, but he could tell from her intrigued expression that some tiny part of her wondered if he was telling the truth.

"It's because of its decaying properties. When the elderly tribe members are getting ready to pass to the other side, a ritual is held. The elderly are given blue cheese to help speed up the decaying process and hurry them along their journey."

The look of shock and outrage on her face was too much. He couldn't hold back the laughter. Her eyes widened, and then narrowed when she realized he was teasing her.

Her lips turned down, and she gave him a self-deprecating grin. "I can't believe I semi-fell for that."

"Oh, you fell for it—hook, line, and sinker, darling. You should've seen the look on your face."

She slapped his arm. "You're such a dork," she muttered, but there was a hint of admiration in her voice as she smiled. "The cheese of the dead?" Her hand went to her hip. "I don't know how you come up with this stuff."

He winked. "I'll be here all day."

She gave him a quizzical look. "How do you do it?"

"What?"

"One minute you're talking about how we almost lost our lives. The next, you're telling me some cockamamie story about Papua New Guinea and cheese." She pinned him with a look. "Which one are you? The comedian or the diehard warrior?"

The comment jolted him as he let out a dry chuckle. "Both, I guess." Something in her expression shifted, and he got the feeling there was a lot more to her questions than what was on the surface. "Does it have to be one or the other?" He stepped closer and peered into her jade eyes. In them, he saw what he thought was pain or regret or uncertainty. Maybe it was none of the above. He wasn't sure what she was thinking. "I understand very well the gravity of the situation. I guess I use humor to deal with it. Everyone has layers—the surface and everything going on underneath."

She offered a strained smile. "I guess I'm not as good as you are at jumping back and forth between the two extremes."

The temptation to be close to her was too great. More than anything, he wanted to pull her into his arms and kiss her until neither of them could think straight. "Addie," he uttered, caressing the line of her cheek with his thumb. She drew in a halting breath, and he feared for one agonizing moment she would retreat. When she didn't, it gave him courage to continue. He swallowed, trying to figure out how to explain how he felt. "When you do what I do," he cleared his throat, "um, I've seen things—horrific things." He cringed inwardly when her face grew pinched. "But I've also seen amazing things. I've seen the good a few people, sometimes even one person can do. Look at Sutton and the difference he makes in people's lives. He helps people in impossible situations, gives them hope when no one else can." His voice caught. "To be part of that. To know my life makes a difference. Well, it means everything."

She nodded. "I understand."

He could tell that she didn't, however. He touched her hair. "Life is made up of moments." Tenderness welled in his chest. "Wonderful moments that take your breath away. Those are the moments I hold onto." His gaze moved over her features, savoring every detail. "Take, for example, the moment we shared this morning. Our kiss," he murmured. He caught a flicker of desire in her mesmerizing eyes, sending a blaze of heat blowtorching through him.

Her lips parted expectantly as he encircled her waist, pulling her closer. This time, he didn't wait for her to kiss him, he crushed her lips with his. She melted into his arms, her fingers slipping like silk up his back and through the hair on the nape of his neck. A tiny moan of acceptance escaped her throat when she arched her back. Her lips were a bewitching mixture of softness and demand. As their lips moved together in a tumultuous river of fire, lightning, and thunder, one word kept blazing through Maddox's mind—perfection. Just when he thought he would lose himself to the aching need of her, she pulled back, ending the kiss.

A smile tugged at his lips. "Wow, you are something," he uttered.

Her brows drew together, her eyes turning to hard, green marbles, as she gave him a death glare.

"What?" Raw confusion burst through him like shards of glass. Addie had wanted the kiss as much as he, hadn't she? Her body went rigid as she stepped back. Not sure what to think, he dropped his arms to his side, letting her go. Out of the corner of his eye, he saw her hand go up and realized she was going to slap him. Pain streaked through him as the flat of her palm connected with his jaw. His eyes rounded, his voice rising. "What're you doing?"

"That's for Felicity," she said savagely.

A startled laugh rumbled in his throat. "W—what?"

Her eyes shot fire as she got up in his face. "The second you got home from Syria, you took up with another woman."

"I didn't take up with another woman," he fired back.

She threw back her head, nostrils flaring. "Date another woman, take up with another woman. It's all the same to me." Her jaw turned razor sharp. "Then, as if that weren't bad enough. You're with her now, and you're here kissing me!" She shook her head. "Despicable."

Maddox's hand went to his jaw, still feeling the sting of her slap. He could've sworn he saw steam coming out of Addie's ears. "Are you bi-polar?"

"Not hardly," she scoffed.

"Your moods shift faster than a speed skater with greased blades. One minute we're kissing, and then a second later, you go on the rampage over something ridiculous."

"Ridiculous?" Her voice escalated. "I'll bet poor Felicity doesn't think it's ridiculous! You're supposed to be with her and yet you're kissing me."

"Darling, from where I was standing, you were doing your fair share of kissing too. In fact, you were about to kiss me like you did this morning. I just beat you to the punch." He felt a rush of triumph when her face flamed. He could tell from the embarrassed look in her eyes that she knew it was true. "For the record," he continued, punching out the words in hard hits. "You broke up with me, remember?" The all-too-familiar hurt poured over him like scalding water.

She gasped, her hand going over her chest. A second later, tears misted her eyes. "Breaking up with you was the hardest thing I've ever done." Her voice went hoarse. "You can't imagine what it was like."

"Oh, I think I can," he chuckled darkly.

She lifted her chin, eyes sparking fire. "No, I don't think so." She jabbed a finger into his chest. "Otherwise, you wouldn't have found my replacement a day later."

This whole situation was ridiculous! Addie was getting ticked about a non-issue. An incredulous laugh built in his throat. He tried to hold it back, but it came rolling out like a mudslide. He saw her shocked expression before it twisted into resentment. Once he started laughing, however, he couldn't contain it. He doubled over, holding his stomach, his shoulders shaking.

"Stop!" she demanded through clenched teeth. She shoved his shoulder. "It's not funny," she growled.

Finally, he straightened up, mopping his eyes. He took in a breath to regain control of himself.

She folded her arms tightly over her chest, her fingers tapping out a quick beat, as she gave him a look that could stop an army in its tracks.

He touched his jaw. "Was slapping me really necessary?"

"You're lucky I didn't punch you," she muttered, "you two-timing sleaze ball."

"Really? You're saying that to me? What about your boyfriend?"

She frowned. "I don't have a boyfriend." Her eyes narrowed.

"Unlike you, I didn't find your replacement faster than you could blink."

He rubbed his neck, trying to decide if he wanted to tell her about the guy he'd seen her with at the resort. If he did, the jig was up. She'd know that he came here to see her, and the sight of her with another man sent him running back to San Diego faster than a tucked-tail dog. Then again, would it be so bad if Addie knew? She obviously still had feelings for him. The kisses were evidence of that. No way could he have felt those things if Addie hadn't felt them too. The two of them were dynamite together. Maybe it was better to just come clean, lay it all on the line and see what Addie did with it. "Addie, the thing with Felicity ..." He paused, trying to figure out the best way to continue.

She paddled a circular motion with her hand. "And?" she prompted. "Spit it out."

Her phone rang. She looked toward the phone, but stayed rooted to the floor.

"You'd better get that," Maddox said. "It might be important."

She sighed heavily as she retrieved it from the counter. "It's Sadie, probably wondering about the award ceremony tomorrow for the Watermill conference." She held up a finger, giving him a warning look. "This conversation is not over. Hey, Sadie," she said sweetly, putting the phone up to her ear and turning her back to him. "What's up?"

As Maddox watched her talk, he couldn't help but smile. Addie had more grit than a pound of cornmeal. She was outspoken, impulsive, harsh on the outside and yet, so delectably sweet and tender on the inside. His eyes followed the trail of tangled, milk chocolate curls cascading down her back. The ends were tipped with blonde highlights, reminding him of morning sunlight kissing the ocean horizon. He wanted to slide his arms around her thin waist, bury his head in her thick mane of hair, and kiss the delicate skin on her tantalizing neck. He laughed to himself. If his SEAL buddies could see him now, they'd say he was a pathetic sap. Well, maybe he was. Addie was in his blood, and there seemed to be no way of getting her out.

His phone buzzed. He fished it out of his pocket. It was a text from Sutton letting him know the ETA for the jet. Less than two hours from now. *Crap!* He'd not yet broken the news to Addie. Considering her demeanor at present, he'd better hold on tight because it was bound to be a rocky ride.

A few minutes later, she ended her call. Her eyebrow arched as she launched right back into their previous conversation. "You were saying something about your thing with Felicity?" A dark cloud shadowed her face.

"Yeah." He rocked on the balls of his feet. "I'm afraid that's gonna have to wait."

Her brows furrowed as she wagged a finger, her voice going school-girl sassy, her hips swaying. "Oh, no, Superman. You're not getting out of this."

No time to beat around the bush. Better to just dive in. If he were Catholic, he would've crossed himself before continuing. "We have to hop a plane to New Jersey in less than two hours."

Her mouth dropped. "What?"

"The local authorities are going to arrest Brent Barrett tomorrow afternoon on the charge of your attempted kidnapping. Sutton thinks it's a good idea for me—us—to get there first to question him. That way, we can learn for ourselves how heavily Barrett's involved in this. Also, I'd like to question Blanche Richey, the woman Jordan had the affair with."

She pushed her hair back from her face. "Less than two hours?" She motioned at the salad, her voice rising, hands flying. "That doesn't even give us enough time to eat and get packed! I told Sadie I'd be there tomorrow to help with the award ceremony! I want to go to San Diego to check on Corbin and Delaney before the funeral!"

He caught hold of her hands. "Whoa, take a breath."

She jerked, her lips clamping shut.

He kept his tone calm. "One thing at a time. First of all, as much as I'd love to try that blue cheese—" he couldn't help but smile at the mention of it "—we can forgo the salad and pick up something on the way. Second, your assistant has been handling the conference up to this point. One more day won't tip the turnip truck."

"Turnip truck," she grumbled. "I don't even know what that means."

"I'm sure you get the idea," he chuckled.

She rolled her eyes. "What about the most important part— Corbin and Delaney?"

She reminded him of a kid, pouting to get her way. She was so darn cute that it made him want to give her everything she asked for. "After our trip to New Jersey, we'll take Sutton's private jet to San Diego."

The words *private jet* had the magical effect of shifting the tide in his favor. The lines on her face smoothed, and he caught a hint of excitement glowing in her eyes. "Are you sure Sutton won't mind?"

"No, not at all."

She let out a breath, her shoulders relaxing a fraction. "Okay, it would be nice to get to the bottom of this ordeal, so we can put closure on it." She tipped her head like she'd suddenly thought of something. "Do you think we'll be able to find out if Brent Barrett's the one who stole the hard drive?"

"That's the hope."

"If we could get it back, Piper would be elated."

"That would be great." Maddox wasn't holding out hope that they'd ever see the hard drive again. Even if Brent Barrett took it, the chance of him handing it over was slim to none. However, he didn't want to dash Addie's hopes.

"You know, you never cease to amaze me." Disappointment rang heavy in her voice.

Uh, oh. Maybe he'd called the shifting of the tide too soon. "What?"

A deviant giggle bubbled from her lips. "All this to get out of eating blue cheese."

He laughed in surprise, sticking his finger in his mouth and gagging. "You mean the cheese of the dead?"

"So dramatic," she purred.

"You're calling me dramatic? Seriously! Says the woman who laid a big kiss on me and then slapped me."

Her cheeks reddened. "Uh, for the record, you kissed me that time, Bama boy." She straightened to her full height. "Any self-respecting woman would've done the same." Her eyebrow arched. "By the way, don't even think this gets you off the hook. As soon as we get on that plane, I wanna hear all about this Felicity thing."

There was no mistaking the bite in her voice.

He sighed heavily. "Fine, but only because you're pulling it out of me."

She patted his jaw. "Since you're pretty much already packed, I'll leave the kitchen clean-up to you, while I get ready."

He watched as she traipsed out, her hair moving in rhythm to her steps. *Talk about a long, lean stick of dynamite. They broke the mold when they made Addie.* He glanced at the ingredients of the unmade salad, spread over the counter. He reached for a diced tomato and plopped it into his mouth. "This is the second time today you've waltzed out, leaving me with clean-up duty," he said mostly to himself.

"I heard that," she chimed from the hallway.

"The vixen has owl ears too," he said loudly, then grinned when he heard her grunt in response.

15

Addie rubbed an appreciative hand over the vanilla leather upholstery on the plush seat as her gaze trailed over the patterned, monochromatic carpet and glossy, mid-toned wood accents of the sleek private jet. Maddox was sitting across from her, a small table separating them. She reached for her glass of ginger ale and stirred her straw through the ice before taking a drink. Had they not been traveling to New Jersey to question the man who most likely killed Jordan, Addie might've thought she was in a dream. Working for Sutton certainly had its perks.

She placed her drink back on the table and sat back in her seat, pulling a travel magazine from a nearby rack. She spread it over her lap to appear as though she were reading it, while surreptitiously glancing at Maddox. He was staring out the window as if lost in thought. She smiled inwardly at his unruly curls that went in all directions. A lock fell over one eyebrow, giving him an adventurous, boyish look. Mentally, she circled a dot on the spot on his cheek where his dimple appeared when he smiled. She allowed herself one glance at his muscular biceps before her eyes swept to his torso. His t-shirt formed to the definition of his pecs and flat abdomen.

Heat simmered through her as she looked at the clean lines of his chiseled jaw. Then her eyes settled on his lips, remembering the burn of them against her own. She felt a smidgen of guilt for slapping him. Mostly, it was a knee-jerk reaction when she realized that she'd let her guard down, once again, and was kissing him with reckless abandon that would've made Madonna blush. *Geez.* Did she have no self-restraint whatsoever where Maddox was concerned? She knew he had a girlfriend, meaning that she'd been relegated to the role of the "other woman." When Maddox was kissing her, that meant he was two-timing Felicity.

Maddox felt her gaze and gave her a slow, leisurely smile that unleashed butterflies in her stomach. She was hyper aware that the only other person on the plane, besides the two of them, was the pilot. Dang Maddox! All he had to do was smile and she turned to a puddle of mush. This had to stop! She took a deep breath, mustering up her resolve. It was time to talk turkey.

"How ya doing?" Maddox asked.

"Okay." She homed in on him with a laser focus. "You were going to tell me about your thing with Felicity." She didn't try to hide the accusation in her voice. It was the make-or-break moment in the game when all gloves were off.

He scratched his forehead. "Um, yeah." He motioned at the sofa to their right. "Shall we?"

Her pulse bumped up a few notches. The idea of sitting beside Maddox in a private jet was the stuff dreams were made of. Him having another woman—the stuff of nightmares. She frowned, a thundercloud of irritation rolling over her. "I'm fine where I am."

He stood and came around the table. "Come on." He reached for her hand.

She tried to jerk it away, but he held on tight. Her eyebrow shot up as she gave him a questioning look.

"Come on," he urged. "I don't bite."

"It's not biting that I'm worried about," she retorted.

He pulled her to her feet and to the sofa. She gave him a hard look. "I'm only going along with this because I want to give you the benefit of the doubt. I figure I owe you that much for protecting me."

An amused grin slid over his lips. "That's mighty noble of you, Adelaide Spencer."

The taunting edge in his voice came at her like a thousand needles pricking her all at once. "You think this is funny?" She gritted her teeth. "I don't appreciate being made a fool of."

Concern filled his eyes, all joking vanishing in an instant. "What're you talking about?"

She balled her fist. "You have no right to kiss me the way you did when you have a girlfriend."

He rubbed his neck, blowing out a long breath. "It sounds like my thing with Felicity's getting under your skin."

She rocked back, hardly believing the words that had come out of his mouth. "Now you're taunting me about it?" The nerve! Heat burned up her neck, making her feel like her head would explode as she jumped up. "You think this is all a big joke?"

He sprang to his feet. "No, I don't think it's a joke." His jaw tensed. "I didn't think it was a joke when you dumped me."

"Well, you couldn't have taken it too hard because you found another woman a day later!"

"Sit down, so we can talk about this like rational adults."

She slung back her head as she barked out a laugh. "Ha! You would pull the adult card!"

"Addie, sit down, please."

They stood there eyeing one another until finally Addie sat back down, mostly because she had no place else to go. "I'm listening," she huffed, crossing her arms over her chest.

Maddox rubbed his jaw, laughing humorlessly. "I don't under-stand you, Addie. You're acting like you're the one who was wronged, when you're the one who broke up with me."

She tried to interject a comment, but he held up a hand. "Let me finish."

She clamped her lips shut, glaring at him.

"You act like I'm the only one who found someone else, but that's not true."

"I don't have anyone else," she countered, her voice escalating.

His eyes burned into hers. "You sure about that?"

"Of course!" Had he lost his freaking mind?

"Can you sit there and honestly tell me that you haven't gone on any dates in the past few weeks?"

She went hot all over, then stone cold.

"Yep, just as I thought," he said, giving her a vindicated look.

"T—that's not fair," she sputtered. "Going on a few dates is not the same as going steady." The need to defend herself was all-consuming. Her throat went impossibly small as she swallowed.

The hurt in his eyes darkened them to indigo, his voice taking on a musing tone. "Let's see if I can paint a picture for you. You're standing in the resort. Your curls piled high on your head, sporting that green dress I got you for your birthday—the one that hugs your figure in all the right places. Your long legs showcased in sleek, high heels." His jaw hardened, eyes searing into her soul. "A guy approaches. Hands you roses. Leans in and says something. You laugh and look at him with moon eyes." Disgust coated his voice. "Need I continue?"

Her lungs shriveled to the size of Tic Tacs, and she had the feeling of tumbling off a cliff into thin air. Somehow, she managed to find her voice. "There's no way you could know that unless—"

"I came to see you?" Condemnation burned in his eyes. His voice took on a reflective quality. "Two days after I got back to the states, despite the fact that you dumped me, I came."

Guilt gnawed at her gut as her mind whirled like a tornado. "I thought you were dead."

His voice was as unyielding as the packed snow on the Black Diamond ski trail in February. "No, by that time, I'm pretty sure word had gotten out that I was still alive."

She shook her head, trying to explain. "Yes, I know. But before that, I thought you were dead. Sadie, my assistant—"

"I know who Sadie is," he cut in. His voice was frigid, exact. "I met her today, remember?"

"Quit interrupting me!" she sneered, jerking a hand through her hair. "I'm trying to tell you why I was on a date."

His eyes glittered with a hard amusement as he sat back and folded his arms over his chest. "I'm listening."

She drew in a breath, her chin going high as she pushed out the words. "Sadie, whom you met—" she enunciated the words, giving him a scathing look— "was worried about me. She set me up on a date with her cousin. The date had been set for a few weeks by the time I realized you were still alive." She sighed heavily, throwing her hands up in the air. "Anyway, I don't know why I'm trying to explain myself to you. We weren't a couple then."

"Exactly. Meaning you have no right to keep throwing Felicity in my face." He smirked. "Not to sound like a broken record, but you dumped me, remember?"

Her stomach hardened with the gloom of that knowledge. "Yes, I did," she said quietly. *Because you're a coward!* her mind screamed. "It was the biggest mistake of my life," she uttered.

He cocked an ear. "I'm sorry? I didn't catch that."

"Never mind," she mumbled, waving a hand. Maddox had come back for her! She felt the ridiculous urge to jump up and pump a fist in the air. He'd come for her and saw her with another man. The one time she went on a date and Maddox happened to stop by at the same time. Cruel, stupid, idiotic fate! She looked at him, her eyes lingering on the lines of frustration carved over his features. A smile tugged at her lips. "For the record, my date that night was a total disaster."

He flinched in surprise. Then, a smile pulled at his lips, giving her a glimpse of those adorable dimples. "I'm glad."

Time seemed to stand still as warmth spread through her. She felt such a deep connection to Maddox that, for a split second, she could almost believe the two of them had never been apart.

But they had been apart. They were still apart.

She frowned. "I felt you there. I went to find you and came across the yellow calla lilies. Why did you leave without saying anything to me?" A lump of emotion lodged thick in her throat. "I thought I was imagining things, that the calla lilies were a cruel coincidence." She hesitated. "I assumed that because I'd broken it off you didn't want anything else to do with me." Her eyes misted as she gave him a wan smile.

He placed a hand over hers. "Nothing could be further from the truth." He exhaled a long breath, his eyes going murky. "The truth is, I was a mess at that time—inside and out." He chuckled dryly. "I looked like a half-starved, yard chicken."

"From your imprisonment and torture in Syria," she uttered, the horror of it causing a shiver to slither down her spine. She couldn't imagine what Maddox had been through.

"Yes." He paused, swallowing. "When I saw you with that other guy..." His voice hardened as he released her hand. "I wanted to rip him apart limb by limb."

She flinched, the darkness in him scaring her a little. There it was —the undercurrent that Maddox managed to keep hidden most of the time with his charm and wit. Still, it was there. Could she live with that? The dark side of things Maddox dealt with on a daily basis?

He forced a smile. "I figured it was better for both of us if I left. In retrospect, us being apart was a good thing. It gave me space to sort things out."

She gave him an intense look. "And have you? Sorted things out?"

He looked surprised. "Yeah, I mean, I'm working on it." He grinned, becoming his charming self once more. "I'm like the Sistine Chapel, a work in progress," he teased.

Addie wasn't ready for him to get playful. She needed more answers, needed to understand the man he truly was. "So, after you saw me with my date, you high-tailed it to San Diego?"

Wariness seeped into his eyes. "Yes."

She leaned forward. "When did you start dating Felicity? The day you got back?" She cringed inwardly at the jealousy in her voice. Even to herself, her feelings weren't making sense. One second, she thought she could never be with Maddox. The next, she was irate because he'd found another woman. Maybe she was the one who needed counseling!

He rubbed his neck, a nervous laugh escaping his lips. Then he gave her a perceptive look, his eyes sparkling with laughter. "It really sticks in your craw that I'm with Felicity."

The taunting edge in his voice made her want to slap him. She drew back. "On the contrary. I don't give a flying flip who you date. Like I said this morning, I feel sorry for her," she sniffed.

The corners of his lips pulled down. "I'm glad you brought that up. I wanted to ask you about that." He scooted close and leaned in, closing the space between them. "What do you mean? Why on earth would you feel sorry for Felicity?" His eyes moved over hers in that leisurely way that made her blood pump faster. He was so close she could feel his warm breath on her face. Her breath caught when he trailed a finger down her cheek.

"Maddox," she protested.

"Huh?" His finger moved to her neck. With tantalizing lightness, he skimmed her collarbone lingering on the throbbing indention at the base of her throat. Then he wrapped a finger around one of her curls.

He brushed her lips with his. "What do you mean?" he implored.

Delicious tingles circled down her spine. *Geez.* How was she supposed to think clearly with him this close?

"Because ..."

He kissed the side of her mouth. "Hmm?" he murmured, his lips moving to her ear.

She closed her eyes, anticipation singing through her veins, as he trailed a string of soft, shivery kisses down her neck.

All Addie could think about was Maddox and how he consumed her heart and soul. Finally, she couldn't stand it any longer. She took his face in her hands and pulled him closer. When their lips connected, fire leapt through her veins and sizzled through her with a tantalizing persuasion that zapped her strength, melting her to him. Her heart soared infinitely higher than the altitude they were flying as his lips explored hers. His hands tumbled through her hair with an eager intensity that left her breathless.

When the kiss was over, he pulled back, giving her a quirky grin. "You were saying about Felicity?"

The comment was a frigid splash of water dashing all residual desire as she stiffened. "You're such a jerk." She moved to get away from him, but he caught her arm.

"You love me and you know it," he laughed.

Yes, she did love him, but a thousand armies couldn't drag it out of her. Her eyebrow shot up. "You certainly have a high opinion of yourself, Bama boy." No one could rile her faster than Maddox. She stopped, a thought occurring to her. "You're enjoying this, aren't you?"

"The kiss? Yes, I enjoyed it very much." His eyes danced. Lightly, he fingered a tendril of her hair. "Thanks for initiating it ... again."

Her eyes rounded as she lightly slapped his arm. "I'm such an idiot," she groaned. "I promised myself that I wouldn't kiss you again." Her brows furrowed. "Not while you're with *her*," she spat.

He laughed. "Felicity?"

"Yes." Addie scooted back and clamped her arms over her chest. "You shouldn't be kissing me either. Unless you enjoy being a two-timing snake."

A deep, warm bubble of laughter left his throat. "You're really cute when you're jealous," he teased.

She flinched. "I'm not jealous," she countered. "Just concerned about your behavior towards Felicity." Even as the words left her mouth, she felt like an idiot. Concerned about his behavior towards Felicity. Really?

He brought his lips together and held up a finger, his voice holding a hint of mockery. "It's nice of you to be so concerned about a woman you've never met."

"Yeah, I'm altruistic that way. Just call me Mother Teresa," she quipped.

He gave her a boyish grin that turned her insides to warm caramel. She couldn't help but smile back. She straightened her shoulders, pulling in a breath. "Okay, are you going to tell me about your thing with Felicity? When you started dating her? How serious it is?" Her heart tightened a little at that. She couldn't stand the thought of Maddox being with another woman.

"All right. I'll tell you what you want to know. But first, you've gotta tell me why you feel sorry for Felicity."

There was no way around it. The elephant in the room was always there. She might as well get it in the open. "Fine, but you go first." She eyed him, daring him to disagree.

He rubbed his neck. "I started dating Felicity as sort of a rebound thing." He gave her a sharp look. "I'm sure I don't have to spell it out for you. Some curly haired vixen broke my heart."

She shifted, giving him a nervous laugh. "Hah! With hair like yours I don't think I'd be talking about mine."

He pumped his eyebrows. "Think of the kids we'd have together —all that hair. Maybe I'd better call my broker and order stock in a gel company."

Heat crept up her neck as she giggled. "Stop with the side notes and get on with the story already."

"Hold your horses, woman," he drawled. "I'm working my way into it."

She chuckled, tucking her leg underneath her. "What does that expression even mean? What type of horses do you have?"

He flexed his bicep. "Clydesdales, of course."

Yeah, his muscles were impressive. Too impressive. She forced her eyes to his face, grunting. "More like Shetland ponies."

He burst out laughing. "That was good," he said admiringly, sending a warm glow over her.

She made a circular motion with her hand. "Back to the story."

He sighed. "Oh, yeah. Let's see ... I was talking about my broken heart." His face pulled down in mock sadness. "It was terrible. I couldn't eat. Couldn't sleep. I wandered the streets, barefoot in ragged clothes, searching for my purpose. Trying to figure out how I could possibly forget about the green-eyed, curly haired vixen who'd bewitched me."

She rolled her eyes. "All right. I get the point." Secretly, however, she enjoyed the thought of him pining away for her. She'd certainly done her share of pining away for him.

"Anyway, I met this girl who lives in my condo complex. She seemed nice enough, so we started going out."

He said it casually like he was discussing the weather. She leaned forward, her heart picking up its beat. "How serious is it?"

Time seemed to stop as his eyes held hers. "Do you really have to ask after our kisses?"

An inexplicable feeling of joy rose in her chest, a stupid grin spilling over her lips. "So, you're not serious," she said, stating the obvious.

"There's only one woman who has claim to my heart." His expression grew serious. "The question is—what will she do with it?"

She saw the cautious hope in his eyes and wanted more than anything to tell him that she could be the woman he needed her to be. She wanted to be brave, to love him fiercely in the moment. She wanted to come to terms with the high risk of losing him to the constant danger of his job.

How? How could she do it? Thinking he was dead nearly did her in, and that was *after* they'd broken up. Didn't she tell herself then that not having him in her life was worse than living with the constant fear of losing him? Now that the moment was upon her, however, she was torn and confused. She clasped her hands tightly in her lap, trying to make herself small.

"Addie?" He caressed her hair, a sad smile touching his lips. "You wouldn't make a good poker player. Why do you feel sorry for Felicity?" he asked quietly, even though she could tell he already knew the answer.

"Do you want me to say it out loud?" Her heart ached. "I love you," she admitted. A tear rolled down her cheek. "I never stopped loving you."

Lightly, he brushed the tear away, his thumb lingering on her cheek.

"I wish I could tell you that I could be that woman, the one who will stand by your side—" her voice choked "—the woman who will give her whole heart, not knowing if you'll come back when you walk out the door in the morning." She gave him a pleading look. "The truth is, I'm not sure that I can." Panic fluttered in her stomach when she saw his anguished expression.

"We're back to square one, huh?"

The hurt and accusation in his tone tore at her heart.

Her voice went hoarse. "I don't know what else to tell you. I'm just trying to be honest about my feelings."

He nodded, his lips clamping into a thin line. "I appreciate your honesty," he clipped.

She could feel a wall going up between them.

"I'm so sorry," she uttered, jumping to her feet and rushing to the bathroom before he could see her lose it.

16

The next morning, on the drive to Barrett Medical, all Maddox could think about was that he'd overreacted. After all, Maddox knew how Addie felt. The reason she'd broken up with him to begin with was because she couldn't stomach his life as a SEAL. Now that he was retired, it wouldn't be any different. He couldn't promise her that when he went into dangerous situations that he'd come back. No one could promise that. Things had been going so well between him and Addie—the chemistry between them set him on fire—that he hoped she would come around. Who was he kidding? He'd known from the minute he stepped foot in Birchwood Springs how this would end. Maybe this was the reality check he needed to cut bait and move on with his life.

Soon, Addie would no longer need protecting, and it would be time to go to the next assignment. Maddox hoped, that when he questioned Brent Barrett and Blanche Richey shortly, he'd get the validation he needed to put closure on the situation. By the end of the day, the authorities would have Brent Barrett in their custody. Brent already had the hard drive, meaning no one had any further reason to bother Addie. Like he promised, Maddox would accompany her to San Diego so she could see Corbin and Delaney. After that, they'd go their separate ways. Despondency settled like glue in his gut. Oh, how he wished things could be different, but wishing didn't make it so.

THE LIMOUSINE PULLED up in front of Barrett Medical. Maddox looked up at the modern, high-rise complex of glass and metal, gleaming like a self-important jewel in the midday sun. He glanced at Addie's stony expression. After they'd arrived in New Jersey the night before, they went to a hotel that had two queen-sized beds and got some rest, speaking to each other only when necessary.

This morning, the coolness continued. It was better this way. Maddox couldn't keep opening himself up to her, only to get shot back down. He reached for the door handle. "You ready?"

She nodded, squaring her jaw. "Yep."

A couple minutes later, they walked across the shiny, hard floor of the cavernous foyer to the front desk where a suit-clad woman with a cap of straight-blonde hair sat staring at a computer screen, punching keys. When she realized Maddox and Addie were there, she reluctantly pulled her eyes from the screen and shifted her attention to them.

"Welcome to Barrett Medical, how may I help you?" she said in a nasally tone. Her words were all the same pitch like she was reading from a script.

Maddox leaned into the counter, resting his arm on the lip at the top as he flashed a conversational smile. "We're here to see Brent Barrett."

Her eyes widened. "Your name?"

"Maddox Easton."

She looked at her screen and began furiously typing. Her fingers paused. "I'm sorry, but I don't have you listed. Mr. Barrett doesn't see people without an appointment."

Maddox figured they'd have to go through a song and dance

before getting past the gate keeper. "Brent will want to see me." He looked the woman in the eye, not flinching.

After a second, she blinked and looked back at her screen.

"Call him and tell him I need to speak to him about Jordan Phelps and PZT." He watched the woman's expression to see if it would change at the mention of those two topics. It didn't. She obviously didn't have a clue to what he was referring. He might as well have told her he wanted to talk to Brent about gorillas and balloons for all she cared.

"I'm afraid I don't have the authorization to contact Mr. Barrett personally," the woman said.

"Then call his personal secretary. It's important," he added. He glanced at the metal detectors in front of the elevators. Good thing he'd left his gun in the limousine. Two security guards stood in front of the detectors, checking I.D.s. Maddox had no doubt he could take them both. If the nice way didn't work, he'd have to do things the hard way. One way or another, he was getting in to speak to Brent Barrett. He forced a smile that felt more like a grimace. "Make the call," he ordered.

The woman picked up the phone. "I have a Mr. Easton and ..." she looked at Addie.

"Adelaide Spencer," Addie supplied.

"Adelaide Spencer," the receptionist repeated, "here to see Mr. Barrett." She made a face. "Yes, that's what I told them, that Mr. Barrett doesn't see people without a prior appointment." She shot them a vindicated look.

"Say it's about Jordan Phelps and PZT," Maddox prompted, leaning forward.

The woman gave him an exasperated look. "It's something about Jordan Phelps and PZT," she said, not bothering to hide her irritation over having to bother with them.

Maddox could tell from the woman's surprised look that the conversation had shifted.

"Okay, I'll send them right up." The woman ended the call. A brief smile came over her lips as she reached in her desk and pulled out two visitor badges. "Show these to the guards. Take the elevator up to the twenty-seventh floor. Mr. Barrett's secretary will be waiting for you."

He offered a curt nod. "Thanks."

"You've been so kind," Addie said in a saccharine-sweet voice, her green eyes throwing daggers at the receptionist.

"Come on." Maddox tugged at her arm, chuckling inwardly at her grit. "Save the claws for Brent Barrett," he whispered.

Addie arched an eyebrow, giving him a blistering look. She jerked her arm away from his grasp, straightening her shoulders as she walked stiffly towards the guards. The sting of her rejection hit full force as he followed behind her. How in the heck was he going to get Addie out of his system? Even now, when she was being hateful and stubborn, he was mesmerized by her.

"Let me do the talking," Maddox said quietly as they rode in the elevator.

"Sure, as long as the conversation progresses as it should."

He tightened his jaw. "I'm the one who's trained to handle these types of situations."

She gave him a doe-eyed look, a hard smile stretching over her lips. "Of course, Superman." She winked. "You got it."

"Would you stop being so belligerent?" he seethed.

The elevator door opened. Quickly, Addie stepped out, as if to put as much distance between them as possible. Addie was so dang frustrating! Her curls bounced haughtily on her proud shoulders as she walked. She stepped up to Brent Barrett's secretary and extended her hand. "I'm Addie Spencer." She jerked her thumb behind her. "This is Maddox Easton." She spoke his name like it was a curse word.

The woman gave Addie's hand a quick shake before releasing it and turning her attention to Maddox. He took a quick assessment. The woman was tall and skinny, more like a runway model than secretary, wearing a sleek, black dress that hit her at the mid-thigh. Her glossy hair was chin length, her makeup a touch too heavy to be professional. She wore silver earrings that dangled a good two inches below her hair. Interest lit her eyes as she smiled, shifting her complete focus to him. "Hello."

He glanced at Addie who was glaring at the secretary like she might squeeze her neck until her eyeballs popped out.

Maddox looked back at the woman, flashing a disarming smile. "How ya doing?"

The secretary just stood there, smiling at Maddox until Addie impatiently cleared her throat, spurring the woman into action.

"This way please," she said briskly, like she'd just now remembered she was supposed to be a professional. She led them through an upscale sitting area with giant pieces of abstract art covering the walls. When they reached the large corner office in the back, she motioned.

The man sitting behind the desk, stood. "Please, have a seat," he said in a cultured voice as he flashed a blinding-white smile.

Maddox and Addie took their seats in the chairs across from his desk. Brent Barrett looked to be in his early sixties, although he appeared to be trying to hold onto his youth. He was sporting a California surfer tan, his strawberry-blonde hair streaked with professional highlights. His skin was tight and smooth like he'd had more than a few Botox treatments, possibly a few surgeries. Maddox looked at the bookshelf lined with medical journals. His eye caught on a framed picture, presumably Brent and a much-younger wife, cheesing for the camera as they stood aboard a yacht. Everything about Brent Barrett screamed elegance and comfort. That would all change in a few hours when he was arrested for attempted kidnapping and suspicion of murder.

Brent sat back in his seat and crossed his legs, adjusting his pants so that the crease was straight. "What can I do for you?"

Maddox leaned forward in his seat, jumping straight to the heart of the matter. "We're here to talk about the thug you hired to kidnap Addie."

Brent's face paled, and he looked genuinely confused. "I beg your pardon?"

Men like Brent Barrett disgusted Maddox, sitting in their lavish office buildings behind armies of lawyers, while they destroyed people's lives. "Don't play dumb with us. We know you hired John Wilson to kidnap Adelaide Spencer in the hope she would lead you to the hard drive containing the formula for PZT." Maddox clenched his teeth. "Did you also kill Jordan Phelps?"

An ugly red seeped into Brent's face. "I don't know what you're talking about, but you're way out of line. I don't even know who Adelaide Spencer is."

"I'm Adelaide Spencer." Addie said, glaring at him.

Brent shook his head in bewilderment. "Why would I want to kidnap you? You're a complete stranger."

Either the man was one heck of an actor or all of this was really taking him by surprise. Maddox figured it was the first. A person didn't get where Brent Barrett was without playing the game, knowing how to cover his rear end.

"You can drop the act. The money trail leads straight back to you."

Outrage flashed in Brent's eyes. "I've never heard of John Wilson. I don't know who you think you are to come into my office and accuse me with such outrageous allegations." He stood. "I suggest you leave before I call security."

"Sit back down," Maddox ordered. "This conversation isn't anywhere near being over."

He pressed a button on his phone. "Sheila, call security. Have them come to my office immediately."

"You sure you want to do that?" Maddox countered. He motioned with his hand. "Better yet, why stop with your security? Why don't you call the police as well? Explain to them how you were in cahoots with your VP of operations, Blanche Richey. How you stole the formula for PZT so you could undercut Therapia, your primary competitor, and be the first to market the revolutionary drug that will cure Alzheimer's."

The muscles in Brent's jaw quivered. He pressed the button again. "Sheila, cancel that request."

"Mr. Barrett, are you sure?" came her hesitant voice.

"Positive," he barked, sitting back down.

Maddox could tell he had the man's undivided attention.

"What do you know about PZT?" Brent asked, the interest in his voice outweighing the anger.

"Enough to know it could be worth billions," Maddox said.

"If it works," Brent countered.

"Believe me, it works," Addie inserted. "I've seen the proof."

Brent cocked his head. "What sort of proof?"

"That's not important," Maddox said.

"A video of an Alzheimer's patient who was given PZT," Addie blurted. "She was as lucid as me and you."

Maddox tugged at Addie's arm and leaned close to her. "Let me do the talking," he warned in a low tone.

She rolled her eyes. "What difference does it make what we tell him? Mr. Barrett already knows PZT works or he wouldn't have killed Jordan and stolen the hard drive."

Maddox felt like punching through a brick wall. Really? She was doing this now? Making this a power struggle over their failed relationship. Addie was beyond a doubt the most exasperating woman he'd ever met.

"I did not kill Jordan Phelps, nor did I steal a hard drive," Brent asserted.

The man was determined to deny his crimes till the bitter end. Not uncommon. Maddox switched gears in the hope of tripping him up. "What about your VP, Blanche Richey?" He watched as Brent's nostrils flared. Yep, Maddox had hit a nerve. "Call Blanche in right now. Let's get her take on the situation. You and Blanche were in collusion. She had an affair with Jordan and tried to persuade him to sell Barrett Medical the formula for PZT. When that didn't work, you resorted to more drastic measures, had Jordan killed and eventually stole the hard drive containing the formula."

Brent's face turned blood red as he let out a disbelieving laugh. "These allegations are preposterous. I know nothing about an affair between Blanche and Jordan. Furthermore, Blanche no longer works here. I let her go when I learned she was embezzling company funds."

Maddox held Brent's eyes, not backing down an inch. "And yet, there's no mention of a police investigation or report."

"In the interest of the company, I kept it quiet and handled it privately," Brent countered, breaking eye contact.

"Where's Blanche now?"

"I have no idea." Brent shrugged. "Nor do I care," he added dourly. He spread his hands, letting out a sigh. "Look, the only reason I haven't thrown you out on your ear is because I have an interest in PZT." He looked at Addie, eagerness lighting his eyes. "If it does, indeed, work." He sat back, rubbing his jaw. "For decades, we've been trying to find something that would stop Alzheimer's progression. Reversing it is a whole new ball game. The possibilities are endless."

Maddox could almost see the dollar signs turning in the man's eyes. "Do you deny that you were trying to steal the formula?" Maddox pressed.

"Absolutely." Brent gave Maddox a withering look. "I resent your assertion that I would stoop so low as to try to steal a drug formula from a colleague. I have nothing but the highest respect for Jordan Phelps. His death was not only a blow to me personally, but to the medical community as a whole." His voice shook with righteous indignation.

The guy was good, Maddox had to give him that. Even he was starting to believe Brent's performance.

"What was your affiliation with Jordan?" Addie asked.

Maddox had to admit, it was a decent question. He waited, interested in what Brent had to say.

Brent's jaw worked like he was trying to contain his emotion. "He was my friend."

"Your competitor," Maddox fired back.

"Yes," Brent admitted. "That too." He paused, looking thoughtful. "When I first got wind of PZT and its potential, I met with Jordan, tried to form an alliance between our companies to fast-track the drug to the market. Jordan, however, was territorial and determined to maintain complete control of his creation." He spread his hands in defeat. "At the end of the day, we were unable to come to terms."

"And you left it at that?" Maddox smirked. Somehow, he didn't believe it was that simple.

Brent nodded. He propped his elbows on his desk, his fingers forming a triangle. "Yes."

Uncertainty clouded over Maddox. He'd come here hoping to resolve this matter. Maybe Brent Barrett was guilty as sin, but there were still too many loose ends, such as the whereabouts of Blanche Richey. Had Brent killed her too to silence her? Maybe Brent Barrett was a psychopath, so justified in his own reasoning that he came across as being truthful. At any rate, after the authorities and Sutton's interrogators got through with Brent, the truth would come out.

Brent's secretary stuck her head in the door. "Um, Mr. Barrett. I'm sorry to interrupt, but the police are here."

Brent's face drained. "Why?" Anxiety filled his eyes as he looked at Maddox. "W-what's this all about?"

Maddox and Addie stood.

"I didn't kill Jordan Phelps." His lower lip went limp like spaghetti noodles as he looked at Addie. "I certainly didn't hire anyone to kidnap you." A crazed look came into his eyes. "You have to believe me. I'm innocent. Please." He clutched the arms of his chair.

"Do you think he's telling the truth?" Addie asked in a low tone, her eyes radiating concern.

"Yes! I'm telling the truth," Brent cried.

"Tell it to the police," Maddox said tonelessly, leading Addie out the office. "He's all yours," he said to the police officers waiting outside.

When they got back into the limousine, Addie turned to Maddox. "Do you think he's guilty. He seemed so shocked by our accusations."

Maddox wanted to be able to answer a resounding *yes*, but he wasn't sure. "The evidence certainly points to him. He had motive, opportunity."

"Yes, it was convenient that he let Blanche go."

"That she's nowhere to be found." Maddox made a mental note to ask Sutton have his guys try to locate Blanche. Her testimony could put closure to the whole situation, if she were still alive, that is. He offered a reassuring smile, but could tell it did little to ease Addie's concern. "The good news is that it's in the hands of the authorities now." Maddox didn't add that Sutton was working closely with them to uncover the truth. The idea of interrogation didn't sit well with Addie. No sense adding fuel to that fire. Things were tense enough between them as it was.

She leaned back against her seat with a weary sigh. "Is it really over?"

"It would seem to be the case."

She balled her fist. "I just wish we could've gotten Brent Barrett to admit to killing Jordan and stealing the hard drive. Or that we could've spoken to Blanche Richey."

"Me too," he agreed.

Addie's phone rang. She pulled it from her purse. "It's Corbin, probably wanting to know how it went. Hello?"

Maddox cringed at the stricken look on her face.

"What?" she gasped. "When? Okay, we'll get there as soon as possible." She ended the call. Her lower lip trembled, tears filling her eyes.

Maddox's stomach twisted. "What's wrong?"

"Delaney's blood pressure spiked. She's being rushed into emergency surgery. Corbin asked us to keep her and the baby in our prayers." Her voice quivered. "Corbin didn't sound good." Tears spilled down Addie's cheeks as Maddox gathered her into his arms. "If anything goes wrong...with Delaney or the baby...Corbin will be devastated."

"Take us to the airfield," Maddox instructed the limo driver. "Hurry!"

17

All sorts of horrible scenarios ran through Addie's mind on the plane ride to San Diego. What if something bad happened to Delaney? Or the baby? Or both? By the time she and Maddox arrived at the hospital, she was a nervous wreck. Her body shook like Jell-O, her heart pounding out a ragged beat as she rushed into the family waiting area with Maddox by her side. It was empty except for Pops. He was sitting in a chair against the back wall with his hands clasped in his lap, head leaned back against the wall, and mouth open, snoring loudly.

Addie halted in her tracks, looking sideways at Maddox.

He shrugged, an amused smile tugging at his lips. "Everything must be going okay if he's relaxed enough to sleep."

"Pops can sleep anywhere," she retorted, scrunching her hair.

She hurried across the room and sat down in the chair next to Pops, touching his arm. "Pops," she said loudly, "wake up."

He jerked, then snorted.

She shook his arm. "Hey, it's me." Her emotions bubbled to the surface, and she had to fight the tears pressed against her eyes.

Pops opened his eyes. For a second, he appeared dazed with sleep. Then his gaze focused on Addie, a large smile overtaking his features and emphasizing the leathery wrinkles around his eyes. "Hi, Squirt. I'm glad you're here."

Addie cringed at Pops' nickname for her, especially when she saw the flash of amusement in Maddox's eyes, which turned them a blue so brilliant it would've put the summer sky to shame. A crooked grin tugged at Maddox's cheek, creasing his dimple. Yeah, he certainly enjoyed watching her squirm, she thought sourly. She was struck by how incredibly handsome he was, making her even more irritated at him. Sure, she'd hedged earlier on the plane, but she was trying to be honest. Couldn't he understand that this thing with him was tearing her up inside?

Pops held out his arms and embraced Addie in a tight hug. She buried her nose in his shirt, his familiar scent of Old Spice cologne and cinnamon wafting over her, reminding her of home. A moment later, he pulled back and lumbered to his feet when he saw Maddox.

"These old bones aren't as nimble as they used to be," Pops explained with a self-deprecating chuckle. He extended his hand and gave Maddox a hearty shake and pat on the back. "Thanks for taking such good care of my girl," he said warmly.

Maddox smiled. "Hey, Wallace. Good to see you again. I'm glad I could be of help."

Glad he could be of help? Seriously? He'd relegated her to a project. Addie shot Maddox a dark look. He saw it, but gave her an indifferent expression as he turned his attention back to Pops. So, this was how it was going to be between them—cool and impersonal. Her heart clutched as she drew in a calming breath. She couldn't think about that right now.

Pops motioned as he held onto the back of the chair and sat back down. "Have a seat."

Addie sat beside Pops, and Maddox pulled up a chair in front of him.

"How're Delaney and the baby?" She swallowed, hoping for good news, but fearing the worst. Then again, like Maddox said, Pops seemed pretty relaxed. That was a good sign.

"She and the baby came out of surgery a few hours ago." Gratitude lit his eyes. "Our prayers were answered. All went well. Hope Angelica Spencer is her name," he said, a touch of pride in his voice. "She's in the NICU. Delaney's in her room, and Corbin's with her."

Tears sprang to Addie's eyes as she put a hand over her chest. "I'm so glad everything's okay." She frowned. "Why didn't you call and tell me? I've been worried sick."

He rubbed a hand across his forehead. "I'm sorry, honey. My phone's dead. I forgot to bring my charger to the hospital." His lips formed a grim line. "Corbin's been beside himself with worry, operating on a few hours of sleep. He probably didn't think about it."

"Well, somebody should've called me," Addie grumbled, smarting from the sting of being left out. She was sure she was overly sensitive because her nerves were shot, but still. Someone should've thought to call her. "Can I see them?"

"You bet. They may be asleep, but you can at least see them."

"How much did Hope weigh?" Maddox asked, ingratiating himself into the conversation.

"Three pounds and eleven ounces."

Apprehension sliced through Addie. "That's tiny. Is she okay?"

"She'll have to stay in the NICU for a few weeks, which is to be expected. All in all, Hope is doing great. She's a fighter," Pops finished, pride shining in his eyes.

"I'm so glad," Addie breathed in relief.

"Before we go into the room, I want to hear how everything's going." Concern sounded in Pops' voice as he gave Addie a probing look. "How ya holding up?"

She swallowed the lump of emotion in her throat as she faked a smile. "I'm surviving."

"I'm so sorry about Jordan." Pops shook his head, remorsefully. "I just can't believe someone would kill him."

"Me neither," she said softly. Silence settled between them. Addie glanced at Maddox whose expression was unreadable. She hated the emotions warring inside her. She loved him, no doubt about that. She wanted Maddox in her life. She'd been miserable without him. Why couldn't she come to terms with the danger of his profession? It was the dark cloud forever looming over them. She was glad the ordeal with PZT was over, but that meant she would no longer need Maddox's protection. Her heart hurt just thinking about it. How was she going to manage without him?

"How's Piper doing?" Pops gave Addie a probing look.

She let out a long breath. "Not good. Did Corbin tell you about the hard drive that got stolen?"

Pops nodded, his lips forming a grim line. "Yes, by a masked man with a gun." His expression was one of shock and disbelief as he continued. "Was the drive recovered?"

A glum feeling settled over Addie as she looked at Maddox who spoke for them both. "Not yet, unfortunately."

"Do you think the CEO of the other medical company—" Pops scratched his head "—What was the name of it?"

"Barrett," Addie supplied.

"That's right." Pops held up a finger like the answer had just come to him. "Is the CEO of Barrett Medical the one behind it?"

Maddox spread his hands. "It's looking that way."

Pops tipped his head sideways, looking thoughtful. "You don't sound convinced."

"Brent Barrett was arrested today. He'll be ..." he swallowed "... questioned. Hopefully, we'll get some answers."

Addie could tell Maddox was tip-toeing around the subject. She looked him in the eye. "You mean interrogated."

He didn't flinch. "Yes."

The air between them grew thick enough to cut.

Pop chuckled. "Trouble in paradise," he said dryly.

The words flew at Addie like a match igniting brittle straw. "Pops, how many times do I have to tell you?" she exploded. "Maddox and I aren't a couple!"

"You made that very clear a few hours ago," Maddox said, his eyes turning to balls of ice.

Her voice rose. "Do we have to do this now? At the hospital?"

Maddox shook his head, his voice going flat. "Nope. We don't." He shot her a withering look. "In fact, we don't have to ever discuss it again." He stood.

Panic fluttered like a trapped butterfly against Addie's ribs. "Where are you going?"

"To get some air," he barked, striding away.

Addie growled, balling her fists. "He drives me crazy!" she lamented. Her eyes bugged when she saw the amused grin on Pops' face. "You think this is funny?" Heat blazed over Addie to the point that she thought she might burst into flames. "You know what? I'm done talking about this!" She moved to stand, but Pops caught hold of her arm.

"Sit down," he ordered.

She jerked. "What?" Her hair slung back. "I'm not ten."

His eyebrows raised, wrinkling his forehead. "Oh, really? Then stop acting like it. Sit down," he instructed in a tone Addie recognized well—his fatherly tone that told her she was about to get a lecture.

"Fine," she huffed, her brows furrowing.

Pops laughed under his breath as he assessed her with perceptive eagle eyes.

"What?" She pushed her hair out of her face. Yes, she felt like a moron for losing her temper. The truth was, she was a wreck—so confused she didn't know which way was up. Traitorous tears misted her eyes, but she dried them instantly as she gulped in a breath, holding her hands tightly in her lap.

Pops touched her hair. "Remember when Lou Ella and I went out of town for a weekend getaway? You were so upset that we left you and Corbin with a sitter."

She remembered it well. It had only been a year after her parents had been killed. She had an intense fear, that if Pops and Gram left, something terrible would happen to them too. "Yeah," she said warily when she realized he was awaiting her response. Where was this going?

He chuckled, remembering. "We were halfway to Jackson Hole, Wyoming when we got a call from Mary Bellamy. The poor woman was beside herself, telling us how you were sitting in her front yard under a tree in the same spot you were when we dropped you off, refusing to come in." He shook his head. "You turned down all water and food she offered you."

"I remember," she countered.

"We turned around and came home."

She rolled her eyes. "I know. I told you a gazillion times how sorry I was that I ruined your trip. Geez. I was a kid. Can we let it go already?"

He laughed, holding up a wrinkled hand. "I hold no grudge whatsoever. The only reason I'm bringing it up is because I'm looking at you right now, and I see that same stubborn girl who will hold her ground even if it hurts her to do so." He gave her a look of reproof. "Mary was a nice woman. She would've taken good care of you had you given her a chance and not been so determined to prove your point. You love Maddox, and he loves you. Quit being so stubborn and give him a chance."

She felt like her head would break into pieces. "You don't get it, Pops. It's not about my stubbornness, it's about my—" *fear*, she was about to say, then stopped herself. It wasn't stubbornness that kept her out under that tree all day, but fear. Her heart began to pound. Fear kept her and Maddox apart. She was afraid of losing him like she'd lost her parents. She was afraid of being left behind when he went on his jobs. She was afraid of giving her heart to him, not knowing how she'd survive if anything happened to him. When she thought he was dead, it had nearly been her undoing. How could she live 24/7 with that possibility hanging over her head?

"It's about your what?" Pops prodded.

"Never mind." She bit down on her lower lip, standing. "I don't want to talk about this anymore. Can we just go and see Corbin, Delaney, and the baby now?"

He gave her a long look as he stood, his eyes tinged with pity. "All right."

ADDIE'S first thought when she entered the room was that Corbin and Delaney looked exhausted. "Hey," she said going to Corbin first and giving him a hug.

"Hey, sis. I'm glad you made it."

His eyes were bloodshot, a layer of stubble across his jaw. He looked past her. "Where's Maddox?"

"Getting some air." The bite in her voice came out stronger than she intended. Corbin glanced at Delaney, a look passing between them.

"What?" Addie asked, eyes narrowing.

"Nothing." Corbin pushed a hand through his hair.

Addie approached Delaney's bedside and leaned over, giving her a tight hug. Delaney's normally shiny, blonde tresses looked dull and stringy. She had on no makeup, her face pale. Still, she was beautiful. "How are you doing?"

Delaney offered a weak smile. "Good." A sparkle lit her eyes. "Did you see Hope?"

"Not yet. I thought I'd come and say hello to you both first."

Delaney's smooth, melodic voice sounded so much like Maddox's accent. Understandable, considering both were from Alabama. She and Corbin used to laugh, thinking how ironic it was that two siblings from Colorado had fallen for Southerners. Of course, it was Corbin's friendship with Maddox that brought Maddox into her life. Corbin struck up a friendship with Maddox partially because he felt a kinship with him, being from the same state as Delaney. Around and around they went. None of that mattered now, however. She and Maddox were through. The knowledge settled like stone against her chest.

Addie looked toward the door. Pops was leaning against the doorframe, watching her so intently that she felt like he'd burn a hole through her. *Stop looking at me!* she wanted to scream. Instead, she gave him a steely look before pulling a chair next to Delaney's bed. "How did the surgery go?"

Delaney made a face. "Ugh!"

Addie giggled. "That good, huh?"

"I'm just glad it's over, and we have an adorable baby girl to show for it." She gave Corbin a look of such complete adoration that it evoked a longing in Addie. She wanted what they had—to be so fiercely devoted to one another that nothing, not even Corbin's profession, would stand in their way. Delaney was so petite and dainty, yet she was strong and resilient.

"Are you okay?" Delaney asked, concern touching her features.

Addie forced a smile. "Yeah."

Corbin stepped up beside her and sat down on the edge of the bed. "Maddox and Sutton have been keeping me up to speed on the situation with Jordan and PZT. I'm cautiously optimistic that it's over. I guess we'll know for sure if Brent Barrett was the one behind everything after he's interrogated."

Her mind hung a little on the word *interrogated*. She looked at Delaney whose expression didn't change, as if it were the most common thing in the world for a man to be arrested and interrogated for attempted kidnapping and possible murder. She hugged her arms. "I'll be glad when it's over."

Corbin nodded in understanding. "I'm glad you've had Maddox to keep you safe."

"Yes, he's done his job well," she quipped. "Now that this one's wrapped up, he can move onto bigger and better jobs."

Corbin raised an eyebrow, a teasing grin tugging at his lips. "Is it my imagination? Or do I detect some hostility?"

She half stood and shoved him.

"Hey," he yelped, catching himself before he slipped off the bed. He straightened his shoulders. "In all seriousness, Maddox is crazy about you, sis." He paused, holding her with piercing green eyes identical to her own. "It would be a shame to let petty grievances stand in the way of what the two of you have." He gave Delaney an intimate smile as he reached for her hand. "If you play your cards right, sis, you might just end up finding something wonderful." He raised Delaney's hand to his lips and planted a kiss. He grinned like a lovesick schoolboy at Delaney. "Isn't that right?"

"Absolutely," Delaney exclaimed, breaking the word into syllables like Pops did. She looked at Pops who beamed. Color refilled Delaney's face, making her look radiant.

Addie scowled, the mushiness getting to be a little much. "Please tell me you're not gonna break into song." Pops' favorite catch-phrase was "absolutely." Delaney had been so impressed by it that she'd written a song about it that topped the charts, staying at number one for a record number of weeks.

Corbin chuckled. "Nah, Delaney's had a rough day. We'll give her a few days rest before she has to start earning her keep," he winked.

Delaney shook her head, laughing. "Yeah, yeah. That's mighty kind of you," she said dryly.

"Well, you know, I'm kind that way," Corbin drawled, mimicking a Southern accent.

A few lyrics from the song rushed through Addie's mind.

I'll absolutely love you ... for the rest of my life ... until
    the stars fall from the sky.

They say I'm damaged goods, and I admit it absolutely,
    but baby you give me more hope than a person
    ever should.

Damaged goods. That's what Addie was. Her stupid fear kept her apart from the man she loved, and she was too chicken to rise above it. A tear escaped the corner of her eye. Quickly, she brushed it away, embarrassed for anyone to see her crying. She glanced at Delaney and could tell from her concerned expression that she knew something was wrong.

"Hey," Delaney began, glancing at the clock. "They're bringing Hope in for me to bottle feed in about twenty minutes." She looked at Corbin. "Why don't you go and find Maddox?"

Corbin frowned. "Hey, are you trying to get rid of me?"

A smile broke over her lips. "Absolutely."

Everyone laughed at the reference.

Corbin stood. "All right. I hear ya." He ruffled Addie's hair, planting a kiss on her cheek. "Love ya, sis."

Addie flashed a mischievous smile. "I love you too, Dad."

He straightened to his full height. "Hmm ..." he mused. "*Dad*. I like the sound of that."

"Fatherhood looks good on you," Delaney added, a secret smile passing between her and Corbin.

Addie wrinkled her nose. "Enough of the lovey dovey junk. You're making me want to puke."

Corbin patted her cheek, pursing his lips, his voice going taunting. "Don't worry, sis. Your time will come."

She slapped his hand away. "Don't touch me." Corbin got great delight out of pestering her.

He just laughed. "All right, Pops. Let's go find Maddox, so Delaney and old sour puss can have some girl time."

"Thank you," Delaney chimed, blowing him a kiss.

"I'm not a sour puss," Addie grumbled, then stuck out her tongue as he left the room.

18

"Okay, what's going on?" Delaney asked when it was just the two of them.

Addie let out a long sigh, shifting in her seat. "Oh, you know. Life."

Delaney laughed. "Yep, it can be a real kick in the pants sometimes, huh?"

A giggle gurgled in Addie's throat. Man, she liked Delaney—how real and down to earth she was, calling it like it is. "Yes, it can be."

"I'm glad you've been safe. Corbin and I've been worried about you."

Guilt soured her stomach. "With all you've had going on, I'm sorry I added to your stress."

She waved the comment away with a flick of her wrist. "That's what family's for."

A wave of tenderness went through Addie. "Corbin and I may give each other grief," her voice caught, "but I'm so grateful for him. I don't know what I would've done if he hadn't stepped in to help during all this."

"He only wished that he could be there himself." Delaney gave her a perceptive look. "Knowing he couldn't, he sent the next best man to do the job—someone who loves you as much as Corbin."

Addie choked out a strangled cough.

Delaney smiled. "You've got it bad for Maddox, don't you?"

It was on the tip of Addie's tongue to deny it sheerly out of spite, but she knew the answer was written all over her face. "Yes," she admitted, "I'm in love with him." It felt good to say the words out loud.

"Okay, you love him. From what Corbin says, Maddox is madly in love with you. What's the problem?"

Tears gathered in Addie's eyes. "Everything." She clenched her fists. "How do you do it?"

"What?" Delaney frowned.

The intensity of her feelings shook her body as she rattled out the words. "You and Corbin have a baby together. How do you live each day, not knowing for sure when he walks out the door to some dangerous situation that he'll come back?" She looked at Delaney, desperation clawing at her. She needed reassurance, something she could hang onto.

Understanding seeped over Delaney's features. "I don't," she said simply.

Addie's heart dropped through her chest and spilled onto the floor in a tattered heap. "That's what I was afraid of," she said hoarsely, looking down at the bed.

Delaney reached for her hand. "Addie, look at me," she commanded.

Despite her best effort to hold them back, tears dribbled down Addie's cheeks. "I'm sorry," she muttered, "you must think I'm a complete idiot." She gritted her teeth, hating herself right now. She hated her fear, hated her weakness. And hated that she couldn't be more like Delaney.

"No, I don't think you're an idiot at all. Of course I worry about Corbin. I'd be stupid not to." She paused. "The thought of losing Corbin tears me up inside. Don't you see? None of us has any guarantees. Any of our lives could end tomorrow—today, including yours, Addie."

"Yeah, believe me," she chuckled darkly. "I've got that reality cemented in my brain after Jordan's death."

A shadow crossed Delaney's features. "As you know, my growing up years were rough. Before I met Corbin, I feared I was so damaged by my past that I'd never be able to love anyone again." Her eyes misted. "I was at my lowest when Corbin entered my life. Not only did he save me physically, but also emotionally. My life started anew when I met Corbin." A tender smile curved her lips. "Then I met Wallace, you, and now we have Hope."

Delaney's eyes held such wisdom that Addie felt like she was seeing into her soul.

"Yes, Corbin and Maddox have dangerous jobs." Delaney let out a sardonic laugh. "Life is dangerous."

"Amen," Addie quipped.

"You can't spend your life mourning the hypothetical. You need to learn to be happy in the moment, for those moments are the stuff life is made of."

Addie jerked, remembering the card on her refrigerator. "What did you say?"

"You need to learn to be happy. Trust Maddox. Trust yourself."

Be happy. It always came back to that. "I don't know if I can do it," she lamented. "I'm not brave like you. I can't knowingly enter into a relationship that's so risky." She shuddered. "As much as I want to, I just don't think I can go there."

Delaney gave her a wise smile. "That's just it, Addie. You keep talking about your relationship with Maddox as if it's something that's going to happen in the future. The truth is you're already there."

"Huh?"

"You're in love with Maddox."

"Yes," she said, feeling like she was stepping into a trap.

"It has already happened. You're in a relationship with him now.

You keep questioning if you're brave enough to handle whatever may come—dreaming up all types of scenarios in which you lose. We have a saying for that in the South. It's called borrowing trouble." She gave her a pointed look. "Stop borrowing trouble." She shrugged. "So you're afraid? Big whoop. We're all afraid." Her voice quivered with intensity. "Do you not think I was scared out of my mind to give birth to Hope? I was a high-risk pregnancy." Her eyes softened. "No amount of fear could compare with the joy I felt when I held my little girl in my arms for the first time. The bravest of heroes are scared. They push forward into action, leaving the fear behind. Then comes the victory." She gave Addie a pointed look. "Are you happy without Maddox in your life?"

"No, I'm absolutely miserable," she muttered.

"You can't imagine your life without him, right?"

"Right."

She smiled. "There you go. That's your answer."

There was a knock at the door. They turned as a nurse entered the room, holding Hope in her arms.

A sense of awe came over Addie as she looked at the red-faced bundle, swaddled in a pink blanket. She stood and scooted her chair back. "She's beautiful," she uttered, looking at Hope's squinty, determined face. She was unprepared for the swift feeling of love that rushed through her.

Hope went stiff, belting out a whiny cry.

"She's hungry is what she is," the nurse said with a laugh. "You should probably sanitize your hands before you take her."

"Of course. Would you hand me that?" Delaney asked, pointing at a bottle of hand sanitizer on the nearby table. When Addie gave it to her, Delaney liberally rubbed the solution over her hands, up to her elbows. Meanwhile, Hope's cries became more insistent. Delaney held out her hands as the nurse placed Hope in her arms.

"There," Delaney said soothingly as she held her against her chest. Gently, she rubbed a finger across Hope's cheek. Hope turned her mouth to Delaney's finger, the rooting instinct taking over as she sucked Delaney's finger.

"Look at that," the nurse cooed in delight. "Preemies normally have a hard time learning to suck, but Hope's catching on fast. I'll be right back with the bottle of breast milk that you pumped earlier." She turned, walking briskly out of the room.

It was amazing how natural the instinct of motherhood seemed to come to Delaney as she rocked Hope, making shushing sounds to calm her. Addie had the feeling of witnessing utter perfection.

Delaney seemed to be reading Addie's thoughts as she looked up and flashed an unencumbered smile so joyous it brought tears to Addie's eyes.

Be happy. The words swirled through Addie's mind, finding their place in her heart. Just like that, the muddy water cleared. She laughed inwardly. She'd been borrowing trouble for a long time. When real trouble came knocking, Maddox was there for her. Delaney was right. It was time to stop mourning the hypothetical. As much as she wanted to stay here with Delaney and Hope, she needed to find Maddox. "I have to go."

"You've got this," Delaney said, giving her a reassuring nod.

She touched Delaney's arm. "Thank you."

A smile ruffled Delaney's lips. "You bet. That's what family's for."

When Addie got to the door, she paused for one last look at Delaney, who was peering down at Hope, totally consumed in the softness and wonder of her new baby.

"One of those perfect moments that life is made of," she uttered softly, gently closing the door behind her.

Addie found Corbin and Pops standing in the hall. "Where's Maddox?"

"He went home," Corbin answered.

The words came at her like an invisible punch to the stomach. Her hand went to her throat. "He left? Without telling me goodbye?"

Corbin gave her a funny look. "Just to get some rest. He said he'd come back in the morning to check on you and see Hope."

"Seeing as how you treated him earlier, he probably thinks you don't want anything to do with him," Pops added, reproof sounding in his voice.

"We hope to have information soon on Brent Barrett," Corbin said. "Then we'll know for sure if the threat against you is over."

Meaning Maddox would then go onto his next assignment, she thought glumly. For an instant, the old familiar despair settled over her like a boulder around her neck. *No!* She straightened her shoulders. She couldn't lose Maddox again. She held out her hand to Corbin. "I need your car keys."

His eyes rounded. "What?"

"I'm going to talk to Maddox. I'll be back in a few hours."

"Do you even remember where he lives?" Corbin asked, looking at her like she'd grown another head.

"I can figure it out," she snapped.

Corbin gave her a probing look. "What's this about, Addie?"

She lifted her chin. "None of your business."

A new light came into Corbin's eyes, a smile tugging at his lips. "You're going after him, aren't you? That little heart-to-heart with Delaney must've done you good," he taunted. He wiggled his eyebrows. "Addie's in love."

Heat crawled up her neck as she shoved him. "You're such an idiot," she growled.

Pops gave Corbin a warning look. "Stop teasing her." His eyes smiled. "Time to finally come out from underneath that tree, huh, Squirt?"

"What?" Corbin asked dubiously.

Addie rolled her eyes. "Never mind. Your pea-sized brain's not big enough to comprehend it, even if I explained it to you."

Corbin shook his head and chuckled. "I can tell you one thing— Maddox has got to be one tough cookie to put up with you. Or a long-suffering sucker."

She was about to tell him off, then saw the laughter in his eyes. He tipped a smile. "Love you, sis."

"I love you too," she admitted. She held out her hand, eyeing him. "The keys please?"

"Go ahead and give them to her," Pops urged, "before she changes her mind."

A laugh rumbled in Addie's throat. "I'm not changing my mind." She lifted her chin. "Not this time."

"If I give you my keys, we'll be stuck here," Corbin lamented.

Pops chuckled. "What're you talking about? You haven't left here for days. A few more hours won't hurt you."

Addie leaned forward, sniffing. "I thought I smelled something."

"Hey," Corbin protested.

When Pops gave him *the look*, he sighed. "Fine. But don't be gone too long. And whatever you do, be careful with the Lexus. Delaney's particular about her car."

She laughed, rolling her eyes. "Delaney's particular? More like you are. Don't worry. I'll be careful," she chimed. When she got a few steps away from them, she turned. "Hey, would you be a good boy and text me Maddox's address?"

"Ah-ha! I knew you couldn't remember how to get there." He smirked. "You can't find your way out of a bathtub."

It was true. She was terrible at directions. "Oh, put a cork in it." She stuck her tongue out at him. "I need it for backup, just in case." She turned to rush away.

"Hey, Addie."

She stopped and glanced back over her shoulder. "Huh?"

"Good luck." Corbin gave her a genuine smile. "You've got this."

Those were the same words Delaney had used. They had the power to melt her heart as she returned his smile, realizing in that moment how much she truly loved her big brother. "Thank you."

Anticipation licked through her veins. Delaney and Corbin were right. She had this! For the first time in a long time, she felt like she was running to something instead of running from it. She smiled a little, remembering how those were Maddox's words about joining the SEALs.

She quickened her pace, anxious to get to Maddox as soon as possible.

19

Maddox was bone tired, every inch of his body aching. Part of his weariness was from physical exhaustion. The other, larger part, was his frustration over Addie. Now that the job was wrapping up, he would have to come to terms with the fact that he'd lost her. He'd stayed at the hospital long enough to say a few words to Corbin and Wallace before darting out. The truth was, Maddox hated hospitals. They reminded him of B. J. and how helpless he felt watching his childhood friend fade away to his death. Added to that was the guilt of it being his fault because he'd dared B. J. to jump the creek. He pushed aside the dark memories, knowing they weren't helping matters.

His condo had an empty, lonesome feel. *Well, better get used to it Maddox*, he told himself. *It's your life now*. His phone buzzed. For a split second, he hoped it might be Addie, but it was his mama. He'd not spoken to her in a week. She had no idea that he'd left San Diego and gone to Colorado and back. He made a practice of keeping the details of his job to himself so as not to worry his family.

"Hello," he clipped as he reached into the fridge and pulled out a water bottle.

"Maddox, darling," she drawled. "How are you?"

"Good." Not true. He was lousy. Life sucked right now! He plopped down on the couch and removed his shoes. "How are you?" he asked mechanically.

That's all it took for his mama to launch into a ten-minute monologue about the club, how busy Maddox's daddy was at the firm, and every detail she could think of about his siblings' lives. "What're you up to?" she asked a few minutes later.

"Oh, nothing much. You know, just work."

"When are you planning to come home for a visit? We miss you."

He reached for the remote, turned on the TV, and began flipping through channels. "Christmas, maybe."

"I was hoping you'd come for Thanksgiving too."

"Okay, I'll try to do that."

She paused. "Maddox. Are you sure you're okay? You don't sound like yourself."

"I'm just tired."

"Have you spoken to Addie?"

He sat up, clutching the phone tighter. "What kind of question is that? You know we broke up." The bitterness in his tone sounded in his ears. Did his mama have some sort of radar on him? It was like she instinctively knew, somehow, that he'd been with Addie.

"I was just hoping that maybe the two of you could, you know, work things out." Her voice grew intense. "You should've seen her at your funeral, honey. The poor girl was devastated."

An incredulous laugh broke through his throat. "Do you hear yourself, Mama? I didn't actually die."

"I know that," she responded impatiently. "But we thought you were dead. Going through that had to be tough on her."

Yeah, so tough that she couldn't get over it, he thought, acid churning in his gut.

"You should bring Addie for Thanksgiving."

Sometimes it was like his mama didn't listen to a thing he said. "We're not together anymore."

"Text me her number, and I'll invite her."

"I'm not going to text you her number." This conversation was getting ridiculous. He punched the remote and switched through more channels, finally stopping at a basketball game. His stomach rumbled. That's right, he'd not eaten anything in a few hours. He had very little food in the house. Maybe he'd order a pizza.

"If you won't text me Addie's number, then I suggest you call her. A girl like her doesn't come along every day."

"All right," he interrupted. "I'll talk to her tomorrow."

His mama's voice instantly brightened. "Fantastic," she cooed. "Be sure and tell her I said hello."

The doorbell rang. Maddox sat up, hope bubbling in his chest. Was it Addie? "I've gotta go, Mama. There's someone at the door."

"Okay, I love you. I'll talk to you soon."

He glanced back at the door. "Love you too." He ended the call and tossed the phone on the couch as he stood. Had Addie come to find him? He peered through the peephole, his stomach tightening.

"Hello." Felicity knocked insistently on the door. "I know you're there. I saw your lights."

He opened the door, plastering on a smile. "Hey."

"Hey." She flashed a large smile as she slid her arms around his neck and drew close, pressing her lips to his. All he could think about was how her perfume was too strong, her hair too stiff, her face too made up.

"Whoa!" He drew back, removing her skinny arms from his neck. "What was that for?"

Her face fell, her lips forming a petulant pout. "I thought you'd be happy to see me," she sniffed. She strode past him, walked around the couch, and sat down. She draped an arm over the back and looked at him with a come-hither expression. "Come over here," she purred. "I've missed you. You didn't even tell me you were going out of town."

"Now's not a good time," he began.

"Oh, come on," she urged. "It's not like you were doing anything besides watching a stupid game."

"I happen to like basketball," he countered, raising an eyebrow.

"We'll watch it together then." She squared her jaw. "I'm not leaving, so you'd might as well come over here. Please," she added, giving him a seductive smile.

His shoulders slumped. He didn't know which was worse—sitting alone and wallowing in his sorrows or sitting with Felicity. *Would you rather be (a) drowned or (b) burned to death? Can I choose option (c)? Oh, and can you throw Addie into the mix?*

He grunted. Fat chance of that happening. "Are you hungry? I was thinking of ordering a pizza."

Her face fell. "Can you get a thin, gluten-free crust?" She shuddered. "I can't stand the thought of eating all those carbs."

He laughed to keep from crying. "Sure, why not?"

ADDIE TURNED off the engine and got out of the Lexus. She rubbed her sweaty hands on her jeans. Maddox's lights were on. She was relieved he was home. A part of her had feared that he'd left town on a job and she wouldn't see him again. "You've got this," she repeated. She took in a breath and scrunched her hair as she strode up the curved sidewalk leading to his condo.

She rang the doorbell. No answer.

Her heart leapt into her throat. She knocked. "Maddox?"

No answer. She tried the door handle. It was unlocked. Tentatively, she pushed open the door. "Hello?" She stepped inside and looked around at Maddox's sparse living room. It looked the same as it had when she'd been here last. There were the basics—a sofa and TV. Large prints of Maddox's landscape photographs covered the walls, taken in places he'd traveled. The scent of pizza lingered in the air.

She stiffened when she saw movement on the sofa.

"Maddox?" Her heart was beating so wildly, she felt dizzy. *Geez.* This was hard. Maybe it was better to get it out when he couldn't see her. "Don't stand up." She held out a hand. "Just let me get this out while I can. I was a fool to break up with you." Her words lost air as she tried again. "The truth is, I was so afraid of losing you that I pushed you away." She let out a nervous laugh. "Part of me is still afraid. I'd be lying if I said your job doesn't scare me. Quite frankly, it scares the bejeebies out of me." Dang it, this was so hard! She was rambling, not making a lick of sense. She raked a hand through her curls. "What I'm saying here is that I love you." Her voice caught. "I never stopped loving you, not for one second. When I thought you were dead...well, I wanted to die too. I don't know how this will work, Maddox, but I'm tired of being afraid. I want you in my life. I don't care if you're a SEAL or private contractor." She chuckled. "Whatever the heck you call yourself. I can't imagine my life without you. I want us to try again." There. She'd said it. She breathed a sigh of relief.

"I'm sorry. Who are you?" a woman asked.

Addie jerked as a blonde stood. That she was the epitome of style and gorgeousness didn't help matters.

"W—what?" Addie gurgled, feeling like a noose had encircled her throat. "I must have the wrong condo. S—sorry." She felt like she was in the middle of a nightmare when Maddox popped up. He rubbed his eyes like he'd just woken up.

He blinked, all trace of sleep instantly leaving him. "Addie? What're you doing here?"

The blonde glared at him, her hand going to her hip. "Evidently baring her soul. Telling you how much she loves you. How breaking up with you was the biggest mistake of her life. How she wants to get back together." She twirled her hand. "Blah, blah, blah," she finished in a languid tone as she looked down at her acrylic nails.

Maddox's eyes bugged. "Huh?"

It all came together in a hard punch that took Addie's breath away. "You're Felicity," she croaked.

"In the flesh." Felicity tossed her hair, her eyes radiating disdain as she looked Addie up and down like she was sizing up the competition. She turned back to Maddox. "Who in the heck is this woman? You never told me you were a SEAL." She twirled her hand. "I thought you were a personal trainer."

Fire raged in Addie's gut as she glared at Maddox, tears stinging her eyes. "I never meant anything to you, did I?" She was a fool coming here, opening her heart to him.

Maddox bounded around the couch. "What're you talking about? You mean everything to me."

"What?!" Felicity growled. "Surely, you don't mean that. Look at her over-stretched, last season sweater and her crazy hair." She looked at Addie like she was Medusa. "You know, they do have something called a flat iron. It would do wonders for you."

Addie had a good mind to grab the over-processed Barbie by her bleached hair and punch her lights out. She slung back her head, her hair flying, aiming her venom at Maddox instead. "Yeah, it's obvious you care. You left the hospital and fell straight into Malibu Barbie's arms."

"This isn't Malibu, honey. This is San Diego," Felicity quipped.

Addie's mind raced out of control like a bolting deer. "Have a nice life," she growled as she turned on her heel, stomping out.

"Addie, wait!" He ran after her, pulling her arm.

"Let go of me!" She jerked her arm out of his grasp, detesting the traitorous tears that wet her eyes. She'd already wasted one too many tears on Maddox Easton. Time to move on!

A crazed look came into his eyes. "I had no idea Felicity was coming here tonight. She just showed up."

"That was mighty convenient for you," she seethed. "You certainly didn't waste any time cuddling up with her on the couch. Or maybe you were doing more than cuddling." A hot shame covered her. To think those lips that had kissed her were kissing that bimbo. Her anger rose to new heights when a grin slid over Maddox's face.

"Is it true?"

"What?" she fired back.

"That you love me. That you want to get back together," he said softly, stepping closer.

"*Loved* you!" she heaved through gritted teeth. "Wanted to get back together. That was before I discovered you were a lousy, two-timing slime ball." She growled. "I can't even think of foul enough words to describe you!" Her hand came up to slap his jaw, but he was faster, grabbing her wrist.

"Addie, stop."

She fought against him. "Let go of me! You jerk! Cheat!"

He spun her around so that he was behind her. He hugged her arms in an iron grip. "For the record, I love you too."

"What?" Felicity screamed, clenching her fists. "You're choosing her over me?"

"There was never any choice," Maddox said in Addie's ear. "Felicity and I were never a thing. We just went out on a few dates."

Addie gurgled in disbelief, craning her neck to look at him. "Huh?" All this time, she'd been so worried about Felicity...and there was nothing there. Were it not for the bubble of happiness that rose in Addie's chest, she would've socked Maddox in the gut.

A sheepish grin stole over Maddox's lips. "I made it out to be more than it was to make you jealous."

Felicity shook her head in disbelief. "How can you say there was nothing between us?" Her face hardened as she eyed Addie. "What do you even see in her?"

Maddox laughed. "Well, let's see...she's feisty, stubborn. She gets under your skin to the point where you can't think of anything else. The kind of woman who drives you so berserk you want to pull your hair out one minute, and fight wars for her the next. Or kiss her until you can't see straight," he murmured in Addie's ear.

"This is ridiculous!" Felicity screeched, eyes blazing. "You'll regret this, Maddox Easton."

"I highly doubt that," Maddox responded.

"You stupid, Alabama redneck!"

Addie sniggered. She tried to hold it back when she saw Felicity's indignant expression, but it was too much to hold in and she burst out laughing.

"I should've known better than to get mixed up with you," Felicity huffed. "Good luck with granola girl," she sneered as she marched away.

Maddox turned Addie around to face him. "Hey," he countered, his eyes taking on a mock wounded look. "Do you think I'm a redneck?"

"Oh, yeah. That high-society, country club, gentleman thing you've got going on the surface is just a facade. Deep down, you're really just a—" she cocked her head, amusement dancing inside her "—what were the words? A stupid, Alabama redneck." Her eyes held his, a smile quivering on her lips. "I could add BMX riding, adrenaline junkie, ex-Navy SEAL, trivia master, photographer...Superman." She tipped a smile. "I think I'll stop there for now."

He gave her a crooked grin. "That's a good idea, Squirt."

"Ugh! I wish Pops would've kept his big, fat mouth shut. I hate that nickname."

He pulled her closer, his blue eyes going a shade deeper in their intensity. "Do you really love me?"

Tingles of anticipation circled down her spine as his eyes caressed hers. "Yes," she uttered. "Heart and soul," she managed to add before his lips took hers in a long, demanding kiss that left her breathless.

20

P ops leaned against the Lexus, folding his arms over his chest. He'd driven Addie and Maddox to a private airfield where they were about to get on Sutton's jet and head back to Birchwood Springs. "I wish you didn't have to leave so soon," Pops said, the corners of his lips pulling down into a frown. "You just got here."

Addie sighed. "I know. I was hoping we could stay until Tuesday, but I need to make sure Piper's okay." Her shoulders tensed thinking about the call she'd gotten from Hamilton Gentry a few hours ago, telling her that Piper had attempted suicide the night before. She'd taken a bunch of pills. Luckily, Hamilton realized what she'd done before it was too late. He rushed her to the hospital and had her stomach pumped. He explained that normally, Piper would've been kept in the hospital for a few days of psych monitoring. However, since Hamilton was a doctor, Piper was released into his care and was at home resting. Hamilton not only called to update Addie on the situation, but also to tell her that Piper had been asking to see her.

"I've never seen her this distraught before," Hamilton said, the strain in his voice coming through the call. "The grief of losing Jordan coupled with the fear of who might now have the formula for PZT... it's too much for her to handle."

Addie's heart hurt for Piper and Hamilton. She wished she knew what to say, but there were no words sufficient to heal this. All she could do was tell Hamilton that she was so sorry, and she would get there as soon as possible. The least she could do was be there for Piper in her time of need.

Concern touched Pops' features. "Are you okay?"

His question brought her back to the present as she faked a smile. "Yeah, it's just hard to see Piper go through this."

"I understand," he said grimly.

Maddox went around to the trunk and retrieved their luggage.

Addie touched Pops' arm. "Will you be back in time for the funeral on Wednesday?"

Pops nodded. "Yes, I'm flying back Tuesday evening."

"Okay, we'll pick you up at the airport." She looked at Maddox for confirmation.

He grinned as he turned to Wallace. "She's the boss," Maddox joked, slipping an arm around Addie's shoulders and pulling her close.

"You're a smart man," Pops chuckled.

"My mama didn't raise no dummy," Maddox quipped in an exaggerated drawl.

Addie rolled her eyes. "Yeah, right!"

Maddox's face fell as he turned to her. "You think I'm a dummy?"

Heat flamed her face as she giggled. "No, I meant that I'm not the boss," she explained, then saw the look that passed between Maddox and Pops. She realized they were teasing her. She shook her head, grinning. "Maddox Easton, what am I gonna do with you?"

"I'm sure you'll think of something," he winked.

She knew Maddox was trying to keep the mood light to get her mind off Piper. She reveled in how wonderful it was to be with the man she loved. After they made up at his condo the night before, they'd gone inside. Addie munched on leftover pizza, and they talked into the wee hours of the morning about their future. Maddox invited her to have Thanksgiving with his family, saying that his mama would be thrilled. Maddox was even considering renting one of Pops' cabins, so he and Addie could be together as often as possible. It was hard to believe that everything had changed so quickly. She still didn't like to think about Maddox being in constant danger, but she was going to have to take that one step at a time. *Don't borrow trouble. Don't mourn the hypothetical.* The more she kept repeating those phrases, the more peaceful she felt about the situation. She'd just have to keep moving forward with faith and keep a running prayer in her heart that all would be well.

Just when Addie felt herself dancing on air, she'd gotten the call from Hamilton and everything came crashing back down. It was ironic and so very unfair that the very event—Jordan's death—which had destroyed Piper's life, brought Addie and Maddox back together.

Maddox motioned with his head towards the plane. "You ready?"

"Yep." She gave Pops a tight hug. "I love you."

"I love you too, Squirt. I'm proud of you." A smile filled his face. "I'm so glad the two of you are finally back together." He sighed in contentment. "My work is done."

Addie laughed. "Nah. You've still got lots left to do. You have a granddaughter to take care of." Corbin and Delaney were practically glowing when they left them at the hospital this morning, both ecstatic to be parents.

"That's right." Pops hugged Maddox. "Have a safe trip. I'll see you both Tuesday evening." His lips formed a grim line. "Give Piper my love. Tell her I'm praying for her."

An unexpected lump formed in Addie's throat. "I will. It sounds like she needs all the prayers she can get."

JUST BREATHE, Addie kept repeating to herself as she and Maddox drove through the gates of the Gentry Estate. She glanced at Maddox, who was driving the car, as she rubbed her sweaty palms on her pants. "I'm so glad you're here with me."

"Me too." He smiled, his right hand letting go of the steering wheel as he reached for her hand, linking his fingers through hers. His brows knit together. "You're as cold as ice."

A shiver ran through her. "I know." She looked out the window at the passing evergreens lining the driveway. It had been sunny and warm in San Diego, but they had landed in Colorado to fog and cold drizzle. "It feels like déjà vu, doesn't it?"

"Yeah, it does," Maddox agreed as they lapsed into silence.

When they pulled up to the house, Addie turned to Maddox, her stomach churning. "I don't know what to say to Piper." She'd been floored by Hamilton's phone call, never dreaming in a million years that Piper would try to commit suicide. She and Maddox talked about it on the plane ride over with Maddox explaining that, given the right or wrong set of circumstances, anyone could be driven to that point. Piper had been slammed with so much during such a short period of time that she was understandably fragile. But suicide? Addie still couldn't fathom it. She had no training for this. Needles of desperation pricked at the base of her skull, and she felt a sense of foreboding.

"It's not about what you will say, but the fact that you're here that matters," Maddox reassured her.

Her heart squeezed. "I've got a bad feeling about this."

Maddox frowned. "What do you mean?"

"I don't know. I can't explain it." The foreboding had started on the plane ride and steadily increased. It had built to the point of frenzy. She forced a smile. "I guess I'm just stressed to the max." Tears pooled in her eyes. "I lost Jordan, one of my closest friends." She swallowed. "Yesterday, I almost lost Piper." Her lower lip trembled and she bit down to stay it. "I just keep thinking about what would've happened if Hamilton hadn't found her in time …"

"He did find her." He gathered her hands in his and cradled them. He peered into her eyes. "You're a strong woman, Addie Spencer. You've got this."

She jerked in surprise, a smile tugging at her lips.

He cocked his head. "What?"

"*You've got this.* That's what Delaney and Corbin both said to me last night before I went to find you." The large smile that filled his face sent warmth rushing through her, dispelling some of the gloom.

"See? They were right."

She nodded, trying to psych herself up for the task ahead as she looked at the large front door, which seemed too imposing to pass through. "Okay." She took a deep breath. The next second, her brows shot down. "I wish we had some information for Hamilton and Piper." They'd hoped to hear something from Sutton about Brent Barrett's interrogation. She cringed just thinking of the word *interrogation,* then forced her mind to move past it. She couldn't get hung up on that right now. It was good that Barrett was being questioned. At this point, however, she and Maddox didn't know any more about Barrett's involvement than they did before they left for New Jersey. They didn't know who killed Jordan—had no idea who'd stolen the hard drive and if it contained the formula for PZT. *Geez.* So many unanswered questions. No wonder Piper was wigging out. "Maybe you should call Sutton again."

He pushed out a breath. "I've already left several messages. He'll call me as soon as he knows something."

She nodded, knowing Maddox was right. Blood thrashed against her temples like the incessant surf against the seashore as Maddox came around and opened her door. Her legs were wobbly as she got out. She took in a breath, willing herself to remain calm. It was ridiculous getting this worked up about going in there. Piper was okay. She was recouping. Like Maddox said, there was nothing profound Addie could say to help the situation. It was being here that counted the most.

Breathe.

One step...two steps...a few more and they were to the door.

Maddox punched the doorbell.

A couple minutes later, Hamilton answered the door. His face was pale and drawn, a deep sadness in his eyes.

"Thanks for coming," he said in a somber, subdued tone as he stepped back and motioned. "Please, come in."

"How's Piper doing?" Addie asked in a quiet tone.

"Resting in her room."

They followed Hamilton into the family room where they'd sat when they came the time before.

Hamilton looked at Maddox. "Have a seat." He hesitated, rubbing his jaw. "It's probably better for you to remain in here with me... under the circumstance."

A trickle of unease went through Addie. She understood Hamilton's reluctance to bombard Piper with Maddox too, but she needed him by her side right now. She had no idea how to deal with this on her own. Her apprehension must've been written all over her face because Maddox offered a reassuring smile. "I'll be right here."

She nodded, feeling a little better. "Okay."

"You've been a great friend to Piper," Hamilton added. "It means the world that you would drop everything and fly back here to help her."

"Thank you." Hamilton's words added to her confidence, making her feel like she could do this. Even so, her heart pounded out a wild beat as she knocked on Piper's door.

No answer.

She swallowed, knocking again. "Piper. It's me, Addie." She placed the flat of her hand against the door. "May I come in?"

Nothing.

Finally, she tried the doorknob. It was unlocked. She opened the door and stepped into the bedroom. Piper was lying in her bed, pillows propped against her back. At first glance, she didn't look much different from normal, except for the fact that she was wearing pajamas and very little makeup. However, as Addie approached the bed, she noticed the shadows beneath her red-rimmed eyes and the hard, gaunt lines of her cheekbones, more prominent because she'd lost weight. Piper's vacant stare was what unsettled Addie the most.

She sat down on the bed and touched Piper's arm. "Hey," she began gently.

Piper seemed to realize she was there. She looked at Addie, a weak smile touching her lips. "Hey." Her voice had a gravelly edge. She coughed to clear her throat.

"How are you holding up?" Addie cringed. That was a stupid question. It was obvious how Piper was doing, not well.

Piper's lower lip trembled. Then her shoulders shook. A second later, tears spilled down her cheeks. "Jordan's gone." She spoke the words with a pitiful whine, reminding Addie of a child. "I loved him," she added.

"I know you did." Tears rose in Addie's eyes. "I'm so sorry."

"Everything I've worked so hard to build is being ripped away faster than I can put it back together."

"It'll be okay," Addie soothed.

Piper's dark eyes flashed with anger. "No, it won't," she snapped. "Nothing will ever be okay again."

Addie was taken aback by the sudden change in Piper's behavior. A chill clutched her heart. She wasn't sure how to answer, so she just sat there. Maybe it was better to just listen.

"I don't want to go on without Jordan." Piper let out a brittle laugh. "It's ironic, isn't it? When I found out about Jordan's affair, I hated him for it. Then, just when we were working through our issues, he left me."

"He didn't leave you by choice. He was killed."

A sob broke through Piper's throat. "I know. That's what I meant. It's not fair."

"No, it's not," Addie agreed.

Piper wiped her eyes with the palms of her hands, a shaky laugh escaping her throat. "You probably think I've lost my mind."

"I don't think that at all. You've been through a lot, and it has taken its toll. Anyone would have a hard time under these circumstances." Her gut tightened at how unfair life could be.

"Without Jordan and my company. There's no reason to continue." Her voice broke, a thick silence descending between them.

"That's not true. You've got your dad ... me," she said fiercely. More than anything, she wanted to be as good of a friend to Piper as Piper had been to her. Memories of Addie's critical time came rushing back as her voice grew reflective. "When I found out Gram had brain cancer." A ball of emotion lodged in her throat as she coughed to clear it. She offered Piper a pained smile. "Well, you remember how distraught I was. I was furious with God, wondering how a woman who'd been stripped of everything—her memories, her identity—could then have cancer." She gritted her teeth. "It was so unfair." She paused, giving Piper a meaningful look. "Remember the rest?"

A faint smile graced Piper's lips. "You were in bad shape...sitting by your grandmother's bed, bawling your eyes out. She'd been given a heavy sedative, didn't even know anyone was there."

"You came in and put a hand on my shoulder." Addie couldn't hold back the tears that slipped down her cheeks in thin ribbons. "You told me how strong I was, reminded me that I needed to be there for Pops." She chuckled. "You also told me to dry my eyes because the two of us were going to lunch."

A wry grin formed over Piper's mouth. "Oh, yeah. I'd forgotten about that part."

"Well, I never will." Determination fired in Addie's blood as she sat up straight and took Piper's hand. "This is where I tell you to get your butt out of bed and get a shower, so we can go and grab something to eat." She clapped her hands two times briskly. "Chop, chop."

Piper reached for the sheet and twisted it around her hands. Her eyes clouded, turning them a dark, muddy brown. "I appreciate what you're trying to do, but it won't work." Her voice went flat, and any residual vitality seemed to drain out of her. "Not this time," she said quietly.

Addie was about to grab the sheet and pull it off Piper, demanding that she get up, when a knock sounded at the door. She and Piper looked as Hamilton entered, holding a tray. He spoke to Piper. "I brought you some herbal tea with chamomile. It'll help you relax. I didn't know if you wanted tea, so I brought you a glass of ice water," he explained to Addie, his tone apologetic.

"Water's great," Addie said as he placed the tray in Piper's lap.

"Where's Maddox?" She didn't like the idea of him being left alone in the living room, while the three of them were in here.

"He got a phone call and stepped into the hall to answer it." Hamilton gave Piper a fatherly smile. "I figured it was a good time to bring your tea."

"Thanks, Dad," Piper said in a small voice as she reached for the handle and lifted the cup to her lips.

Hamilton handed Addie the glass of water.

"Thank you," she responded, taking a sip. She was about to place the glass on the nightstand beside the bed when Hamilton spoke.

"Drink up," he encouraged them both, bringing his hands together.

Piper took another drink of her tea, her eyes taking on a hint of laughter as she looked at Addie. "Better do as he says, or else he'll stand here hovering over us all day."

It was a relief to see a spark of life coming back into Piper's eyes. Addie laughed, feeling like they were teenagers again. Out of politeness, she downed a few large swallows.

A couple minutes later, Piper placed the half-empty tea cup on the tray and leaned back against the pillows. She stifled a yawn. "All right, Dad. We drank it. You can go now."

"Thanks for the water." Addie lifted the glass to her lips and took another couple of sips, then placed it on the bedside table. Hamilton stepped forward and retrieved the tray and Addie's glass. "Can I get you a snack?" he asked.

Piper waved a hand. "No, Dad. We're fine. Thank you."

He nodded, leaving the room.

Piper looked at Addie. "Thank you for accommodating him."

"Of course. It's nice of him to take such great care of you."

"Yes," she responded, her tone going listless. Addie could almost see her slipping back into the depression. She fingered the sheet. "So, Maddox is here with you?"

"Yes," Addie couldn't help but smile as she answered. Since last night, she'd felt like she was wrapped in a protective blanket of bliss, secure in the knowledge that the two of them were together for good this time.

"I take it things are going well?"

She was about to launch into a detailed description of just how wonderful things were, then caught herself. Now was not the time to bask in her own happiness. She cringed, imagining how tacky that would be with Piper's loss. "Things are going okay," she said in a monotone voice.

"It's all right," Piper said as if reading her mind. "You've got enough joy shining on your face to light up Manhattan."

The note of irony in Piper's voice was faintly irritating. Addie's first instinct was to point it out. Then again, Piper wasn't thinking clearly.

"I'm glad things are working out for one of us." Piper scrunched her eyebrows, her tone brooding.

Addie could feel the sadness oozing from Piper, flowing onto the floor where it climbed like gooey slime up the wall. She felt so guilty that things were working out for her when everything was going wrong for Piper. The timing was rotten. "I'm sorry."

A tight smile stretched over Piper's lips. "No, I'm the one who's sorry." She sighed resolutely. "I'm glad you're happy, Addie." Interest lit her eyes. "Are you and Maddox officially back together?" When Addie didn't answer, she reached for her hand. "It's okay."

A heat wave blasted over Addie. "Is it hot in here to you?" She pulled her hand from Piper's and tugged on the neck of her shirt. Something was wrong.

"Are you okay?"

She looked at Piper whose expression radiated concern.

"What's wrong?"

Piper's voice came at Addie from a distance like she was under water. The room began to spin. A cold sweat broke over Addie's forehead. She clutched her chest, finding it difficult to breathe. She coughed and sputtered, clutching her throat. "I've got to get to Maddox," she slurred, staggering to her feet.

Blackness closed in around her as she fell to the floor.

21

Maddox had been sitting in the living room with Hamilton, attempting to make conversation with the excruciatingly awkward man when Sutton called. He excused himself and stepped into the hall to take the call.

"Sorry I've been hard to reach," Sutton began. "I wanted to make sure I had as much info as possible before we spoke."

"I understand." Maddox braced himself, sensing that what Sutton was about to say was significant.

"Brent Barrett came up clean."

The breath left Maddox's lungs. "What? Are you sure?" His mind raced in circles like a dog chasing its tail.

"I'm sure," Sutton answered in a tone so matter-of-fact that it left no room for doubt.

"To be clear, you're saying Barrett didn't kill Jordan and that he didn't steal the hard drive?"

"That's precisely what I'm saying."

"What about Addie's attempted kidnapping?"

"The money trail leads to Brent Barrett. From the outside, looking in, it's a slam-dunk case against him."

"Meaning you think he was framed."

"Bingo."

Something Addie said came rushing back to Maddox. She questioned why a criminal would use his bank account to finance a kidnapping. She made a good point, but most transactions were done electronically as opposed to cash. Maddox also figured that Barrett wanted to do things remotely to keep as much distance between himself and his henchman as possible. The trail that led them to Brent Barrett had been twisty, going through various accounts before it was finally linked to an offshore account owned by Barrett Medical. He spoke, thinking out loud. "Are you saying that someone made the transactions convoluted enough to avoid suspicion, but clear enough for us to follow back to Barrett?"

"That's my thought."

A bitter disappointment rose in Maddox's throat. He swallowed, tasting acid. If Brent Barrett was innocent, then they were back to ground zero.

"I do have some other information that might prove useful."

Maddox's ears perked up.

"When we did the initial round of questioning at Therapia, everything came up squeaky clean. However, we did more digging— offered a reward for information—and received an anonymous call from a woman asserting that PZT wasn't all it was cracked up to be. We were able to track the call to a pharmaceutical scientist who worked alongside Jordan Phelps."

Maddox tightened his hold on his phone. "How trustworthy is this woman? Is it possible she's blowing smoke to get a reward?" Maddox thought about the video he and Addie watched of the Alzheimer's patient in the care center who'd been given PZT. Addie knew the woman, knew firsthand the state the patient was in before taking PZT.

"Yes, it's possible. At this point, I don't have enough information to make a clear assessment."

Maddox's thoughts were a jumble. Even though he and Addie

weren't a hundred percent sure Barrett was guilty, they were both cautiously optimistic that they were getting to the bottom of this thing. Maddox knew from sad experience that no mission or job ever went as planned, but this was like finishing Hell Week only to be told you had to do it all over again. If Barrett was innocent, then who was behind all of this? Addie was going to flip her lid when she realized they were back to square one. He forced himself to push aside his personal feelings to think analytically. "What's the woman saying?"

"That Jordan and his wife, Piper, were at odds about PZT. The drug had gone through several rounds of company testing. It passed the initial tests with flying colors. However, when it got to the beagle phase, some abnormalities were detected."

"What sort of abnormalities?" he asked carefully.

"Radical cell division."

"Cancer." Maddox said flatly.

"Yes."

"Why were Jordan and Piper at odds?" Maddox asked. "Was Jordan trying to cut corners to fast-track PZT to the market?"

"Not according to the researcher. Piper was the one who wanted to push forward. She was concerned about looking bad to the investors. Jordan was the one holding back. He'd given the drug to a handful of patients at a care facility. It shook him up badly when one of his test subjects developed cancer."

Maddox gasped like he'd been sucker punched. Addie's grandmother! Had Jordan given her PZT? "What kind of cancer?"

"Let me check my notes." The sound of rustling papers came over the line. "Brain."

Blood fired through Maddox's veins like a rocket launcher. The answer had been staring him in the face the whole time. He'd suspected Piper from the beginning, but Addie had been so adamant about her innocence. Then, after he saw the video with the Alzheimer's patient, the hard drive was stolen and the trail led to Barrett Medical. So, he assumed Addie was right, and Piper was the victim. A warning bell went off in his head, his only thought to get to Addie.

"You need to question Piper Phelps and her father, Dr. Hamilton Gentry."

"I'm here now. I'll let you know what I find out." He'd just ended the call when he heard movement. At the same instant, he felt a sharp stab of pain in his neck. He grunted as he collapsed to the floor, the phone falling out of his hand.

ADDIE'S HEAD felt like a gargantuan watermelon as she tried to swim through the darkness surrounding her. Voices swirled around her like hissing serpents.

"Time to wake up," a woman said.

She tried to raise her eyelids, but they wouldn't budge. Rough hands shook her arm. Her head dropped forward, her chin resting against her neck.

The voice became more adamant. "Addie!"

"My head," she moaned, pain throbbing across the bridge of her nose. Some of the fog lifted as she opened her eyes. She tried to brush her hair out of her face, then realized her hands were caught behind her back. Panic rose in her throat as she twisted, realizing she was sitting in a chair—no, tied to a chair! Her eyes shot open wide. She looked around wildly, trying to orient herself. She'd been sitting beside Piper when something happened ...

"She's awake," a voice snapped.

Piper's voice. The room came into focus. Addie realized she was in Piper's family room. She looked down at the kitchen chair, her heart racing. She jerked, trying to free her hands. Then it occurred to her that Piper was standing in front of her, watching with a curious expression as if Addie were a lab rat. "What's going on?" she managed to squeak. "Maddox!" she shouted, a wave of dizziness assaulting her. "Hamilton put something in my water" she asserted, glaring at Piper. Right after she drank it, she passed out. She looked at Piper, now dressed in jeans and a pullover shirt. She didn't look weak or suicidal. She looked perfectly normal. Well, except for her hostile expression. Addie tried to grapple with what was happening. "Why are you doing this?" Nausea swept over her, making her want to puke. She tried to swallow but couldn't. Where was Maddox? "Maddox!" she screamed, terror clawing at her like the talons of an eagle, picking apart its prey.

Piper sat down on the arm of an overstuffed chair, folding her arms over her chest, an amused smile washing over her face. "Don't worry. Loverboy can hear you." A cruel smile overtook her lips. "But I'm afraid he can't do much about it."

Heat flushed over Addie's body as she glared at Piper. "What did you do to him?" She couldn't believe this! She was still so floored by what was happening that she could hardly process it.

Piper laughed. "All in good time." Her eyes turned a deep black, malice twisting over her features. She leaned forward. "First, you're going to tell me what you did with the formula for PZT."

Somehow, Addie managed to find her voice. "W—what?"

"Don't play dumb, Addie. I know you have it."

Terror—swift and mind-numbing—raced through Addie as she tried to make sense of what Piper was saying. A hysterical giggle bubbled in her throat. "Do you think I stole the formula?"

"No, I don't think you stole it," she sneered. "Jordan gave it to you."

Addie's eyes narrowed. "Did you kill Jordan?"

Piper grunted. "If you mean, did I hit him with the car? Yes." Piper rattled out a hard laugh. "But I didn't kill him." She shot Addie a look of malice. "You did." She clenched her teeth. "You took Jordan from me and destroyed any chance we had for happiness." A sadistic look came into her eyes. "It's time for me to repay the favor."

Addie's heart slammed against her ribs like a caged animal. Repay the favor? Meaning hurt Maddox? Her heart shrank in despair as a prayer rose in her mind. *Please, help me and Maddox.* Piper wasn't making any sense. "I don't understand." Addie got the feeling that none of this was real, that she was in the middle of a nightmare. Tears rose in her eyes. "Why're you doing this?"

Piper sighed. "Determined to play Miss Innocent, huh? Fine, I'll play along. Everything was going along just fine until Jordan gave PZT to your precious grandmother," she spat.

"No, he didn't give PZT to Gram, remember? That's why he asked me to forgive him." Maybe Piper was insane. Why had Addie not noticed the signs before?

"No, stupid! Jordan gave PZT to your grandmother. As my rotten luck would have it, she was the one in fifty who developed a brain tumor."

The only sound in the room was Addie's sudden intake of breath. An invisible fist squeezed her lungs. "I can't breathe," she uttered.

"You can give it a rest, Addie. Your tricks won't work."

Addie felt like her head would explode. Jordan had given Gram PZT. She died because of him. Piper killed Jordan! She would kill Addie, had possibly killed Maddox already. Addie willed herself to relax. The only chance she had to make it out of this was to keep her wits about her. *Breathe!* she commanded herself. Her lungs expanded, allowing in a margin of blessed air. She tried to rise above the tide of hysteria threatening to sweep her into oblivion.

"Jordan felt guilty because of your grandmother and suddenly developed a conscience. He wanted to pull the plug on PZT." She wrinkled her brows. "Do you think he gave a crap that Dad and I had hocked everything to finance the research of PZT? That we had investors breathing down our necks, threatening to pull their backing? No!" she barked. "Not in the slightest."

Addie tried to connect the dots. "Does PZT really cure Alzheimer's?"

"Or course," Piper snipped. "You saw the video."

"But it causes brain cancer."

"In one out of fifty patients."

Addie exerted her strength, trying to break free of the band that bound her hands together with a spindle of the chair. It felt like hard plastic cutting into her wrists. Probably a zip tie. "When Jordan realized it caused cancer, he wanted to stop the process, which is why you killed him." Her mind raced to something else. "Are you the one who ransacked my house and hired the man to kidnap me?"

A hard light streaked in Piper's eyes. "Well, duh. It would've been so much easier to handle this if your SEAL hadn't stepped back into the picture. Now we'll have to do things the hard way."

"Why did you want to kidnap me?"

A raucous laugh issued from Piper's throat. "That's the ironic part. I was trying to find out what Jordan had given you the day he came to see you." Accusation shot from her eyes like arrows. "I figured Jordan would run to you. You were his true love." She spoke the words nastily.

"No, that's not true. What Jordan and I had was over a long time ago. Jordan loved you." The urge to charge out of her chair and wipe the smirk off Piper's face was overwhelming. "He trusted you." Her stomach churned acid in her throat as she eyed the woman she'd thought was her best friend. "How could you kill your own husband?" she seethed. Piper was lower than low.

"You took Jordan from me!" Piper screamed, rage filling her eyes. She clenched her fist and raised it at Addie. "You knew Jordan loved you when you introduced him to me." She snorted in disgust. "That's how you are, Addie. You rack up hearts, pining away for you, while pretending to be oblivious."

Addie realized that any argument she put forth would be shot down by Piper. It was better not to waste her breath. "You were looking for the item that Jordan gave me—the key."

"Yes."

"Maddox and I handed it to you on a silver platter."

Piper lifted her eyebrows, her eyes dancing in amusement. "Pretty much."

Addie connected the rest. "Dr. Gentry said he had to meet with the funeral director, but he's the one who stole the hard drive." It all came rushing back with a hard slap in the face. She'd thought the voice of the masked gunman was familiar, but had pushed it to the back of her mind. Regret punched through her. Maddox had been suspicious of Piper the entire time, but she'd dismissed his assertions, confident Piper was innocent. The sting of betrayal hit her so strongly she felt like her chest might collapse. "Jordan was never having an affair with Blanche Richey, was he?"

Piper giggled like a teenager. "That's the part I was most surprised about—your willingness to believe that. Your opinion of Jordan was almost as high as his opinion of you. I'm sure the two of you would've ridden off happily into the sunset had it not been for your SEAL." An expression of mock pity masked her face. "Poor Jordan. He never did get over you falling in love with another man." She sighed. "He tried to make do with his consolation prize—" she touched her hair "—me. That was so kind of you to throw your leftovers in my direction," she pouted.

"The money trail that led to Brent Barrett, you framed him."

"See, you're getting it, Addie. You're not as dumb as you look. Blanche was all too happy to help implicate her former boss."

"Because Brent Barrett fired her for embezzlement."

"Yes."

"Blanche was in cahoots with you."

"Blanche got a hefty payment for her assistance. She's living it up in Mexico." She frowned. "Too bad she's greedy, always wanting more money to keep quiet." She pursed her lips, cocking her head. "I guess I'll have to deal with her when the time comes."

It was at that moment that a chilling realization swept over Addie. Piper wouldn't be telling her all this if she planned to let her go. She didn't want to die! Not now, when she'd finally found happiness. She forced away the fear, willed her mind to concentrate on the details. Piper still needed something from Addie or she'd already be dead. She'd said earlier that Maddox could hear her, but that he couldn't do anything about it. Hopefully, that meant he was still alive. *Even if I have to die here today, please let Maddox be okay*, she prayed. "What was on the hard drive?"

"I'm so glad you asked," Piper answered gleefully. "Because I'm about to show you." She grabbed the remote from the coffee table and turned on the TV. A video of Jordan came on.

Tears rose in Addie's eyes when she realized he was speaking to her.

"Hey, Addie," he began, offering a slight smile into the camera. "If you're seeing this, then it must mean that the situation has escalated."

A sense of horror rose in Addie's chest as she listened to him outline the events in a dispassionate, cool tone—telling her everything Piper just had. When he got to the part about giving PZT to Gram, his voice choked. "I can't begin to tell you how sorry I am," he uttered.

Tears rolled down Addie's cheeks.

"How touching," Piper cooed, her voice dripping with venom.

A scorching indignation pulsed through Addie's veins as she glared at Piper.

Piper fast-forwarded the video. "You already know all of this part," she explained. "This is the part I want you to see." Her voice hardened to flint. "That way, you won't waste my time trying to deny that you don't have the formula." The video slowed to normal speed, Jordan's voice commanding Addie's attention.

"Addie, you're the only one I can trust. This drive contains Therapia's lab results for PZT, including how the damaged tissue samples were switched. I'm putting this into your hands because I trust you will get it to the right people to stop PZT from hitting the market in its current form." A pained look came over him. "I'm so sorry I failed you." He smiled thinly. "My intentions were good. You have everything you need, including the formula for PZT. I suppose a part of me hopes that you can get it in the right hands, so the formula can be refined." His face radiated optimism. "Think about what it would mean to the world, Addie, if we can cure this horrible disease once and for all." A boyish smile tugged at his lips as he pushed on his glasses. "You were my hope and inspiration. I love you."

"How sweet," Piper purred, turning off the TV. Her face went hard. "Where's the formula?"

Confusion swirled around Addie. "You said you kept the formula for PZT on a single computer, locked in a vault. You killed Jordan, stole the hard drive. You already have everything you need to move forward. Why am I here? Unless ..."

"Jordan broke into the vault and messed up the formula." Piper smirked. "Yeah, unfortunately, I didn't realize that part of the equation when I killed him." She stepped forward and got in Addie's face. "Where's the formula?"

"I don't know," Addie admitted.

The hard slap against her jaw took her by surprise as she yelped in pain, the force of the hit jerking her head sideways.

Piper eyed her. "I was afraid that might be the case." She sighed. "Well, let's see if I can jog your memory." Piper left the room and returned a minute later, holding a gun in one hand and a knife in the other.

Revulsion swelled over Addie like something rotten as she swallowed. She had no idea where the formula was. Even if by some miracle she found it, Piper would kill her. She prayed silently for help. Piper stepped behind her. Addie realized she was using the knife to cut the zip tie.

As she stood, Addie felt the cold press of metal in her back. "One wrong move, and you die," Piper growled. "Hands up where I can see them!"

Addie complied, raising her hands into the air.

"Move," Piper ordered, pushing her forward.

Addie's wrists burned, and her legs felt like wobbly toothpicks. Her thoughts rushed back to when she was kidnapped as the same feeling of desperation cloaked her. Maddox had rescued her then. Not likely to happen this time. The notion sank like lead in her gut.

"We're going to my bathroom," Piper said.

Piper's bathroom? Fear iced down Addie's spine. A strangled cry sounded from Addie's throat when she saw him. Maddox was lying in a large Jacuzzi tub filled with water up to his face. His eyes were open, his body motionless. For an instant, Addie feared he was already dead, then saw the distress in his eyes. "What did you do to him?" She moved to rush to his side, but Piper grabbed her sweater, yanking her back.

"Not so fast." Piper jabbed the gun in her back.

Trembles started in Addie's hands and rippled through her body, snaking down to her toes. "Oh, my gosh," she uttered, her hand going over her mouth.

Piper stepped around to face Addie, pointing the gun at her.

Rage trumped the fear as Addie glared at Piper. "What did you do to him?"

"I gave him a nice cocktail of drugs to render him motionless but allow him to comprehend everything with excruciating detail. Don't worry, if you do exactly as I say and get me the formula, the drugs will wear off and Loverboy will be just fine. If you don't ..." A vicious smile twisted her lips as she went over to the tub and turned on the faucet.

Addie screamed as the water rose higher. "Stop!" The water was an inch shy of entering Maddox's nose and mouth. She could feel his despair spilling out between them. It couldn't end like this! Maddox was a kick-butt, former Navy SEAL who'd survived torture and imprisonment by ISIS. Addie couldn't let Piper do him in.

"Of course, if the threat of drowning isn't enough to sway you, there are other means." Her voice had the controlled hiss of a viper about to strike. She reached for her blow dryer, resting on the nearby vanity. Addie followed the trail of the cord and realized there was an extension cord leading from the bathroom to the bedroom.

"I know what you're thinking," Piper said with a laugh. "I thought about just plugging the blow dryer in here. Then I realized all the outlets in the bathroom have GFCI switches, hence the extension cord."

Addie felt like she was having an out-of-body experience when Piper turned on the blow dryer. Keeping her hand with the gun trained on Addie, she held the blow dryer with the other hand. "One drop is all it will take," she taunted.

"Okay," Addie screamed, tears pooling in her eyes. "I'll give you the formula." She squared her jaw, her eyes burning with wrath. "Know this though, if you kill Maddox, you'll never get it no matter what you do to me."

After what seemed like an eternity, Piper turned off the blow dryer and placed it back on the vanity. "All right," she said lightly. "Where is it?"

"In the jewelry Jordan gave me," Addie blurted, not knowing what else to say.

Piper studied her with a keen eye, trying to decide if Addie was telling the truth.

Addie didn't flinch. "It's at the cabin."

Piper cocked her head. "Maddox said the jewelry was being examined."

"I lied." She gave Piper an unyielding look. "You're not the only one who can keep secrets."

Piper laughed. "All right. We'll go to the cabin and get the jewelry." Her eyes turned to black slits. "But for your sake and his, she motioned at Maddox, you'd better be telling the truth."

"What's going on here?" Hamilton asked as he came into the bathroom and stepped up beside Addie.

"Dad, you were supposed to be taking a nap," Piper said, giving him an annoyed look.

Shock came over Hamilton's features as he looked at the gun and Maddox in the bathtub. "You said you were only going to hold Maddox so Addie would be more inclined to help us find the formula. This has gone too far."

Piper gritted her teeth, her voice rising. "I told you to let me handle this!"

Hamilton's voice was heavy with regret as he continued. "I went along with your plan because I felt like a cure for Alzheimer's outweighed the negative effects of PZT. But this," he shook his head, his face draining, "it's too much. You need to put the gun down and stop this before more people get hurt."

"Shut up!" Piper screamed. Rage boiled in her eyes as she zeroed in on Hamilton. "You're weak, just like Jordan. I'm the only one who has the courage to do anything!"

Act now! Addie's mind screamed. Adrenaline rushed through her veins as she lunged forward and attacked Piper. They toppled to the ground, wrestling for the gun. A shot went off. Piper let out a cry of anguish as Hamilton fell to the floor.

Addie wrenched the gun out of Piper's hand. She scuttled back, holding it with both hands, aiming it at Piper as she got to her feet.

"You shot Dad," Piper croaked, a crazed look coming into her eyes. She crawled to Hamilton's side as she cradled him in her arms. "Oh, no." she cried. "What do I do? How do I fix this?"

Hamilton fought to get a breath. His hand was over his chest, a pool of red spreading in a large circle over his white dress shirt.

"Dad, tell me what to do?" Piper screamed, hysteria coating her voice. "Oh, my gosh!" she kept repeating.

"I think my artery has been hit," Hamilton breathed, then coughed, wincing in pain. "Use my cellphone. In my pocket." The words came out in gasps. "Call 911 before I bleed out."

"I'd do what he says," Addie demanded. "Better yet, hand me his phone."

Piper's upper lip curled, making her look more monster than human. "Or what? You're gonna shoot me?" She let out a derisive chortle. "You don't have the guts."

Time seemed to slow as Addie saw herself clearly for the first time. Yes, she had the guts to shoot Piper, or anything else it required to save Maddox. Addie flinched as she pulled the trigger, the bullet firing into the wall just to the right of Piper's head. Piper jumped, her head slumping into her shoulders. "The next time, I won't miss," Addie said savagely. "The phone. Now!" she barked.

Piper reached in Hamilton's pocket, then handed her the phone.

"4348 is my passcode," Hamilton managed to get out in halting breaths before closing his eyes.

"Dad!" Piper screamed. "Dad!"

"911. What is your emergency?" the operator asked.

"A man has been shot." Addie glanced at Maddox. "Another man has been drugged. We're at the Gentry Estate in Liberty Falls. Hurry!"

Piper's anguished wails echoed off the hard wall of the master bath. "Dad's dead! You killed him!"

"No, you killed him," Addie replied softly. She wanted to feel pity for Piper, but the bitterness of her betrayal was too overshadowing. She glanced at Maddox. "It's okay," she assured him, "the police and paramedics are on their way." She wasn't sure but thought she saw relief in his eyes.

"I love you," she added, gratitude welling in her chest. Her prayers had been answered. It was a miracle that they'd made it through this. Her heart clutched. Hopefully, the drug cocktail wouldn't have any lingering effects on Maddox.

He blinked, the corners of his mouth twitching.

Intense relief surged through her when he made a noise. At first, it was guttural grunts. Then finally, he got the words out in slurred groans. "I love you too."

22

The three of them stood silently, looking out at the gentle sloping hills framed by trees donning their finery of brilliant yellow, orange, and cinnamon brown. Addie's gaze trailed up to the jagged line of silvery blue mountains, their tips touched with ribbons of pink from the setting sun. A light breeze ruffled her hair, bringing with it the crisp scent of fall.

"Lou Ella loved it here," Pops said quietly, his declaration interrupting the stillness of the evening.

"Yes," Addie agreed.

Maddox stepped closer, concern coloring his eyes a deep blue as he assessed her. "Are you okay?"

"Yeah," she sighed, offering a dim smile. After Jordan's funeral, they decided to go to one of Gram's favorite places to honor her life. Maddox slid an arm around her shoulders as she snuggled into the curve of his arm, appreciating his warmth. "I'm just glad you're here with me."

He kissed the top of her head. "Me too." He chuckled dryly. "You're stuck with me now. It'll take a lifetime to repay you for saving my life."

"No repayment necessary." She turned and looked into his eyes. "I mean that."

The effects of the cocktail Piper concocted to temporarily paralyze Maddox wore off in less than twenty-four hours, leaving his physical body whole. However, Addie could tell that he blamed himself for being taken unaware and not being able to protect her. She shivered, knowing it would take a long time before she would stop seeing the tortured look in Maddox's eyes when he was in that wretched bathtub, unable to move. "I'm sorry I didn't listen to you when you tried to warn me about Piper." Remorse filled her throat, seeping down and tightening her chest. It would take a lifetime to get over her best friend betraying her—both of them, actually. At least Jordan meant well. Still, it didn't erase the fact that he'd caused Gram's death.

Piper was arrested and being held without bail, awaiting trial. Hamilton died before the paramedics arrived. Addie still had no idea if Jordan had given her the formula for PZT. At this point, it hardly mattered.

"You know what I think?" Pops asked, eyeing them.

Addie was the first to speak. "What?" She could feel a lecture coming on.

"It's time for the two of you to let bygones be bygones. You've been given a great gift—the chance to start over fresh." A smile tugged at his lips as he laughed softly. "If Lou Ella were here, she'd tell you to be happy."

Addie jerked in surprise, tears glistening in her eyes. There it was, that same advice ... again.

Maddox tightened his hold on her, giving her a significant look. "Be happy," he uttered.

She tipped her head. "That seems to be a recurring theme, doesn't it?" As she looked at the handsome face of the man she loved more than life, a feeling of pure and undiluted joy bubbled in her chest.

"Maybe it's time we took it to heart," Maddox said, his face splitting into a wide grin that showcased his dimples.

"Absolutely," she proclaimed, winking at Pops.

EPILOGUE

THREE WEEKS LATER

Addie looked sideways at Maddox. "Where are we going?"

A lopsided grin tugged at his lips. "You'll see."

She groaned. "You know I hate being kept in the dark," she lamented. "Give me a hint."

He pursed his lips, tightening his hold on the steering wheel. "Hmm ... let's see ... a hint. Okay, how about this? I think it's time we took our relationship to the next level."

Electricity zinged through her when he reached for her hand, bringing it to his lips. Anticipation licked through her veins. Was he talking about proposing?

When they pulled up to a pet store a few minutes later, she frowned, her hopes of an impending proposal going down the drain. "You're getting a pet?"

He laughed lightly. "Don't look so enthusiastic."

She wrinkled her nose. "Are you seriously considering getting a pet? What kind?"

"A fish."

"Oh, okay." She scrunched her hair, a thought occurring to her. "Who's gonna take care of it while you're gone on your jobs?"

He wiggled his eyebrows. "I was thinking you could help with that. Please."

"Just because you're handsome, doesn't mean you get the world handed to you on a silver platter," she grumbled. It was fine for Maddox to get a fish if he wanted, but why make a big deal about it? Why tell her he was taking their relationship to the next level? She folded her arms over her chest. "You go ahead. I'll just wait for you out here."

"Come on, Squirt. Go in with me. I need you to help me pick out Nemo."

She rolled her head back, hating when Maddox called her that. He'd been teasing her about Pops' nickname for weeks. It was starting to get old.

He leaned closer, his thumb caressing her cheek. "I'll make it up to you," he uttered, his gaze lingering on her lips.

Ribbons of desire swirled through her stomach, making her forget her irritation for a moment. "Fine," she huffed. "I'll go in, but I'm telling you right now that I refuse to take care of Nemo when you go out of town."

He laughed, shaking his head.

Her phone rang. She pulled it out of her purse. "Hello?"

"Hello? Is this Addie Spencer?" a male voice asked.

"Yes, it is."

"This is Frank Steinway."

"Mr. Steinway. Hello."

"I'm calling about your bracelet."

"Yes."

"I just got it back from my nephew in Brooklyn. He was able to repair it for you."

"Oh, thank you." She didn't want anything further to do with Jordan's mother's jewelry. Still, she'd asked Mr. Steinway to do a job and was obligated to pay him for his service.

"It's the darnedest thing. The clasp wasn't working properly because there was some sort of chip wedged into it."

Addie stiffened, looking at Maddox.

"What?" he asked.

She put Mr. Steinway on speaker. "Are you there?"

"Uh, yes."

"What were you saying about a chip being in the clasp of the bracelet?" Addie asked.

Maddox's eyes widened.

"My nephew discovered it. It's so tiny, he didn't know what it was at first."

Addie's pulse increased. "Do you have the chip?"

"Yes, it's here. My nephew thought it might be important, so he sent it back with the bracelet."

She put a hand to her chest. "I'll be there shortly to pick it up. Thank you, Mr. Steinway."

"My pleasure," he said, ending the call.

Her mind raced as she turned to Maddox. "Do you think the chip contains the formula for PZT?"

Maddox shook his head, an ironic grin curving his lips. "When the rest of the jewelry came up clean, it seemed highly unlikely that the bracelet would contain anything."

"Obviously, the odds were better than we thought," Addie chuckled.

He searched her face. "What do you want to do, if it is the formula?"

"I dunno. Maybe get it to someone who can work the bugs out of it?"

Maddox looked thoughtful. "Or sell it to someone like Barrett Medical for a pretty penny."

"No way would I sell it," she countered, giving him a sharp look. "As far as I'm concerned, it would be blood money." Her brows bunched as she glared at Maddox, hardly believing he'd suggest such a thing.

"I don't mean keep the profits. You could stipulate that the proceeds go to help patients with Alzheimer's."

Warmth spread through her chest as she smiled. She reached for his shirt and pulled him close. "That's an excellent idea," she said, her lips taking his in a long, slow kiss that sent shivery tingles circling through her.

A few minutes later, he pulled back. "All right. Are you ready to go inside the pet store?"

She made a face. "Now? But we need to get to the jewelry store," she argued.

"All in good time," he drawled. "Don't you dare open that door," he said as he jogged around and got the door for her.

"My Southern gentleman," she chimed, giving him a doting look. "Thank you."

He nodded. "Of course."

When they stepped inside the store, the teenage girl behind the counter smiled broadly in recognition. "Hello, Mr. Easton. I have your package ready for you."

Addie gave him a dubious look. "Package?" The last time she'd heard the word package it had a bad connotation. Sutton's men had referred to the kidnapper as the *package* they were to pick up.

"I'll be right back," the girl said.

Addie looked at Maddox who had a Cheshire Cat grin on his face. "What're you up to?"

Light danced in his eyes like sunlight sparkling over azure water.

The girl returned a minute later, holding a crate wrapped in a large, red bow. Addie peered inside the crate, surprised to see a cream ball of fur sitting in the middle. She laughed in surprise. "You got me a puppy?"

"Us a puppy," he corrected. He took the crate from the girl and placed it on the floor. He opened the door and pulled out the puppy, cradling it in his arms. The sight of Maddox holding such a cute and cuddly puppy caused her heart to melt. She rubbed the puppy's head, his fur feeling soft against her skin. "He's a golden retriever."

"Yep," Maddox said proudly.

A smile curved Addie's lips. "Much better than a fish."

"Oh, I almost forgot," the girl said. "Here are your instructions." She flashed a large smile as she handed Addie a small, white envelope.

Addie shook her head. "Instructions?"

"For the puppy," the girl answered.

"Go ahead," Maddox prompted, "open it."

"Okay." Addie felt like she was missing something. She ripped open the envelope and pulled out a card. She drew in a sudden breath, tears filling her eyes as she read the words.

Make me the happiest man on earth. Marry me.

She looked at Maddox's sparkling eyes wondering how she'd ever managed to get so lucky. "Yes!" she exclaimed, laughing and crying at the same time.

As she bridged the distance between them, pressing her lips to his, two little words circled through her head. Simple, yet powerful enough to change the course of her life.

Be happy.

"Yes," her mind responded with exultation.

I am.

Don't miss any of Jennifer's Navy SEAL Romances:

The Reckless Warrior

The Diehard Warrior

The Stormy Warrior

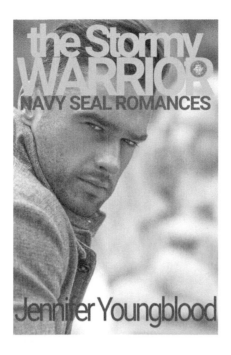

Free-spirited Tess Eisenhart wasn't looking for love when she went to Hawaii for her sister's wedding. Everything changed the instant she met Caden O'Brien, her future brother-in-law's brother. A former Navy SEAL, Caden is a tough-guy who seems oblivious to Tess's charms. When their paths keep crossing, Tess suspects that Caden may be more interested in her than he lets on.

When a lapse in judgment strands Tess and her young nephew on a small, remote island, Caden comes to their rescue. Sizzling sparks kindle to a raging fire as Tess and Caden embark on a new relationship. However, Tess soon learns unsettling details about Caden's past that may prevent him from making a commitment.

An unexpected tragedy throws Tess into the center of a dangerous game of deceit with a powerful, ruthless man who wants Tess for himself.

Will Caden and Tess's love be able to withstand the wounds of the past, or will everything they hold dear crumble in the face of misunderstanding and deception?

Find *The Stormy Warrior* on Amazon.

ABOUT JENNIFER YOUNGBLOOD

Jennifer loves reading and writing clean romance. She believes that happily ever after is not just for stories. Jennifer enjoys interior design, rollerblading, clogging, jogging, and chocolate. In Jennifer's opinion there are few ills that can't be solved with a warm brownie and scoop of vanilla-bean ice cream.

Jennifer grew up in rural Alabama and loved living in a town where "everybody knows everybody." Her love for writing began as a young teenager when she wrote stories for her high school English teacher to critique.

Jennifer has a BA in English and Social Sciences from Brigham Young University Hawaii where she served as Miss BYU Hawaii. Before becoming an author, she worked as the owner and editor of a monthly newspaper named *The Senior Times*.

She now lives in the Rocky Mountains with her family and spends her time writing and doing all of the wonderful things that make up the life of a busy wife and mother.

Made in the USA
Columbia, SC
25 October 2025

72040266R00132